# The Author

D1376414

MARGARET LAURENCE was born in Neepawa, Manitoba, in 1926. Upon graduation from Winnipeg's United College in 1947, she took a job as a reporter for the *Winnipeg Citizen.*

From 1950 until 1957 Laurence lived in Africa, the first two years in Somalia, the next five in Ghana, where her husband, a civil engineer, was working. She translated Somali poetry and prose during this time, and began her career as a fiction writer with stories set in Africa.

When Laurence returned to Canada in 1957, she settled in Vancouver, where she devoted herself to fiction with a Ghanaian setting: in her first novel, *This Side Jordan,* and in her first collection of short fiction, *The Tomorrow-Tamer.* Her two years in Somalia were the subject of her memoir, *The Prophet's Camel Bell.*

Separating from her husband in 1962, Laurence moved to England, which became her home for a decade, the time she devoted to the creation of five books about the fictional town of Manawaka, patterned after her birthplace, and its people: *The Stone Angel, A Jest of God, The Fire-Dwellers, A Bird in the House,* and *The Diviners.*

Laurence settled in Lakefield, Ontario, in 1974. She complemented her fiction with essays, book reviews, and four children's books. Her many honours include two Governor General's Awards for Fiction and more than a dozen honorary degrees.

Margaret Laurence died in Lakefield, Ontario, in 1987.

# THE NEW CANADIAN LIBRARY

General Editor: David Staines

Margaret Laurence

# THE TOMORROW-
# TAMER

*With an Afterword by Guy Vanderhaeghe*

M&S

First published in 1963 by Macmillan & Co. Ltd.

Reprinted 1993

**Canadian Cataloguing in Publication Data**

Laurence, Margaret, 1926-1987
The tomorrow-tamer

(New Canadian library)
ISBN 0-7710-9894-4

I. Title. II. Series.

PS8523.A86T6 1993   C813'.54   C93-093520-9
PR9199.3.L39T6 1993

Series design by T.M. Craan
Typesetting by M&S, Toronto
The support of the Government of Ontario through the
Ministry of Culture and Communications is acknowledged.
Printed and bound in Canada

McClelland & Stewart Inc.
*The Canadian Publishers*
481 University Avenue
Toronto, Ontario
M5G 2E9

For
NADINE AND KWADWO

# Contents

# Acknowledgements

These stories have appeared in the following publications:

The Drummer of All the World – *Queen's Quarterly*, 1956.

The Perfume Sea – *Winter's Tales 6*, 1960; *Saturday Evening Post*, 1961; *Post Stories*, 1962.

The Merchant of Heaven – *Prism*, 1959.

The Tomorrow-Tamer – *Prism*, 1961 (awarded President's Medal, University of Western Ontario, 1962).

The Rain Child – *Winter's Tales 8*, 1962.

Godman's Master – *Prism*, 1960.

The Pure Diamond Man – *The Tamarack Review*, 1963.

The Voices of Adamo – *Saturday Evening Post*, 1962.

A Gourdful of Glory – *The Tamarack Review*, 1960 (awarded President's Medal, University of W. Ontario, 1961).

# The Tomorrow-Tamer

# The Drummer of All the World

**M**Y father thought he was bringing Salvation to Africa. I, on the other hand, no longer know what salvation is. I am not sure that it lies in the future. And I know now that it is not to be found in the past.

The mission where I was born was in a fishing village between Accra and Takoradi, on Africa's salt-steaming west coast. I lived there all my early boyhood. A missionary — how difficult it was to live down my father's profession. I almost wish I had not tried.

A missionary had to have a genuine calling in those days. Nothing less would have withstood the nagging discomfort of the place. Our bungalow was mudbrick, dank and uncleanable. Our lights were unreliable hurricane lamps, which my father always forgot to fix until the sudden surging arrival of night. Our bath was a cement tub where grey lizards flattened themselves for coolness. A green fur of mould grew over everything, especially over my father's precious books, irritating him to the point of desperation. Diarrhoea was a commonplace, malaria and yellow fever only slightly less so.

I did not notice these things much. For me it was a world of wonder and half-pleasurable terror. Our garden was a jungle of ragged banana palms and those giant leaves called 'elephant's ears'. In front of the bungalow the canna lilies stood, piercingly scarlet in the strong sunlight. Sometimes the nights were suffocating, and the mosquito net over my bed showed scarcely a tremor of breeze. Every lizard nervously hunting for insects, every cockroach that scuttled across the floor, seemed to me the footsteps of *asamanfo*, the spirits of the dead. Then the rains would come, and at night the wooden shutters would slam against the house like untuned drums, and the wind would frighten me with its insane laughter.

The chief thing I remember about my mother is that she was always tired. She was very pale and thin, and often had malaria. In a sense, she even welcomed it.

'It is God's way of trying us, Matthew,' she would say to me. 'Remember Job.'

She never gave in. She went on, thumping the decayed hand-organ in the little mud church, chalking up the week's attendance, so many black souls for Jesus. I think she would have been happier if she had even once admitted that she hated Africa, hated the mild-eyed African women who displayed in public their ripe heavy breasts to suckle their babies, and the brown-skinned men with their slender fingers, their swaggering walk, their bare muscular thighs. I suppose she must have realized her hatred. Perhaps that is why she worked herself to death — trying to prove it was not so.

When I was young I had an African nurse. She was old Yaa, the wife of Kwaku, our cook. I don't suppose she was really old. Her second son, Kwabena, was my age, and the younger ones kept coming for years. But she seemed ancient as stone to me then, with her shrewd seamed face and her enormous body. It was Yaa and Kwabena who taught me Twi, taught it to me so thoroughly that by the time I was six I could speak it better than English.

Kwabena and I used to run, whooping and yelling, beside Yaa as she walked back from the market, her great hips swaying under the thick folds of her best green and mauve

2

cloth, and her wide brass headpan piled high with mangoes and paw-paw, yams and red peppers.

'Ei ei!' she would cry, as the goats and chickens scattered out of her way on the narrow street. 'Another week of this walk and I am finished! The bottom of the hill — that would not have suited God, oh no! If the master had less worry about my soul and more about my feet——'

When Kwabena and I stole eggs to give to the fetish, she whipped us. I would have died rather than tell my father — not for shame, but for love of her.

'A hen treads on her chicks,' she would tell us the old proverb, 'but not to kill them.'

In the rains I used to lie awake, listening to the thunder that seemed to split the sky, and thinking of Sasabonsam, the red-furred Great Devil, perched on his *odum* tree with those weird folk of witchery, the *mmoatia* who talked in whistles. Then I would hear the soft slapping of Yaa's footsteps in the passage, and she would come in and rock me in her arms.

'Do they think he is a man yet?' she would demand angrily, of no one. 'Sleeping in a room by himself! Listen, little one, shall I tell you what the thunder is? In the beginning, when Odamankoma created all things——'

And soon I would be asleep.

I found out accidentally that Yaa had suckled me at her breast when I was a baby. My mother never knew.

'I asked what day I was born,' I told Kwabena. 'It was a Tuesday.'

His face lit up. 'Then we are brothers in one way——'

Kwabena's name was given to the Tuesday-born. Yaa laughed.

'You are brothers anyway,' she said.

And then she told me. I do not know why that should make a difference to me, even yet, when I think of her.

Perhaps because her love, like her milk, was plentiful. She had enough to spare for me.

My father was an idol-breaker of the old school. He hated only one thing more than the heathen gods and that was the Roman Catholic Church.

'Formalism, Latin — all learned by rote,' he would say. 'They have no spontaneity. None at all.'

Spontaneity to my father meant drilling the Mission Boys' Fife and Drum Band to play 'Nearer My God to Thee' until their mouths were sore and puckered with blowing and their heads spinning with the uncomprehended tune.

The mission had a school. My father taught the boys to read and write; and who knows, in the eternal scheme of things perhaps that is all he was meant to do. But he was not a very patient man. Once when a family of rats died in the well, and the merchant cheated him on the price of cement for a new one, he beat six boys in a single afternoon. I cannot say that I blame him. He worked hard and had so pathetically little to show for his toil and his poverty. He would have been superhuman if the light of holiness had not flickered low from time to time.

For twenty years he tried to force, frighten or cajole his flock away from drumming and dancing, the accompaniments of the old religion. He forbade the making of wooden figures. I suppose we have to thank men like my father for the sad fact that there are so few carvers of any merit left in West Africa.

He broke idols literally as well as symbolically. Perhaps it was necessary. I do not know. I heard the story of Moses and the Golden Calf so often that after a few years of almost tasting the powdered gold harsh against my throat, I passed into the stage of boredom.

'I have discovered another fetish hut,' my father announced importantly one day.

I nearly betrayed myself and the whole village by asking which one.

'Where?'

'On the shore, between the palm grove and the fishing beach. I am going to break into it.'

I knew the one. The *obosom* there was a powerful one, Kwabena had told me. I stared at him with wide eyes. My father probably thought I was full of admiration for his zeal. In fact, I was wildly curious.

'He will — of course — die,' Kwabena said when I told him.

My father did break into the fetish hut, and he did not die. He did not even have indigestion or a fever. The fetish inside the little hive of woven palm leaves was part of the vertebrae of an enormous sea creature, possibly a whale. It was very old, and crumbled when he kicked it. I suppose it was a blow for truth. But I was ashamed.

I still am. Moses broke the idols of his own people.

The parades were something my parents organized and bore with, but never liked. They took place on saints' days or whenever the attendance of the Band of Jesus was falling off.

'If only the girls would just walk along,' my mother would complain, 'instead of — what they do. And to the hymns, too.'

'I know,' my father soothed her. 'But it's necessary. We will just have to keep impressing them with the desirability of dignity. But we can't cut out the parades. Remember, they're like children, these people. In order to be drawn to the church, they must have the pageantry, the music — it's better than their own heathen dancing, anyway. Besides, the Roman Catholics have parades.'

My father marched with the parade only once, and that time the District Commissioner's wife happened to see him. He was so humiliated he never went again. I can still see those parades, headed by the mission banner in purple and yellow silk. I wish you could have heard the Mission Boys' Fife and Drum Band playing 'Onward, Christian Soldiers' with a syncopated jazz beat, hot as the forest's pulse. The words, badly translated in Twi, were chanted by the snaking line of girls, their hands outstretched, their shoulders lifting to the off-beat, their whole bodies giving back the rhythm. Dignity! They could no more stop themselves from dancing than they could from breathing. Every sinew, every bone, in their bodies responded to rhythm as to a lover's touch.

One Easter my father discovered that I had gone with Kwabena, as always, and joined the parade at a distance from the church.

'I can't understand,' my father began, more in sorrow than anger, 'why Kofi let you stay. I've told him——'

Kofi was one of the monitors, one of the very few of his flock whom my father trusted.

'He didn't see me,' I replied abruptly.

He could hardly have missed seeing me, turning cartwheels with Kwabena at the head of the parade. But Kofi was the last person who would have tattled. Fortunately for my father, he never found out, as I had done, that Kofi was one of the most renowned fetish priests along the coast.

'We have explained it all to you, Matthew,' my father went on. 'The parades are not — proper — for you in the practice of your faith.'

'Why not?' I was still excited. 'It was fun — why shouldn't I go?'

'Religion is not fun,' thundered my father. 'It is serving God.'

How can I describe Kwabena, who was my first and for many years my only real friend? I cannot think of him as he is now. The reality of him is the little boy I remember, slighter than I but more wiry, braver but less far-sighted. Until my mother objected, he used to run naked, his brown body paled with dust. He had Yaa's aggressive spirit and his laughter was like hers, irreverent, deep, flooded with life. He was totally unlike the charming, indolent Kwaku, his father.

I used to go with him into the village, although my parents had forbidden it, into the mudbrick huts thatched with dried palm leaves, the fusty little dwellings stinking of goats and refuse and yellow spicy palm oil. The filth and the sorrow — I hardly noticed them. I was shown a girl child who had died of malaria, the belly bloated, the limbs twisted with the fever. And what interested me most was that they had left her gold earrings on. Avariciously, I longed to steal those thin bright circles before they were wasted in the earth.

I do not know when Kwabena began to notice suffering. Perhaps the knowledge of it was born in him.

When I was with Kwabena, the world of the mission and Band of Jesus did not exist for me. However powerfully my father preached, he could not stop the drums playing in the evenings. Kwabena and I would sit under the casuarina tree in our garden and listen to the thudding rhythm, the tempo building up and up until you knew the drummer was hypnotized with the sound.

'Ei! That one! It is almost like the voice of Drum himself,' Kwabena would say.

And I would imagine the vast-bellied giant, the Drummer of all the world, drumming on himself, the Drum of drums. For years I thought of the great grinning mask each time the drums pulsed in the moon-grey night, seeming to shiver even the ribboned leaves of the banana palms.

The casuarina tree was a special meeting-place for Kwabena and me. It was there that the wind spoke to us, whispering through the feather fans of the branches like the warning voices of the ancestors themselves. It was there that Kwabena used to tell me stories about Ananse Kokuroko, Ananse the gigantic spider, who desired greedily all power and all wealth, and who wove his web of cunning to ensnare the stupid and the guileless. Whenever I saw a spider I always sidestepped it, out of respect for the Father of Spiders, and for a time I half believed they could understand what I was saying.

There was a deserted palm hut on the shore, a mile from the village. Kwabena said it was where Death lived. We always walked far to the side of it and never looked at it directly. Kwabena was especially mindful of taboos, for he wanted to be a fetish priest when he became a man.

In the sweltering afternoons Kwabena and I would steal away from the bungalow and go to the lagoon. The sea was nearby and clean, and we were allowed to swim there. I suppose that is why we preferred the lagoon. Kwabena would peel off his scanty garb.

'I can dive better than you, Matthew!'

Often I hesitated, some deep English fear of unclean water stirring within me.

'It is forbidden——'

Kwabena would spout brown water from his mouth like a whale.

'You are afraid! If I had such fear I would go and hide myself in the forest, for shame!'

So I would strip also, indignantly, and jump in. I never got bilharzia — some kindly spirit must protect the very foolish.

The shore was ours, with its twisted seashells and moss-hair rocks and stretches of pale sand where transparent crabs scurried like tiny crustaceous ghosts. Ours the thin-prowed fishing boats that impertinently dared the angry surf each day. Ours the groves of slender palms, curved into the wind, and the bush paths with their tangled vines and tree roots torn from the red earth by storms. Ours was the village, too, with its baked mud streets where old gossiping men squatted and children slept and big-breasted women walked with babies slung on their backs and laden brass trays balanced on their heads.

This was my Africa, in the days of my childhood, before I knew how little I knew.

I was ten when I first saw Afua. She was Yaa's niece, and when her mother died she came to live with Yaa and Kwaku. She was a thin and bony little girl, and as though she sensed her ugliness she was very shy. No one ever noticed her except Yaa, who would chatter away encouragingly as the two of them pounded fu-fu in the shade of the mango tree.

'I know — you are a little owl now, but it will not always be so. There is beauty in you. You will fatten and grow tall, and one day all the young men will want you. You will not have to marry a poor man.'

And the child would look at her gravely, not believing.

Afua had been living in our compound for nearly two years before I really saw her. She had changed in that time, without my realizing it. Perhaps I, too, had changed. My childhood was nearly over, although I did not know it then and still longed for the slow years to pass.

It was afternoon and the sun filled the street with its hot orange light, making vividly dark the shadows on the earth and walls. Afua had been carrying a basket of melons home from the market. Now the basket lay forgotten in the festering gutter.

Afua was dancing with her shadow. Slowly, lightly, then faster, until she was whirling in the deserted street, her hands clapping, her hips swaying with a sudden knowledge of her womanhood. I had to stop and watch her. For the first time I saw her ripening breasts under her faded cotton cloth, and the beauty given to her face by her strong fine-shaped bones. When I saw Kwabena coming along the street behind me, I did something totally strange to me. I turned and went to meet him, and led him back the other way, so he should not see her.

My father had forbidden me to take part in the mission parades, and I never went again. I wondered afterwards what he would have thought if he had known what I did instead. When the talking drums sounded in the evening, I got Kwaku to tell me any of their invocations which he understood, or the proverbs and parables which they drummed forth.

> *Odamankoma created the Thing,*
> *The Carver, He hewed out the Thing——*

I learned some of the other names of Nyame — the Shining One, Giver of Rain, Giver of Sun. Once for a whole year I called God by the name of Nyame in my silent prayers. I tried to find out from Kwaku — and was laughed at — the meaning of the saying 'Odamankoma created Death, and Death killed Him'. When my mother was ill for the last time, I invoked Nyankopon's strong name, Obommubu-wafre, not for love of her but as a duty.

God of my fathers, I cannot think You minded too much. If anything, I think You might have smiled a little at my seriousness, smiled as Kwaku did, with mild mockery, at the boy who thought Africa was his.

The year after my mother died, I went back to England to school. It was not until I was seventeen that I returned to Africa on a visit. I had grown very like my father, tall and big-shouldered, and I did not have much difficulty in working my passage out as deckhand on a cargo boat.

Kwabena was at school in Takoradi, but he came home several times to see me. He had grown taller, although he was still a head shorter than I, and his lank child's body had filled in and become stocky. Apart from that, to my unobservant eyes he was the same. I wonder now how I could have thought so. The indications were plain enough, had I not wanted to ignore them. I asked him to come with me to the palm grove one day, to look at the fetish huts. His face became guarded.

'I do not go there any more,' he said.

We passed a man planting cassava in a little field.

'They pour libation to make the crops good,' Kwabena commented, 'and then work the land like that, by hand, with a hoe.'

We saw the District Commissioner one afternoon, his white topee gleaming. He was holding a formal palaver with the local chief.

'We will not always be slaves of the English,' Kwabena said.

'That's stupid,' I replied. 'You're not slaves now.'

'If they own us or own our country, where is the difference?'

'So they will have to go?'

'Yes,' he answered firmly. 'They will have to go.'

'Splendid,' I said ironically. 'And I with them? If I were here in government?'

He did not reply for a moment.

'Perhaps I would not wish it,' he said finally, carefully. 'But there is a saying — follow your heart, and you perish.'

We did not talk of it again, and after a while I forgot.

Afua still lived with Yaa and Kwaku. I thought she had changed more than anyone. I see now that she had changed less than Kwabena, for the difference in her was one that life had brought about, easily, of itself. Her body gave the impression of incredible softness and at the same time a maternal strength. She belonged to earth, to her body's love, to toil, to her unborn children. One evening, after Kwabena had gone back to Takoradi, I fulfilled the promise to myself and went to the palm grove. It was deserted, and the wind ruffled the tops of the trees like fingers through unruly hair. Afua walked quietly, and I did not hear her until she was very close. But she did not enter the grove.

'Why do you stand there?' she asked.

'I don't know. Perhaps to hear the ancestors' voices.'

'You must not.'

'Why?'

'Because it is a sacred place,' she answered simply, 'and I am afraid.'

The beach was only a few yards away. We walked down there.

'You have grown very tall,' she smiled, and she placed one of her hands lightly on my wrist. Then she hesitated. 'Are — are Englishmen like other men?'

I could not help laughing at that, and she laughed too, without self-consciousness or shame. Then, clumsily, I took her in my arms.

She was more experienced than I. I would not have blamed her if she had mocked me. But she did not. For her, it answered a question. Quite probably that is all. But for me it was something else. Possessing her, I possessed all earth. Afterwards, I told her that I had to go back to England soon. Perhaps I expected her to say she would be broken-hearted.

'Yes, it is right that you should return to your own land,' Afua said.

I was about to tell her that I would come back here, that I would see her again. But something stopped me.

It was the sudden memory of what Kwabena had said. 'Follow your heart, and you perish.'

Of course I did go back to Africa after all, but not for another ten years. Africa had changed. The flame trees still scattered their embers of blossoms upon the hard earth. The surf boats still hurtled through the big waves. The market women's mammy-cloths were as gaudy, their talk as ribald as ever. Yet nothing was the same.

The country was to have its independence the following year, but the quality of change was more than political. It was so many things. It was an old chieftain in a greasy and threadbare robe, with no retinue — only a small boy carrying aloft the red umbrella, ancient mark of aristocracy. It was an African nightclub called 'Weekend in Wyoming', and a mahogany-skinned girl wearing white face powder. It was parades of a new sort, buxom market women chanting 'Free — dom!' It was the endless palaver of newborn trade unions, the mushroom sprouting of a dozen hand-set newspapers. It was an innuendo in the slogans painted on mammy-lorries — The Day Will Come, Life Is Needed, Authority Is Never Loved. It was the names of highlife bands — The Majestic Atoms, Scorpion Ansah And His Jet Boys. It was the advertisements in newspapers — 'Take Tiger Liver Tonic for fitness, and see how fast you will be promoted at work.' It was the etiquette and lovelorn columns —'Is it proper for a young lady to wear high heels with traditional African dress?' or 'I am engaged to a girl whose illiteracy is causing me great embarrassment — can you advise?'

The old Africa was dying, and I felt suddenly rootless, a stranger in the only land I could call home.

I drove up the coast to our old village one day to see Afua. I ought to have known better, but I did not. Afua is married to a fisherman, and they have so far four living children. Two died. Afua must have married very young. Her face is still handsome. Nothing could alter the beauty of those strong sweet bones — they will be the same when she is eighty. Yes, her face is beautiful. But that is all. Her body is old from work and child-bearing. African women suckle their children for a long time. Her breasts are old, ponderous, hanging. I suppose they are always full of milk. I did not mind that so much. That is the way of life here. No, I am wrong. I did mind. But that was not what I minded the most.

She came to the door of the hut, a slow smile on her lips. She looked questioningly at my car, then at me. When she saw who it was, she stopped smiling. Around her, the children nuzzled like little goats, and flies clung to the eyelids of the sleeping baby on her back. The hot still air was clogged with latrine stench and the heavy pungency of frying plantains.

'I greet you — master,' Afua said.

And in her eyes was the hatred, the mockery of all time.

I met Kwabena accidentally on the street in Accra. He had grown thinner and was dressed very neatly now in white shirt and grey flannels. He looked disconcertingly serious, but when he smiled it was the same grin and for a moment I thought it was going to be all right. But when I gave him the Twi greeting, he did not reply to it.

'So you have come back after all, Matthew,' he said finally.

'Yes, I've come back.' Perhaps my voice was more emphatic than I had intended. 'This is where I belong.'

'I see.'

'Or perhaps you don't think so——'

Kwabena laughed. Africans quite often laugh when they are not amused.

'What I think,' he commented, 'should not matter to you.'

'For heaven's sake, Kwabena,' I demanded, 'what's wrong?'

'Nothing is wrong,' he replied vaguely. Then, with a show of interest, 'Well, are you with government, as you used to say you would be?'

'Yes. Administration. They're not taking on new European staff any more — I only managed it because I speak Twi. And you?'

'Oh, I am a medical orderly.' His voice was bitter. 'An elevated post.'

'Surely you could do better than that?'

'I have not your opportunities. It is the closest I can get now to real medical work. I'm trying to get a scholarship to England. We will see.'

'You want to be a doctor?'

'Yes——' He laughed in an oddly self-conscious way. 'Not a ju-ju man, you understand.'

Suddenly, I thought I did understand. With me, he could never outgrow his past, the time when he had wanted to be another kind of doctor — a doctor who dealt in charms and amulets, in dried roots and yellow bones and bits of python skin. He knew I would remember. How he must have regretted betraying himself to me when we were both young.

I wanted to tell him that I knew how far he had travelled from the palm hut. But I did not dare. He would have thought it condescension.

He was talking about his parents. Kwaku, he said, was working in Takoradi. He was getting old for domestic work, but he could not afford to retire. None of the sons or daughters had made or married money.

'And your mother?' I asked him.

15

'She died three years ago. She had hookworm for years. She was a Christian, as you know, but she still bought bush medicine and charms instead of going to a doctor. I couldn't persuade her. She became very weak. When she got typhoid she didn't have much chance.'

For a moment I could not speak, could not believe that Yaa was really dead. It seemed wrong that I should learn of it this way, so long afterwards. And wrong, too, that I had thought of her these past years as unchanged, as though I had believed she would keep on during all my lifetime, shouting her flamboyant abuse to the sellers in the market, and gathering each successive generation of children into her arms.

'I — I didn't know,' I stumbled. 'No one told me——'

'Why should they tell you' — he smiled wryly — 'if an old African woman dies?'

Pain and anger spread like a bloodstain over my whole mind.

'You know as well as I do,' I replied harshly, 'that she was more mother to me than my own mother.'

Kwabena looked at me as though he hated me.

'Yes,' he said. 'I shared my mother with you, in exchange for your cast-off khaki shorts.'

There was something in it that shocked both of us, and we were uncomfortably silent.

'I did not mean to say that,' Kwabena said finally, and there was shame in his voice, but no withdrawal.

I could not help thinking of the two boys who had both been born on a Tuesday, and of the woman, immense, bad-tempered, infinitely gentle, who had said, 'You are brothers anyway.' I found I was not angry at Kwabena any more. It was no one's fault that life had allowed us a time of illusion, and that the time was now past.

'Never mind.' I felt very tired. 'It doesn't matter.'

'What do you think of the country' — he seized on the first topic to hand, as Englishmen seize on the weather — 'now that you're back?'

'Mixed feelings,' I said. 'Independence is the new fetish, and political parties are the new chieftains. I'm not sure that much is gained.'

'A chieftain in a Kente cloth — you prefer that to a politician in a business suit?'

Whatever subject we touched seemed to be wrong. But I no longer cared.

'Quite frankly, yes. I think it's more genuine. I don't see anything very clever in all this cheap copying of western ways.'

'So——' Kwabena said thoughtfully. 'You would like us to remain forever living in thatch huts, pounding our drums and telling pretty stories about big spiders.'

I stared at him, hardly able to comprehend what he had said.

'You forget,' he went on, 'that the huts were rotten with sickness, and the tales made us forget an empty belly, and the drums told of our fear — always there was fear, fear, fear — making us pay out more and more to the fetish priest——'

He broke off and looked away. When he spoke again, it was calmly, almost coldly.

'That was one thing about your father. He did not like us — that is true. He did not understand us. And we did not like or understand him. Nearly everything he did was wrong. But at least he did not want us to stand still.'

'As I do?' The words dried my throat, for I had meant them as irony, but they had not come out that way.

Kwabena did not reply. Instead he looked elaborately at his watch, like a doctor dismissing a demanding patient.

'I must not keep you any longer,' he concluded. 'Also, I have to be back at work by one o'clock.'

I did not see him again.

Since then very little has happened to me. I do my job adequately but not brilliantly. My post is to be given to an African soon.

I married on my last leave. My wife is slight and fair, quite good-looking. She does not like Africa much, and she is always telling me that the servants have no idea of cleanliness. I do not argue with her. Quite probably she is right. She is looking forward to the day when we will have a semi-detached house in England's green and pleasant land.

And I? I thought of Kwabena's words for a long time. He was right about me, I suppose. But I wonder if I can ever forgive him for it. No man wants to know that the love in him is sterile.

To reject the way of a lifetime is not easy. It must have been hard for Kwabena, and now in another way it is hard for me. But at last I know, although I shall never be able to admit it to him. It was only I who could afford to love the old Africa. Its enchantment had touched me, its suffering — never. Even my fright had stopped this side of pain. I had always been the dreamer who knew he could waken at will, the tourist who wanted antique quaintness to remain unchanged.

We were conquerors in Africa, we Europeans. Some despised her, that bedraggled queen we had unthroned, and some loved her for her still-raging magnificence, her old wisdom. But all of us sought to force our will upon her.

My father thought he was bringing Salvation to Africa. I do not any longer know what salvation is. I only know that one man cannot find it for another man, and one land cannot bring it to another.

Africa, old withered bones, mouldy splendour under a red umbrella, you will dance again, this time to a new song.

But for me it is different. Now the wind in the casuarina trees is only a wind. The drums at night are only men pounding on skins stretched over wood. The Drummer of all the world is gone. He no longer drums himself, for me. A spider is only an insect, and not the child of Ananse. A deserted hut on the shore is only a heap of mud and dried palm leaves. Death no longer keeps such a simple establishment.

I shall be leaving soon. Leaving the surf that stretches up long white fingers to clutch the brown land. The fetid village enclosed and darkened by a green sky of overhanging palm trees. The giant heartbeat of the night drums. The flame tree whose beauty is suddenly splendid — and short-lived — like the beauty of African women. The little girl dancing with her shadow in the stifling streets. The child sleeping, unmindful, while flies caress his eyes and mouth with the small bright wings of decay. The squalor, the exultation, the pain. I shall be leaving it all.

But — oh Kwabena, do you think I will ever forget?

# The Perfume Sea

'No question of it,' Mr. Archipelago said, delicately snipping a wisp of hair. 'I am flotsam.'

'Not jetsam?' Mrs. Webley-Pryce asked, blinking sharply watchful eyes as the scissored shreds fell down onto her face. 'I always get the two confused.'

Outside, the small town was growing sluggish under the sedative sun of late morning. The one-footed beggar who squatted beside Mr. Archipelago's door had gone to sleep on the splintery wooden steps. Past the turquoise-and-red façade of Cowasjee's Silk Bazaar, in the rancid and shadowy room, the shrivelled Parsee sat, only half awake, folding a length of sari cloth and letting the silk slip through his fingers as he dreamed of a town in India, no less ill-smelling and dirty than this African one, but filled with the faces and speech of home. At the shop of K. Tachie (General Merchant), Tachie himself sat beside his cash register, surrounded by boxes and barrels. Kinglike, he perched on a high stool and roared abuse at his court of counter-clerks, while at the same time he managed to gulp a lurid carbonated grape beverage called Doko-Doko. At the Africa Star Chemists, a young shopgirl dozed, propping her brown arms against a carton of Seven Seas codliver oil. Down the street, in the Paradise Chop-Bar, a young man recalled those arms as he sloshed a rag over the tables in preparation for the customers who would soon be lifting the striped bedspread that hung across the doorway and shouting for beer and

*kenkey*. In the Government Agent's office, and in the offices
of Bridgeford & Knight, Exporters-Importers, Englishmen
sighed and wilted and saw from their watches that they could
not yet legitimately leave for lunch. Pariah dogs on the
road snarled over a cat corpse; then, panting, tongues
dribbling, defeated by sun, they crawled back to a shaded
corner, where their scabrous hides were fondled by an old
man in a hashish dream. Footsteps on the cracked and
scorching pavement lagged. Even the brisk shoes of white
men slackened and slowed. The market women walked
tiredly, their headtrays heavy, their bare feet pressing the
warm dust into ripples and dunes. Babies slung on their
mothers' backs allowed their heads to loll forward and
whimpered at the sweat that made sticky their faces. A
donkey brayed disconsolately. Voices droned low. Laughter
like melted honey poured slowly. Down by the shore, under
a few scattered palm trees, the wives of fishermen drowsed
over their net-mending. Only the children, the fire and
gleam of them greater even than the harsh glint of sun,
continued to leap and shout as before.

Mr. Archipelago riffled a comb through the winter straw
of the lady's hair, and nuzzled his rotundity against her arm
for the lightly spiteful pleasure of feeling her recoil. He
moved back a decent pace. Under his white smock, the red
and gold brocade waistcoat quivered with his belly's silent
laughter.

'Flotsam, dear lady,' he said. 'I looked it up in the Concise Oxford.'

On the other side of the room, Doree glanced up from the
lustrous green with which she was enamelling the fingernails
of her thin white hands, knuckle-swollen from years of
cleansing other women's hair. Her mild myopic eyes were
impressed, even awed. Her mouth, painted to emulate
hardness, opened in a soft spontaneous astonishment.

'Can you beat it?' she said. 'He looks up words all the time, and laughs like the dickens. I used to read the telephone book sometimes, in the nights, and wonder about those names and if they all belonged to real people, living somewhere, you know, and doing something. But I never laughed. What'd it say for flotsam, Archipelago?'

Mr. Archipelago beamed. His shiny eyes were green as malachite. He stood on tiptoe, a plump pouter-pigeon of a man, puffing out his chest until the brocade waistcoat swelled. His hair, black as ripe olives, he only touched from time to time with pomade, but it gave the impression of having been crimped and perfumed.

'Wreckage found floating,' he said proudly. 'It said — "wreckage found floating".'

'The very thing!' Doree cried, clapping her hands, but Mrs. Webley-Pryce looked aloof because she did not understand.

The air in the shop was syrupy with heat and perfume, and the odd puff of breeze that came in through the one window seemed to be the exhalation of a celestial fire-eater. Mrs. Webley-Pryce, feeling the perspiration soaking through her linen dress, wriggled uncomfortably in her chair and tried to close her eyes to the unseemly and possibly septic litter all around her. The shop was not really dirty, although to the fastidious English minds of lady customers it appeared so. Doree swept it faithfully every evening at closing time, but as her sight was so poor and she would not wear glasses, she often missed fragments of hair which gradually mingled with dust and formed themselves into small tangled balls of grey and hazelnut brown and bottled blonde. The curl-papers, too, had an uncanny way of escaping and drifting around the room like leaves fallen from some rare tree. Doree chain-smoked, so the ashtrays were nearly always full. Mr.

Archipelago found her cigarette-butts charming, each with its orange kiss mark from the wide mouth he had never touched. But the ladies did not share his perception; they pushed the ashtrays away impatiently, hintingly, until with a sigh he emptied them into a wastepaper-basket and watched the ashes flutter like grey flakes of dandruff.

Sweat was gathering on Mr. Archipelago's smooth forehead, and his fingers were becoming slippery around the comb and scissors.

'The morning beer,' he announced. 'It is now time. For you, as well, Mrs. Webley-Pryce?'

'I think not, thanks,' she replied coldly. 'Nothing before sundown is my rule. Can't you hurry a little, Mr. Archipelago? At this rate it'll be midnight before my perm is finished.'

'Pardon, pardon,' said Mr. Archipelago, tilting the beer bottle. 'One moment, and we fly to work. Like birds on the wing.'

Out came the solutions, the flasks of pink and mauve liquid, the odour of ammonia competing with the coarse creamy perfumes. Out came clamps and pins and curl-papers, the jumbled contents of a dozen shelves and cupboards. In the midst of the debris, stirring it all like a magic potion, stood Mr. Archipelago, a fat and frantic wizard, refreshing himself occasionally with Dutch ale. He darted over to the mainstay of his alchemist's laboratory, an elaborate arrangement of electrically-heated metal rods, on which he placed the heavy clamps. He waited, arms folded, until the whole dangerous mechanism achieved the dull mysterious fire which was to turn Mrs. Webley-Pryce's base metal, as it were, to gold.

'You should sell that lot,' Mrs. Webley-Pryce remarked. 'Any museum in Europe would give you a good price.'

At once he was on the defensive, his pride hurt.

'Let me tell you, dear lady, there isn't one beauty salon in the whole of Europe could give you a perm like this one does.'

'I don't doubt that for one instant,' she said with a short laugh.

Doree stood up, an emaciated yellow and white bird, a tall gaunt crane, her hair clinging like wet feathers around her squeezed-narrow shoulders. With her long hesitant stride she walked across the room, and held out her green lacquered hands.

'Sea pearl,' she said. 'Kind of different, anyhow. Africa Star Chemists just got it in. Like it?'

Shuddering slightly, Mrs. Webley-Pryce conceded that it was very handsome.

'Pearl reminds me,' Mr. Archipelago said, returning to cheerfulness, 'the Concise Oxford stated another thing for flotsam.'

Mrs. Webley-Pryce looked at him with open curiosity and begged decorously to be told. Mr. Archipelago applied a dab of spit to a finger and casually tested the heat of the clamps.

'Precisely, it said "oyster-spawn". Think of that. Oyster-spawn. And that is me, too, eh?'

Doree laughed until she began to cough, and he frowned at her, for they were both worried by this cough and she could not stop smoking for more than an hour at a time.

'I don't see——' Mrs. Webley-Pryce probed.

'A little joke,' Mr. Archipelago explained. 'Not a very good one, perhaps, but we must do the best with what we have. My father, as I may have told you, was an Armenian sailor.'

'Oh yes,' Mrs. Webley-Pryce said, disappointed, holding

her breath as he placed the first hot clamp on her tightly wound-up hair, 'I believe you did mention it. Odd — Archipelago never seems like an Armenian name to me, somehow.'

'It isn't.'

'Oh?'

Mr. Archipelago smiled. He enjoyed talking about himself. He allowed himself a degree of pride in the fact that no one could ever be sure where the truth ended and the tinted unreality began. With the Englishmen to whom he administered haircuts, Mr. Archipelago talked sparingly. They seemed glum and taciturn to him, or else overly robust, with a kind of dogged heartiness that made him at once wary. But with the lady customers it was a different matter. He had a genuine sympathy for them. He did not chide, even to himself, their hunger. If one went empty for long enough, one became hungry. His tales were the manna with which it was his pleasure to nourish his lady customers. Also, he was shrewd. He knew that his conversation was an attraction, no less than the fact that he was the only hairdresser within a hundred miles; it was his defence against that noxious invention, the home-permanent.

'It would have been difficult for my mother to give me my father's name,' he said, 'as she never knew it. She was — I may have mentioned — an Italian girl. She worked in a wineshop in Genoa. It smelled of Barbera and stale fish and — things you would prefer I did not speak about. I grew up there. That Genoa! Never go there. A port town, a sailors' town. The most saddening city in the world, I think. The ships are always mourning. You hear those wailing voices even in your sleep. The only place I ever liked in all Genoa was the Staglieno cemetery, up on the hills. I used to go there and sit beside the tombs of the rich, a small fat boy with the white marble angels — so compassionate they looked, and so costly — I believed then that each was the likeness of a lady buried beneath. Then I would look over at the fields of rented graves nearby. The poor rent graves for one, two, five years — I can't remember exactly. The body must be taken out if the rent cannot be paid. In death, as in life, the rent must always be paid.'

'How horrible,' Mrs. Webley-Pryce said. 'Look here — are you sure this clamp isn't too hot? I think it's burning my neck. Oh thanks, that's better. It's your mother's name, then?'

Doree glared. Mrs. Webley-Pryce was the wife of the Government Agent, but she had married late and had lived in Africa only one year — she had not yet learned that however eager one might be, the questions must always be judicious, careful. But Mr. Archipelago was bland. He did not mind the curiosity of his lady customers.

'No, dear lady, it is not her name. Why should a person not pick his own name? It sounds Italian. I liked it. It suits me. Do you know what it means?'

'Well, of course,' Mrs. Webley-Pryce said uncertainly. 'An archipelago is — well, it's——'

'A sea with many islands, according to the Concise Oxford. That has been my life. A sea with many islands.'

'This is one of them, I suppose?'

'The most enduring so far,' he replied. 'Twelve years I have been here.'

'Really? That's a long time. You'll go back, though, someday?'

'I have no wish to go back,' Mr. Archipelago answered offhandedly. 'I would like to die here and be buried in my own garden. Perhaps if I were buried under the wild orchids they would grow better. I have tried every other kind of fertilizer.'

'You can't be serious,' Mrs. Webley-Pryce protested. 'About not going back, I mean.'

'Why not? I like it here.'

'But it's so far away from everything. So far from home.'

'For you, perhaps,' Mr. Archipelago said. 'But then, you are not a true expatriate. You may stay twenty years, but you are a visitor. Your husband, though — does he anticipate with pleasure the time when he will retire and go back to England?'

She looked at him in surprise.

'No — he dreads it, as a matter of fact. That's understandable, though. His work is here, his whole life. He's been here a long time, too, you know. But it's rather different. He was sent out here. He had to come.'

'Did he?'

'Of course,' she said. 'If a person goes in for colonial administration, he must go to a colony, mustn't he?'

'Indeed he must,' Mr. Archipelago said agreeably. 'If he goes in for colonial administration, it is the logical step.'

'But for a hairdresser,' she said, 'it's not the sort of place most people would exactly choose——'

'Aha — now we come to it. You are one of those who believe I did not choose to come here, then? That I was, perhaps, forced to leave my own country?'

'I didn't mean that——' Mrs. Webley-Pryce floundered. 'And I suppose it's a blessing for the European women that there's someone in a tiny station like this who can do hair——'

'Even if it is only Archipelago with his equipment that belongs in a museum. Well, well. Tell me, madam — what is the current theory about me? It changes, you know. This interests me greatly. No, please — I am not offended. You must not think so. Only curious, just as you are curious about me. Once, I remember, I was said to have been a counterfeiter. Another time, I had deserted my wife and family. Through the years, it has been this and that. Perhaps one of them is true. Or perhaps not. To maintain dignity, one must have at least one secret — don't you agree?'

Mrs. Webley-Pryce gave him a sideways glance.

'I have heard,' she admitted, 'about there having been some trouble. I'm sure it couldn't have been true, though——'

But Mr. Archipelago neither confirmed nor denied. He tested a curl, and finding it satisfactory, he began to remove the mass of iron from the hair. Mrs. Webley-Pryce, embarrassed by his silence, turned to Doree, who was applying bleach to her own long yellow hair.

'Speaking of names, I've always meant to ask you about yours, Doree. It's rather unusual, isn't it?'

'Yeh,' Doree said, through her mane. 'I used to be Doreen.'

'Oh?' Once more the lilt in the voice of the huntress.

Doree spoke of herself rarely. She did not possess Mr. Archipelago's skill or his need, and when she talked about her own life she usually blurted unwillingly the straight facts because she could not think of anything else to say. Her few fabrications were obvious; she wrenched them out aggressively, knowing no one would believe her. Now she was caught off guard.

'I had my own shop once,' she said in her gentle rasping voice. 'It had a sign up — DOREEN/BEAUTY IN-CORPORATED. Classy. Done in those gilt letters. You buy them separately and stick them up. The state of my dough wasn't so classy, though. So when the goddam "N" fell off, I figured it was cheaper to change my name to fit the sign.'

Gratified, Mrs. Webley-Pryce tittered.

'And just where was your shop?'

Now it was Mr. Archipelago's turn to glare. It was permissible to question him minutely, but not Doree. Customers were supposed to understand this rule. He saw Doree's eyes turn vague, and he longed to touch her hand, to comfort and reassure her. But it was better not to do such a thing. He did not want her to misunderstand his devotion, or to be in any way alarmed by a realization of its existence. Instead, he slithered a still-hot clamp down on Mrs. Webley-Pryce's neck, causing a faint smell of singed skin and a gasp of pain.

'It was in Montreal, if you must know,' Doree said harshly.

Last time someone asked, the answer was Chicago, and once, daringly, Mexico City. Mr. Archipelago himself did not know. She had simply walked into his shop one day, and where she came from, or why, did not matter to him. When they were alone, he and Doree never questioned each other. Their evening conversation was of the day's small happenings.

'Montreal——' Mrs. Webley-Pryce said thoughtfully. 'Perhaps David and I will go to some place like that. There's nothing much left for administrative men in England.'

'You're leaving?' Mr. Archipelago asked, startled. 'You're leaving Africa?'

'Yes, of course — that's what I meant when I said David dreaded — didn't you know?'

'But — why?' he asked in dismay, for recently she had been patronizing the shop regularly. 'Why?'

'Dear me,' she said, with an effort at brightness, 'you are behind the times, aren't you? Didn't you know this colony will be self-governing soon? They don't want us here any more.'

'I knew it was coming,' Mr. Archipelago said, 'but I had not realized it was so soon. Strange. I read the newspapers. I talk with Mr. Tachie, my landlord, who is a very political man. But — ah well, I tend my garden, and try to get wild orchids to grow here beside the sea, where the soil is really much too sandy for them, and I do the ladies' hair and drink beer and talk to Doree. I think nothing will ever change in this place — so insignificant, surely God will forget about it and let it be. But not so. How many will be going?'

'Oh, I don't know — most of the Europeans in government service — perhaps all. I expect some of those in trade will remain.'

Her tone implied that Mr. Archipelago would be left with a collection of lepers, probably hairless.

'There are not enough of them,' he murmured, 'to keep me in business.'

He groped on a shelf for another beer and opened it with perspiring hands. He thought of the sign outside his establishment. Not a gilt-lettered sign, to be sure, but nicely done in black and aquamarine, with elegant spidery letters:

ARCHIPELAGO

English-Style Barber

European Ladies' Hairdresser

'A sea with many islands,' he said, addressing only himself. 'Sometimes it happens that a person discovers he has built his house upon an island that is sinking.'

A large green house by the shore sheltered Mr. Archipelago. Once he had lived there alone, but for the past five years he had not been alone. Doree's presence in his house had been, he knew, a popular topic of discussion at the morning coffee parties in the European cantonment. He did not blame the ladies for talking, but it did give him a certain satisfaction to know that their actual information on the subject was extremely slight. Neither he nor Doree had ever spoken of their domestic arrangements to customers. And their cook-steward, Attah, under the impression that he was protecting his employers' reputations, had never told a living soul that the two shared only living and dining-rooms and that neither had ever entered the private apartments of the other.

Mr. Archipelago's dwelling was not close either to the white cantonment or to the African houses. It was off by itself, on a jut of land overlooking a small bay. The sprawling overgrown garden was surrounded by a high green wall which enabled Mr. Archipelago in the late afternoons to work outside clad only in his underwear and a round white linen hat. He had no wish to tame the garden, which was a profusion of elephant grass, drooping casuarina trees, frowsy banana palms, slender paw-paw, and all manner of flowering shrubs — hibiscus, purple bougainvillaea, and the white Rose of Sharon, whose blossoms turned to deep blush as they died. Into this cherished disorder, Mr. Archipelago carefully introduced wild orchids, which never survived for long, and clumps of hardy canna lilies that bloomed pink and ragged. He grew pineapples, too, and daily prodded angrily with his stick at the speared clusters which consistently refused to bear fruit the size of that sold for a mere shilling in the African market. The favourite of his domain, however, was the sensitive plant, an earth vine which, if its leaves were touched even lightly, would softly and stubbornly close. Mr. Archipelago liked to watch the sensitive plant's closing. Nothing in this world could stop its self-containment; it was not to be bribed or cajoled; it had integrity. But he

31

seldom touched it, for the silent and seemingly conscious inturning of each leaf made him feel clumsy and lacking in manners.

Just as the garden was Mr. Archipelago's special province, so the long verandah was Doree's. Here flew, uncaged, four grey African parrots, their wings tipped with scarlet. Sometimes they departed for a while, and sulked in the branches of the frangipani tree. Doree never attempted to catch them, nor would she even lure them with seeds or snails. Mr. Archipelago believed she almost wished one of them would find itself able to leave the sanctuary and return to the forest. But they had lived inside the verandah for too long. They could not have fended for themselves, and they must have known it. They always came back to be fed.

Mr. Archipelago could well have done without some of the visitors to Doree's menagerie. He did not mind the little geckos that clung transparent to the walls, like lizards of glass, nor the paunchy toads whose tongues hunted the iridescent green flies. But the trays containing all the morsels which Doree imagined to be choice fare for spiders — these sometimes drew scorpions and once a puff-adder. Doree would not kill even the lethal guests. She shooed them carefully out at broom-point, assuring the sweating Mr. Archipelago that they had no wish to harm anyone — they wanted only to be shown how to escape. Perhaps her faith protected her, or her lack of fear, for within her sanctuary no live thing seemed to her to be threatening. In any event, she had never been touched by the venom of wild creatures.

She had a chameleon, too, of which she was extremely fond, an eerie bright green reptile with huge eyes and a long tail curled up like a tape-measure. Mr. Archipelago once ventured to suggest that she might find a prettier pet. Doree's large pale eyes squinted at him reproachfully.

'What do you want me to do, anyway? Conk him on the head because he's not a goddamn butterfly?'

Mr. Archipelago, appalled at his blunder, answered humbly.

'Am I God, that I should judge a creature? It is not the chameleon that is ugly, but I, for thinking him so. And now, looking at him more carefully, and seeing his skin grow darker against that dark branch where he is, I can see that he must be appreciated according to his own qualities, and not compared with butterflies, who are no doubt gaudy but who do not possess this interesting ability. You are right — he is beautiful.'

'I don't get it,' Doree said. 'I never said he was beautiful.'

'Well, then, I did. I do.'

'You're what they call "round the bend", Archipelago. Never mind. Maybe so am I.'

'We suit each other,' he replied.

The evenings were spent quietly. They did not go out anywhere, nor did they entertain. They had always been considered socially non-existent by the European community, while in the Africans' view they were standard Europeans and therefore apart. Mr. Archipelago and Doree did not mind. They preferred their own company. Mr. Archipelago possessed a gramophone which vied in antiquity with the wave-machine. Often after dinner he played through his entire repertoire of fourteen records, mainly Italian opera. He particularly liked to listen to Pagliacci, in order to criticize it.

'Hear that!' he would cry to the inattentive Doree. 'How sorry he is for himself! A storm of the heart — what a buffoon. Do you know his real tragedy? Not that he had to laugh when his heart was breaking — that is a commonplace. No — the unfortunate fact is that he really is a clown. Even in his desolation. A clown.'

Doree, sitting on the mock-Persian carpet whose richness was not lessened for her by its label 'Made in Brussels', would placidly continue to talk to her two favourite parrots. She called them Brasso and Silvo, and Mr. Archipelago understood that this christening was meant as a compliment to him, these being the closest to Italian names she could manage.

After work, Mr. Archipelago's scarlet waistcoat was discarded in favour of an impressive smoking-jacket. It was a pale bluish-green Indian brocade, and the small cockerels on it were worked in thread of gold. Although it was a rather warm garment, Mr. Archipelago suffered his sweat for the sake of magnificence.

'You look just like one of those what-d'you-call-'ems — you know, sultans,' Doree had once said admiringly.

He remembered the remark each evening when he donned the jacket. Momentarily endowed with the hauteur of Haroun al Raschid, he would saunter nonchalantly through the Baghdad of his own living-room.

Frequently they brought out their perfumes, of which they had a great variety, bottles and flagons of all colours and intricate shapes — crowns and hearts and flowers, diamonded, bubbled, baubled, angular and smooth. The game was to see how many could be identified by smell alone, the vessel masked, before the senses began to flag. Mr. Archipelago did not love the perfumes for themselves alone, nor even for their ability to cover the coarse reek of life. Each one, sniffed like snuff, conjured up for him a throng of waltzing ladies, whirling and spinning eternally on floors of light, their grey gowns swaying, ladies of gentle dust.

Mr. Archipelago and Doree got along well with their one servant. Attah regularly told them the gossip of the town, although they cared about it not at all. He tended to be cantankerous; he would not be argued with; he served for meals the dishes of his own choice. They accepted him philosophically, but on one point they were adamant. They would not allow Attah's wife and family to live within the walls of the compound. The family lived, instead, in the town. Mr. Archipelago and Doree never ceased to feel sorry about this separation, but they could not help it. They could not have endured to have the voices of children threatening their achieved and fragile quiet.

Outside the green wall, however, and far from the sugared humidity of the small shop, events occurred. Governments made reports and politicians made speeches. Votes were cast. Supporters cheered and opponents jeered. Flags changed, and newspaper men typed furiously, recording history to meet a deadline. Along the shore, loin-clothed fishermen, their feet firm in the wet sand, grinned and shrugged, knowing they would continue to burn their muscles like quick torches, soon consumed, in the sea-grappling that claimed them now as always, but sensing, too, that the land in which they set their returning feet was new as well as old, and that they, unchanged, were new with it.

In the town, the white men began to depart one by one, as their posts were filled by Africans. And in Mr. Archipelago's shop, the whirr of the hair-dryer was heard less and less.

Late one night Doree came downstairs in her housecoat, an unheard-of thing for her. Mr. Archipelago was sitting like a gloomy toad in his high-backed wicker armchair. He glanced up in surprise.

'It's my imagination again,' she said. 'It's been acting up.'

Doree suffered periodic attacks of imagination, like indigestion or migraine. She spoke of it always as though it were an affliction of a specific organ, as indeed it was, for

her phrenology charts placed the imagination slightly above
the forehead, on the right side. Mr. Archipelago brought
another wicker chair for her and gave her a little creme-de-
cacao in her favourite liqueur glass, a blinding snow-shadow
blue, frosted with edelweiss.

'It's two months,' Doree said, sipping, 'since the Webley-
Pryces left. I don't know how many are gone now. Almost
all, I guess. I heard today that Bridgeford & Knight are
putting in an African manager. The last perm we gave was
nearly a month ago. This week only three haircuts and
one shampoo-and-set. Archipelago — what are we going
to do?'

He looked at her dumbly. He could give her no comfort.

'Could we go someplace else?' she went on. 'Sierra
Leone? Liberia?'

'I have thought of that,' he said. 'Yes, perhaps we shall
have to consider it.'

They both knew they did not have sufficient money to
take them anywhere else.

'Please——' He hesitated. 'You must not be upset, or I
cannot speak at all——'

'Go on,' she said roughly. 'What is it?'

'Did you know,' Mr. Archipelago questioned sadly, 'that
if an expatriate is without funds, he can go to the consulate
of his country, and they will send him back?'

She lowered her head. Her yellow hair, loose, fell like
unravelled wool around her, scarfing the bony pallor of
her face.

'I've heard that — yes.'

Mr. Archipelago pushed away his creme-de-cacao, the
sweetness of which had begun to nauseate him. His
incongruously small feet in their embroidered slippers
pattered across the concrete floor. He returned with
Dutch ale.

'I have never asked,' he said. 'And you have never asked, and now I must break the rule. Could you go back? Could you, Doree, if there was nothing else to do?'

Doree lit a cigarette from the end of the last one.

'No,' she replied in a steady, strained voice. 'Not even if there was nothing else to do.'

'Are you sure?'

'My God——' she said. 'Yes, I'm sure all right.'

Mr. Archipelago did not ask why. He brought his hands together in a staccato clap.

'Good. We know where we stand. Enough of this, then.'

'No,' she said. 'What about you?'

'It is very awkward,' he said, 'but unfortunately I cannot go back, either.'

She did not enquire further. For her, too, his word was sufficient.

'But Archipelago, the Africans won't let us stay if we're broke. We're not their responsibility——'

'Wait——' Mr. Archipelago said. 'I have just remembered something.'

Beside his chair, a carved wooden elephant bore a small table on its back. Mr. Archipelago groped underneath and finally opened a compartment in the beast's belly. He took out an object wrapped in tissue paper.

'I have always liked this elephant,' he said. 'See — a concealed hiding place. Very cloak-and-dagger. A treasure — no, a toy — such as Columbus might have brought back from his travels. He was once in West Africa, you know, as a young seaman, at one of the old slave-castles not far from here. And he, also, came from Genoa. Well, well. There the similarity ends. This necklace is one I bought many years ago. I have always saved it. I thought I was being very provident — putting away one gold necklace to insure me against disaster. It is locally made — crude,

37

as you can see, but heavy. Ashanti gold, and quite valuable.'

Doree looked at it without interest.

'Very nice,' she said. 'But we can't live off that forever.'

'No, but it will give you enough money to live in the city until you find work. More Europeans will be staying there, no doubt, and we know there are several beauty salons. At least it is a chance. For me, the worst would be for you not to have any chance——'

Mr. Archipelago perceived that he had revealed too much. He squirmed and sweated, fearful that she would misunderstand. But when he looked at her, he saw in her eyes not alarm but surprise.

'The necklace and all——' Doree said slowly. 'You'd do that — for me?'

Mr. Archipelago forgot about himself in the urgency of convincing her.

'For you, Doree,' he said. 'Of course, for you. If only it were more——'

'But — it's everything——'

'Yes, everything,' he said bitterly. 'All I have to offer. A fragment of gold.'

'I want you to know,' she said, her voice rough with tears, 'I want you to know I'm glad you offered. Now put the necklace back in the elephant and let's leave it there. We may need it worse, later.'

'You won't take it?' he cried. 'Why not?'

'Because you haven't told me yet what's gonna happen to you,' Doree said. 'And anyway, I don't want to go to another place.'

He could not speak. She hurried on.

'If I wasn't here,' she said, with a trembling and apologetic laugh, 'who'd remind you to put on your hat in the boiling sun? Who'd guess the perfumes with you?'

'I would miss you, of course,' he said in a low voice. 'I would miss you a great deal.'

She turned on him, almost angrily.

'Don't you think I'd miss you?' she cried. 'Don't you know how it would be — for me?'

They stared at each other, wide-eyed, incredulous. Mr. Archipelago lived through one instant of unreasonable and terrifying hope. Then, abruptly, he became once more aware of himself, oddly swathed in Indian brocade and holding in his fat perspiring hands an ale-glass and a gold necklace.

Doree's eyes, too, had become distant and withdrawn. She was twisting a sweat-lank strand of her hair around one wrist.

'We're getting ourselves into a stew over nothing,' she said at last. 'Nobody's gonna be leaving. Everything will be just the same as always. Listen, Archipelago, I got a hunch we're due for a lucky break. I'm sure of it. Once I met a spiritualist — a nice old dame — I really went for that ouija-board stuff in those days — well, she told me I had natural ability. I had the right kind of an aura. Yeh, sure it's phony, I know that. But my hunches are hardly ever wrong. Shall we shake on it?'

Gravely, they shook hands and drank to the lucky break. Mr. Archipelago began to tell stories about the tourists with whom, as a boy, he used to practise his shaky English, and how nervous they always were of getting goat's milk in their tea.

They talked until the pressure lamp spluttered low and the floor beneath it was littered with the beige and broken wings of moths. Doree went upstairs then, singing a snatch of an African highlife tune in her warm raw voice. But later, Mr. Archipelago, queasy with beer and insomnia, heard once again the sound that used to be so frequent when she first came to this house, her deep and terrible crying in her sleep.

They had had no customers at all for a fortnight, but still they opened the shop each morning and waited until exactly four o'clock to close it. One morning Tachie strolled in, prosperous in a new royal blue cloth infuriatingly patterned with golden coins. He was a large man; the warm room with its sweet cloying air seemed too small to hold his brown ox-shoulders, his outflung arms, his great drum of a voice.

'Mistah Arch'pelago, why you humbug me? Two month, and nevah one penny I getting. You t'ink I rich too much? You t'ink I no need for dis money?'

Mr. Archipelago, standing beside his idle transmutation machine and sagging gradually like a scarlet balloon with the air sinking out of it, made one unhopeful effort at distracting Tachie.

'Can I offer you a beer, Mr. Tachie? A light refreshing ale at this time of day——'

Tachie grimaced.

'You t'ink I drink beer wey come from my shop an' nevah been pay at all? No, I t'ank you. I no drink dis beer — he too cost, for me. Mistah Arch'pelago, you trouble me too much. What we do, eh?'

Mr. Archipelago's skin looked sallower than usual. His eyes were dull and even his crisp neat hair had become limp. Doree held out large and pitying hands towards him, but she could not speak.

'In life as in death, the rent must be paid,' he said. 'We have been dreaming, dreaming, while the world moved on, and now we waken to find it so changed we do not know what to do. We wanted only to stay and not to harm anyone, but of course you are right, Mr. Tachie, to remind us it is not enough. One must always have a product to sell that someone wants to buy. We do not have much of anything any more, but we will try to pay our debts before we move on. Perhaps a museum will buy my wave-machine after all.'

Doree put her hands over her face, and Tachie, horrified, looked from one to the other, still unable to grasp the actuality of their despair.

'You no got money — at all? De time wey I come for you shop, I anger too much for you. Now angry can no stay for me. My friend, I sorry. Befoah God, I too sorry. But what I can do?'

'It is not your concern,' Mr. Archipelago said with dignity. 'We do not expect you to let us stay. We are not appealing for charity.'

But Tachie could not stop justifying himself.

'I look-a de shop, I see Eur'pean womans all dey gone, I see you no got lucky. But I no savvy propra. I t'ink you got money you put for bank. Now I see wit' my eye you tell me true, you no got nothing. But what I can do? I no be rich man. I got shop, I got dis place. But I got plenty plenty family, all dey come for me, all dey say "Tachie, why you no give we more?" My own pickin dey trouble me too much. My daughtah Mercy, she big girl, all time she saying "meka you buy for me one small new cloth, meka you buy powdah for face, meka you buy shoe same city girl dey wear it——" '

Mr. Archipelago peered sharply at Tachie.

'Your daughter — facepowder — shoes — she, too, is changed——'

'I tell you true. Mistah Arch'pelago, why you're looking so?'

The balloon that was Mr. Archipelago suddenly became re-inflated. He began to spin on one foot, whistled a Viennese waltz, bounced across the room, grasped Doree's hand, drew her into his comprehension and his laughter. Together they waltzed, absurd, relieved, triumphant.

'Mr. Tachie, you are a bringer of miracles!' Mr. Archipelago cried. 'There it was, all the time, and we did not see it. We, even we, Doree, will make history — you will see.'

Tachie frowned, bewildered.

'I see it happen so, for white men, wen dey stay too long for dis place. Dey crez'. Mistah Arch'pelago, meka you drink some small beer. Den you head he come fine.'

'No, no, not beer,' Mr. Archipelago replied, puffing out his waistcoat. 'Here — a flask kept for medicinal purposes or special celebrations. A brandy, Mr. Tachie! A brandy for the history-makers!'

He and Doree laughed until they were weak. And Tachie, still not understanding, but pleased that they were in some lunatic fashion pleased, finally laughed with them and consented to drink the unpaid-for brandy.

That evening they painted the new sign. They worked until midnight, with tins and brushes spread out on the dining-room table, while Brasso and Silvo squawked and stared. The sign was black and gilt, done in optimistically plump lettering:

### ARCHIPELAGO & DOREE
Barbershop
All-Beauty Salon
African Ladies A Speciality

The men of the town continued, not unnaturally, to have their hair cut by the African barbers who plied their trade under the *niim* tree in the market. The African women, however, showed great interest in the new sign. They gathered in little groups and examined it. The girls who had attended school read the words aloud to their mothers and aunts. They murmured together. Their laughter came in soft gusts, like the sound of the wind through the casuarina branches. But not one of them would enter the shop.

Several times Mr. Archipelago saw faces peeping in at the window, scrutinizing every detail of the room. But as soon as he looked, the curious ones lowered their eyes and quickly walked away.

The hair-straightening equipment (obtained second-hand, and on credit, through Tachie) remained unused. Each day Doree dusted and set back on the counter the unopened packets and jars of dusky powder and cinnamon-brown make-up base which she had hurriedly ordered from the city when she discovered that the Africa Star Chemists, slightly behind the times, sold only shades of ivory and peach.

Another week, and still no customers. Then one morning, as Mr. Archipelago was opening his second bottle of Dutch ale, Mercy Tachie walked in.

'Please, Mr. Archipelago——' she began hesitantly. 'I am thinking to come here for some time, but I am not sure what I should do. We have never had such a place in our town before, you see. So all of us are looking, but no one wishes to be the first. Then my father, he said to me today that I should be the first, because if you are having no customers, he will never be getting his money from you.'

Mercy was about sixteen. She was clad in traditional cloth, but her face was thickly daubed with a pale powder that obscured her healthy skin. She stood perfectly still in the centre of the room, her hands clasped in front of her, her face expressionless. Mr. Archipelago looked in admiration at the placidity of her features, a repose which he knew concealed an extreme nervousness and perhaps even panic, for in her life there had not been many unfamiliar things. He motioned her to a chair, and she sat down woodenly.

'Good,' he said. 'Doree and I welcome you. Now — can you help us to know, a little, the way you want to look?'

Mercy's splendid eyes were blank no longer; they turned to him appealingly.

'I would like to look like a city girl, please,' Mercy Tachie said. 'That is what I would like the most.'

'A city girl——' Mr. Archipelago ran a finger lightly over the chalky powder on her face. 'That is why you wear this mask, eh? Ladies never know when they are beautiful — strange. They must be chic — God is not a good enough craftsman. Fortunate, I suppose, for us. Ah well. Yes, we will make you look like a city girl, if that is what you would like the most.'

Confused by his sigh and smile, Mercy felt compelled to explain herself.

'I was going for seven years to the mission school here, you see, and all my life I am never knowing any place outside this town. But someday, maybe, I will be living in some big place, and if so, I would not want to feel like a bushgirl. So I wish to know how it is proper to have my hair, and what to do for the face. You do not think I am foolish?'

Mr. Archipelago shook his head.

'I think the whole world is foolish,' he said. 'But you are no more foolish than anyone else, and a great deal less so than many.'

Doree, who felt his reply to be unsatisfactory, placed her splay-hands on the girl's dark wiry hair.

'Not to worry,' she said. 'We'll straighten your hair just enough to set it and style it. We'll take that goop off your face. You got lovely skin — not a wrinkle — you shouldn't cover it up like that. We'll give you a complete make-up job. Doll, you'll be a queen.'

And Mercy Tachie, her eyes trusting, smiled.

'Do you think so? Do you really think it will be so?'

The air was redolent once more with the potions and unguents, the lotions and shampoos and lacquers, the nostril-pinching pungency of ammonia and the fragrance of bottled colognes. The snik-snik-snik of Mr. Archipelago's scissors was the theme of a small-scale symphony; overtones and undertones were provided by the throb of the dryer and the strident blues-chanting of Doree as she paced the room like a priestess. Mercy began to relax.

'My friends, they also would like to come here, I think, if they like the way I will look,' she confided. 'Mr. Archipelago, you will be staying here? You will not be leaving now?'

'Perhaps we will be staying,' he said. 'We must wait and see if your friends like the way you look.'

Mercy pursed her lips pensively.

'Will you not go back, someday,' she ventured, 'to your own country? For the sake of your family?'

Doree glared, but Mr. Archipelago was bland. He had never minded the curiosity of his lady customers.

'The charming questions,' he said. 'They begin again. Good. No — I have no family.'

'Oh, I thought it must be so!' Mercy cried.

'I beg your pardon?'

Once more she became self-conscious. She folded her hands and looked at the floor.

'I have heard,' she said apologetically, 'that you were leaving your own country many years ago because you had some bad trouble — maybe because you thought you might go to prison. But I am never believing that story, truly. Always I think you had some different kind of trouble. My

aunt Abenaa, you know, she lost all her family — husband
and three children — when their house burned down, and
after that she left her village and came to live here, in my
father's house, and never again will she go to that village.'

'You think it was that way, for me?' he said.

'I think it — yes.'

Mr. Archipelago straightened his waistcoat over his belly.
In his eyes there appeared momentarily a certain sadness, a
certain regret. But when he replied, his voice expressed
nothing except a faint acceptable tenderness.

'You are kind. Perhaps the kindest of all my ladies.'

At last the ritual was accomplished, and Mercy Tachie
looked at herself in the cracked and yellowing wall-mirror.
Slowly, she turned this way and that, absorbing only gradually the details — the soft-curled hair whorled skilfully
down onto her forehead, the face with its crimson lipstick
and its brown make-up that matched her own skin. Then
she smiled.

'Oh——' she breathed. 'It is just like the pictures I have
seen in *Drum* magazine — the girls, African girls, who know
how everything is done in the new way. Oh, now I will
know, too!'

'Do you think your friends will overcome their shyness
now?' Mr. Archipelago asked.

'I will make sure of it,' Mercy promised. 'You will see.'

They sat quietly in the shop after Mercy had left. They
felt spent and drained, but filled and renewed as well. Doree
stretched her long legs and closed her eyes. Mr. Archipelago
bulged in his carved rocking-chair, and cradled to and fro
peacefully, his shoes off and his waistcoat unbuttoned.

The crash of noise and voices from outside startled them.
They ran to the open door. Spilling down the street was an
impromptu procession. Every girl in town appeared to be
there, hips and shoulders swaying, unshod feet stepping

lightly, hands clapping, cloths of blue and magenta and yellow fluttering around them like the flags of nations while they danced. A few of the older women were there, too, buxom and lively, their excited laughter blaring like a melody of raucous horns. At the front of the parade walked Mercy Tachie in new red high-heel shoes, her head held high to display her proud new hair, her new face alight with pleasure and infinite hope. Beside Mercy, as her guard and her champions, there pranced and jittered half a dozen young men, in khaki trousers and brilliantly flower-printed shirts. One held her hand — he was her own young man. Another had a guitar, and another a gourd rattle. They sang at full strength, putting new words to the popular highlife 'Everybody Likes Saturday Night'.

> *'Everybody like Mercy Tachie,*
> *Everybody like Mercy Tachie,*
> *Everybody everybody*
> *Everybody everybody*
> *Everybody say she fine pas' all——'*

Mr. Archipelago turned to Doree. Gravely, they shook hands.

'By an act of Mercy,' Mr. Archipelago said, 'we are saved.'

They walked along the shore in the moist and cooling late afternoon. The palm boughs rustled soothingly. The sound reminded Mr. Archipelago of taffeta, the gowns of the whispering ladies, twirling forever in a delicate minuet of dust, the ladies watched over by pale and costly marble angels, the dove-grey and undemanding ladies of his insomnia, eternally solacing, eternally ladies.

He watched Doree. She had discovered a blue crab,

clownishly walking sideways, a great round crab with red and comic protruding eyes, and she stooped to examine it more carefully, to enjoy its grotesque loveliness. But it did not know that it need not be afraid, so it ran away.

'Archipelago,' Doree said, 'now that it's over, and we're here to stay, I guess I oughta tell you.'

'No,' he said. 'There is nothing you need tell me.'

'Yes,' she insisted. 'You know when you asked me if I could go back, and I said I couldn't? Well, I guess I didn't give you the straight goods, in a way——'

'I know,' Mr. Archipelago said quietly. 'There was no troubled past. I have always known that.'

'Have you?' she said, mild-eyed, not really surprised. 'How did you know?'

He glanced at her face, at the heavy make-up that covered the ageing features, ravaged and virginal.

'Because,' he replied slowly, 'for me it was the same. I, too, had no past. The white ladies and now the brown ladies — they have never guessed. I did not intend that they should. It is not their concern. But we know, Doree, why we are here and why we stay.'

'Yes,' she said, 'I guess we do know. I guess we both know that. So we don't need to talk about it any more, do we?'

'No,' he promised. 'No more.'

'And whatever happens,' she went on, 'even if we go broke, you won't get any more fancy ideas about me finding a better job somewhere else?'

'The new sign——' he reminded her. 'Have you forgotten what it says?'

'That's right,' she said. ' "Archipelago & Doree". Yeh, that's right.'

Mr. Archipelago sniffed the brine-laden wind.

'Smell the sea, Doree? A perfume for our collection.'

She smiled. 'What shall we call it?'

'Oh, nothing too ornate,' he said lightly. 'Perhaps *eau d'exile* would do.'

The sea spray was bitter and salt, but to them it was warm, too. They watched on the sand their exaggerated shadows, one squat and bulbous, the other bone-slight and clumsily elongated, pigeon and crane. The shadows walked with hands entwined like children who walk through the dark.

# The Merchant of Heaven

ACROSS the tarmac the black-and-orange dragon lizards skitter, occasionally pausing to raise their wrinkled necks and stare with ancient saurian eyes on a world no longer theirs. In the painted light of mid-day, the heat shimmers like molten glass. No shade anywhere. You sweat like a pig, and inside the waiting-room you nearly stifle. The African labourers, trundling baggage or bits of air-freight, work stripped to the waist, their torsos sleek and shining. The airport officials in their white drill uniforms are damp and crumpled as gulls newly emerged from the egg.

In this purgatorially hot and exposed steam bath, I awaited with some trepidation the arrival of Amory Lemon, proselytizer for a mission known as the Angel of Philadelphia.

Above the buildings flew the three-striped flag — red, yellow and green — with the black star of Africa in its centre. I wondered if the evangelist would notice it or know what it signified. Very likely not. Brother Lemon was not coming here to study political developments. He was coming — as traders once went to Babylon — for the souls of men.

I had never seen him before, but I knew him at once, simply because he looked so different from the others who came off the plane — ordinary English people, weary and bored after the long trip, their still-tanned skins indicating that this was not their first tour in the tropics. Brother Lemon's skin was very white and smooth — it reminded me of those sea pebbles which as a child I used to think were the eyeballs of the drowned. He was unusually tall; he walked in a stately and yet brisk fashion, with controlled excitement. I realized that this must be a great moment for him. The apostle landing at Cyprus or Thessalonica, the light of future battles already kindling in his eyes, and replete with faith as a fresh-gorged mosquito is with blood.

'Mr. Lemon? I'm Will Kettridge — the architect. We've corresponded——'

He looked at me with piercing sincerity from those astonishing turquoise eyes of his.

'Yes, of course,' he said, grasping me by the hand. 'I'm very pleased to make your acquaintance. It surely was nice of you to meet me. The name's Lee-*mon*. Brother Lee-*mon*. Accent on the last syllable. I really appreciate your kindness, Mr. Kettridge.'

I felt miserably at a disadvantage. For one thing, I was wearing khaki trousers which badly needed pressing, whereas Brother Lemon was clad in a dove-grey suit of a miraculously immaculate material. For another, when a person interprets your selfish motive as pure altruism, what can you tactfully say?

'Fine,' I said. 'Let's collect your gear.'

Brother Lemon's gear consisted of three large wardrobe suitcases, a pair of water skis, a box which from its label and size appeared to contain a gross of cameras but turned out to contain only a Rolleiflex and a cine-camera complete with projector and editing equipment, a carton of an anti-malarial drug so new that we in this infested region had not yet heard of it, and finally, a lovely little pigskin case which enfolded a water-purifier. Brother Lemon unlocked the case and took out a silvery mechanism. His face glowed with a boyish fascination.

'See? It works like a syringe. You just press this thing, and the water is sucked up here. Then you squirt it out again, and there you are. Absolutely guaranteed one hundred per cent pure. Not a single bacteria. You can even drink swamp water.'

I was amused and rather touched. He seemed so frankly hopeful of adventure. I was almost sorry that this was not the Africa of Livingstone or Burton.

'Wonderful,' I said. 'The water is quite safe here, though. All properly filtered and chlorinated.'

'You can't be too careful,' Brother Lemon said. 'I couldn't afford to get sick — I'll be the only representative of our mission, for a while at least.'

He drew in a deep breath of the hot salty tar-stinking air.

'I've waited six years for this day, Mr. Kettridge,' he said. 'Six years of prayer and preparation.'

'I hope the country comes up to your expectations, then.'

He looked at me in surprise.

'Oh, it will,' he said with perfect equanimity. 'Our mission, you know, is based on the Revelation of St. John the Divine. We believe there is a special message for us in the words given by the Spirit to the Angel of the Church in Philadelphia——'

'A different Philadelphia, surely.'

His smile was confident, even pitying.

'These things do not happen by accident, Mr. Kettridge. When Andrew McFetters had his vision, back in 1924, it was revealed that the ancient Church would be reborn in our city of the same name, and would take the divine word to unbelievers in seven different parts of the world.'

Around his head his fair hair sprouted and shone like some fantastic marigold halo in a medieval painting.

'I believe my mission has been foretold,' he said with stunning simplicity. 'I estimate I'll have a thousand souls within six months.'

Suddenly I saw Brother Lemon as a kind of soul-purifier, sucking in the septic souls and spewing them back one hundred per cent pure.

That evening I told Danso of my vague uneasiness. He laughed, as I had known he would.

'Please remember you are an Englishman, Will,' he said. 'Englishmen should not have visions. It is not suitable. Leave that to Brother Lemon and me. Evangelists and Africans always get on well — did you know? It is because we are both so mystical. Did you settle anything?'

'Yes, I'm getting the design work. He says he doesn't want contemporary for the church, but he's willing to consider it for his house.'

'What did he say about money?' Danso asked. 'That's what I'm interested in.'

'His precise words were — "the Angel of Philadelphia Mission isn't going to do this thing on the cheap".'

Danso was short and slim, but he made up for it in mercurial energy. Now he crouched tigerish by the chaise-longue, and began feinting with clenched fists like a bantam-weight — which, as a matter of fact, he used to be, before a scholarship to an English university and an interest in painting combined to change the course of his life.

'Hey, come on, you Brother Lemon!' he cried. 'That's it, man! You got it and I want it — very easy, very simple. Bless you, Brother Lemon, benedictions on your name, my dear citric sibling.'

'I have been wondering,' I said, 'how you planned to profit from Brother Lemon's presence.'

'Murals, of course.'

'Oh, Danso, don't be an idiot. He'd never——'

'All right, all right, man. Pictures, then. A nice oil. Everybody wants holy pictures in a church, see?'

'He'll bring them from Philadelphia,' I said. 'Four-tone prints, done on glossy paper.'

Danso groaned. 'Do you really think he'll do that, Will?'

'Maybe not,' I said encouragingly. 'You could try.'

'Listen — how about this? St. Augustine, bishop of hippos.'

'Hippo, you fool. A place.'

'I know that,' Danso said witheringly. 'But, hell, who wants to look at some fly-speckled North African town, all mudbrick and camel dung? Brother Lemon wants colour, action, you know what I mean. St. Augustine is on the river bank, see, the Congo or maybe the Niger. Bush all around. Ferns thick as a woman's hair. Palms — great big feathery palms. But very stiff, very stylized — Rousseau stuff — like this——'

His brown arms twined upward, became the tree trunks, and his thin fingers the palm fans, precise, sharp in the sun.

'And in the river — real blue and green river, man, all sky and scum — in that river is the congregation, only they're hippos, see — enormous fat ones, all bulging eyes, and they're singing "Hallelujah" like the angels themselves, while old St. Augustine leads them to paradise——'

'Go ahead — paint it,' I began, 'and we'll——'

I stopped. My smile withdrew as I looked at Danso.

'Whatsamatter?' he said. 'Don't you think the good man will buy it?'

In his eyes there was an inexpressible loathing.

'Danso! How can you——? You haven't even met him yet.'

The carven face remained ebony, remained black granite.

'I have known this pedlar of magic all my life, Will. My mother always took me along to prayer meetings, when I was small.'

The mask slackened into laughter, but it was not the usual laughter.

'Maybe he thinks we are short of ju-ju,' Danso remarked. 'Maybe he thinks we need a few more devils to exorcise.'

When I first met Brother Lemon, I had seen him as he must have seen himself, an apostle. Now I could almost see him with Danso's bitter eyes — as sorcerer.

I undertook to show Brother Lemon around the city. He was impressed by the profusion and cheapness of tropical fruit; delightedly he purchased baskets of oranges, pineapples, paw-paw. He loaded himself down with the trinkets of Africa — python-skin wallets, carved elephants, miniature *dono* drums.

On our second trip, however, he began to notice other things. A boy with suppurating yaws covering nearly as much of his body as did his shreds of clothing. A loin-clothed labourer carrying a headload so heavy that his flimsy legs buckled and bent. A trader woman minding a roadside stall on which her living was spread — half a dozen boxes of cube sugar and a handful of pink plastic combs. A girl child squatting modestly in the filth-flowing gutter. A grinning penny-pleading gamin with a belly outpuffed by navel hernia. A young woman, pregnant and carrying another infant on her back, her placid eyes growing all at once proud and hating as we passed comfortably by. An old Muslim beggar who howled and shouted *sura* from the Qoran, and then, silent, looked and looked with the unclouded innocent eyes of lunacy. Brother Lemon nodded absently as I dutifully pointed out the new Post Office, the library, the Law Courts, the Bank.

We reached shanty town, where the mud and wattle huts crowded each other like fish in a net, where plantains were always frying on a thousand smoky charcoal burners, where the rhythm of life was forever that of the women's lifted and lowered wooden pestles as the cassava was pounded into meal, where the crimson portulaca and the children swarmed over the hard soil and survived somehow, at what loss of individual blossom or brat one could only guess.

'It's a crime,' Brother Lemon said, 'that people should have to live like this.'

He made the mistake all kindly people make. He began to give money to children and beggars — sixpences, shillings — thinking it would help. He overpaid for everything he bought. He distributed largesse.

'These people are poor, real poor, Mr. Kettridge,' he said seriously, 'and the way I figure it — if I'm able through the Angel of Philadelphia Mission to ease their lives, then it's my duty to do so.'

'Perhaps,' I said. 'But the shilling or two won't last long, and then what? You're not prepared to take them all on as permanent dependants, are you?'

He gazed at me blankly. I guess he thought I was stony-hearted. He soon came to be surrounded by beggars wherever he went. They swamped him; their appalling voices followed him down any street. Fingerless hands reached out; half-limbs hurried at his approach. He couldn't cope with it, of course. Who could? Finally, he began to turn away, as ultimately we all turn, frightened and repelled by the outrageous pain and need.

Brother Lemon was no different from any stranger casting his tiny shillings into the wishful well of good intentions, and seeing them disappear without so much as a splash or tinkle. But unlike the rest of us, he at least could console himself.

'Salvation is like the loaves and fishes,' he said. 'There's enough for all, for every person in this world. None needs to go empty away.'

He could hardly wait to open his mission. He frequently visited my office, in order to discuss the building plans. He wanted me to hurry with them, so construction could begin the minute his land-site was allocated. I knew there was no hurry — he'd be lucky if he got the land within six months — but he was so keen that I hated to discourage him.

He did not care for the hotel, where the bottles and glasses clinked merrily the night through, disturbing his sombre slumbers. I helped him find a house. It was a toy-size structure on the outskirts of the city. It had once (perhaps in another century) been whitewashed, but now it was ashen. Brother Lemon immediately had it painted azure. When I remonstrated with him — why spend money on a rented bungalow? — he gave me an odd glance.

'I grew up on the farm,' he said. 'We never did get around to painting that house.'

He overpaid the workmen and was distressed when he discovered one of them had stolen a gallon of paint. The painters, quite simply, regarded Brother Lemon's funds as inexhaustible. But he did not understand and it made him unhappy. This was the first of a myriad annoyances.

A decomposing lizard was found in his plumbing. The wiring was faulty and his lights winked with persistent malice. The first cook he hired turned out to have both forged references and gonorrhoea.

Most of his life, I imagine, Brother Lemon had been fighting petty battles in preparation for the great one. And now he found even this battle petty. As he recounted his innumerable domestic difficulties, I could almost see the silken banners turn to grey. He looked for dragons to slay, and found cockroaches in his store-cupboard. Jacob-like, he came to wrestle for the Angel's blessing, and instead was bent double with cramps in his bowels from eating unwashed salad greens.

I was never tempted to laugh. Brother Lemon's faith was of a quality that defied ridicule. He would have preferred his trials to be on a grander scale, but he accepted them with humility. One thing he could not accept, however, was the attitude of his servants. Perhaps he had expected to find an African Barnabas, but he was disappointed. His cook was a decent enough chap, but he helped himself to tea and sugar.

'I pay Kwaku half again as much as the going wage — you told me so yourself. And now he does this.'

'So would you,' I said, 'in his place.'

'That's where you're wrong,' Brother Lemon contradicted, so sharply that I never tried that approach again.

'All these things are keeping me from my work,' he went on plaintively. 'That's the worst of it. I've been in the country three weeks tomorrow, and I haven't begun services yet. What's the home congregation going to think of me?'

Then he knotted his big hands in sudden and private anguish.

'No——' he said slowly. 'I shouldn't say that. It shouldn't matter to me. The question is — what is the Almighty going to think?'

'I expect He's learned to be patient,' I ventured.

But Brother Lemon hadn't even heard. He wore the fixed expression of a man beholding a vision.

'That's it,' he said finally. 'Now I see why I've been feeling so let down and miserable. It's because I've been putting off the work of my mission. I had to look around — oh yes, see the sights, buy souvenirs. Even my worry about the servants, and the people who live so poor and all. I let these things distract me from my true work.'

He stood up, there in his doll's house, an alabaster giant.

'My business,' he said, 'is with the salvation of their immortal souls. That, and that alone. It's the greatest kindness I can do these people.'

After that day, he was busy as a nesting bird. I met him one morning in the Post Office, where he was collecting packages of Bibles. He shook my hand in that casually formal way of his.

'I reckon to start services within a week,' he said. 'I've rented an empty lot, temporarily, and I'm having a shelter put up.'

'You certainly haven't wasted any time recently.'

'There isn't any time to waste,' Brother Lemon's bell voice tolled. 'Later may be too late.'

'You can't carry all that lot very far,' I said. 'Can I give you a lift?'

'That's very friendly of you, Mr. Kettridge, but I'm happy to say I've got my new car at last. Like to see it?'

Outside, a dozen street urchins rushed up, and Brother Lemon allowed several of them to carry his parcels on their heads. We reached the appointed place, and the little boys, tattered and dusty as fallen leaves, lively as clickety-winged cockroaches, began to caper and jabber.

'Mastah — I beg you — you go dash me!'

A 'dash' of a few pennies was certainly in order. But Brother Lemon gave them five shillings apiece. They fled before he could change his mind. I couldn't help commenting wryly on the sum, but his eyes never wavered.

'You have to get known somehow,' Brother Lemon said. 'Lots of churches advertise nowadays.'

He rode off, then, in his new two-toned orchid Buick.

Brother Lemon must have been lonely. He knew no other Europeans, and one evening he dropped in, uninvited, to my house.

'I've never explained our teaching to you, Mr. Kettridge,' he said, fixing me with his blue-polished eyes. 'I don't know, mind you, what your views on religion are, or how you look at salvation——'

He was so pathetically eager to preach that I told him to go ahead. He plunged into his spiel like the proverbial hart

59

into cooling streams. He spoke of the seven golden candlesticks, which were the seven churches of Asia, and the seven stars — the seven angels of the churches. The seven lamps of fire, the heavenly book sealed with seven seals, the seven-horned Lamb which stood as it had been slain.

I had not read Revelation in years, but its weird splendour came back to me as I listened to him. Man, however, is many-eyed as the beasts around that jewelled throne. Brother Lemon did not regard the Apocalypse as poetry.

'We have positive proof,' he cried, 'that the Devil — he who bears the mark of the beast — shall be loosed out of his prison and shall go out to deceive the nations.'

This event, he estimated, was less than half a century away. Hence the urgency of his mission, for the seven churches were to be reborn in strategic spots throughout the world, and their faithful would spearhead the final attack against the forces of evil. Every soul saved now would swell that angelic army; every soul unsaved would find the gates of heaven eternally barred. His face was tense and ecstatic. Around his head shone the terrible nimbus of his radiant hair.

'Whosoever is not found written in the book of life will be cast into the lake of fire and brimstone, and will be tormented day and night for ever and ever. But the believers will dwell in the new Jerusalem, where the walls are of jasper and topaz and amethyst, and the city is of pure gold.'

I could not find one word to say. I was thinking of Danso. Danso as a little boy, in the evangel's meeting place, listening to the same sermon while the old gods of his own people still trampled through the night forests of his mind. The shadow spirits of stone and tree, the hungry gods of lagoon and grove, the fetish hidden in its hut of straw, the dark soul-hunter Sasabonsam — to these were added the dragon, the serpent, the mark of the beast, the lake of fire and the anguish of the damned. What had Danso dreamed about, those years ago, when he slept?

'I am not a particularly religious man,' I said abruptly.

'Well, okay,' he said regretfully. 'Only — I like you, Mr. Kettridge, and I'd like to see you saved.'

Later that evening Danso arrived. I had tried to keep him from meeting Brother Lemon. I felt somehow I had to protect each from the other.

Danso was dressed in his old khaki trousers and a black mammy-cloth shirt patterned with yellow diamonds. He was all harlequin tonight. He dervished into the room, swirled a bow in the direction of Brother Lemon, whose mouth had dropped open, then spun around and presented me with a pile of canvases.

Danso knew it was not fashionable, but he painted people. A globe-hipped market mammy stooped while her friends loaded a brass tray full of tomatoes onto her head. A Hausa trader, encased in his long embroidered robe, looked haughtily on while boys floated stick boats down a gutter. A line of little girls in their yellow mission-school dresses walked lightfoot back from the well, with buckets on their heads.

A hundred years from now, when the markets and shanties have been supplanted by hygienic skyscrapers, when the gutters no longer reek, when pidgin English has grown from a patois into a sedate language boasting grammar texts and patriotic poems, then Africans will look nostalgically at Danso's pictures of the old teeming days, and will probably pay fabulous prices. At the moment, however, Danso could not afford to marry, and were it not for his kindly but conservative uncles, who groaned and complained and handed over a pound here, ten shillings there, he would not have been able to paint, either.

I liked the pictures. I held one of them up for Brother Lemon to see.

'Oh yes, a market scene,' he said vaguely. 'Say, that reminds me, Mr. Kettridge. Would you like me to bring over my colour slides some evening? I've taken six rolls of film so far, and I haven't had one failure.'

Danso, slit-eyed and lethal, coiled himself up like a spitting cobra.

'Colour slides, eh?' he hissed softly. 'Very fine — who wants paintings if you can have the real thing? But one trouble — you can't use them in your church. Every church needs pictures. Does it look like a church, with no pictures? Of course not. Just a cheap meeting place, that's all. Real religious pictures. What do you say, Mr. Lemon?'

I did not know whether he hoped to sell a painting, or whether the whole thing was one of his elaborate farces. I don't believe he knew, either.

Brother Lemon's expression stiffened. 'Are you a Christian, Mr. Danso?'

Immediately, Danso's demeanour altered. His muscular grace was transformed into the seeming self-effacement of a spiritual grace. Even the vivid viper markings of his mammy-cloth shirt appeared to fade into something quiet as mouse fur or monk's robe.

'Of course,' he said with dignity. 'I am several times a Christian. I have been baptised into the Methodist, Baptist and Roman Catholic churches, and one or two others whose names I forget.'

He laughed at Brother Lemon's rigid face.

'Easy, man — I didn't mean it. I am only once a Christian — that's better, eh? Even then, I may be the wrong kind. So many, and each says his is the only one. The Akan church was simpler.'

'Beg pardon?'

'The Akan church — African.' Danso snapped his fingers.

'Didn't you know we had a very fine religion here before ever a whiteman came?'

'Idolatry, paganism,' Brother Lemon said. 'I don't call that a religion.'

Danso had asked for it, admittedly, but now he was no longer able to hold around himself the cloak of usual mockery.

'You are thinking of fetish,' he said curtly. 'But that is not all. There is plenty more. Invisible, intangible — real proper gods. If we'd been left alone, our gods would have grown, as yours did, into One. It was happening already — we needed only a prophet. But now our prophet will never come. Sad, eh?'

And he laughed. I could see he was furious at himself for having spoken. Danso was a chameleon who felt it was self-betrayal to show his own hues. He told me once he sympathized with the old African belief that it was dangerous to tell a stranger all your name, as it gave him power over you.

Brother Lemon pumped the bellows of his preacher voice.

'Paganism in any form is an abomination! I'm surprised at you, a Christian, defending it. In the words of Jeremiah — "Pour out thy fury upon the heathen!"'

'You pour it out, man,' Danso said with studied languor. 'You got lots to spare.'

He began leafing through the Bible that was Brother Lemon's invariable companion, and suddenly he leapt to his feet.

'Here you are!' he cried. 'For a painting. The throne of heaven, with all the elders in white, and the many-eyed beasts saying "Holy, Holy" — what about it?'

He was perfectly serious. One might logically assume that he had given up any thought of a religious picture, but not so. The apocalyptic vision had caught his imagination, and he frowned in concentration, as though he were already planning the arrangement of figures and the colours he would use.

Brother Lemon looked flustered. Then he snickered. I was unprepared, and the ugly little sound startled me.

'You?' he said. 'To paint the throne of heaven?'

Danso snapped the book shut. His face was volcanic rock, hard and dark, seeming to bear the marks of the violence that formed it. Then he picked up his pictures and walked out of the house.

'Well, I must say there was no need for him to go and fly off the handle like that,' Brother Lemon said indignantly. 'What's wrong with him, anyway?'

He was not being facetious. He really didn't know.

'Mr. Lemon,' I asked at last, 'don't you ever — not even for an instant — have any doubts?'

'What do you mean, doubts?' His eyes were genuinely puzzled.

'Don't you ever wonder if salvation is — well — yours to dole out?'

'No,' he replied slowly. 'I don't have any doubts about my religion, Mr. Kettridge. Why, without my religion, I'd be nothing.'

I wondered how many drab years he must have lived, years like unpainted houses, before he set out to find his golden candlesticks and jewelled throne in far places.

By the time Danso and I got around to visiting the Angel of Philadelphia Mission, Brother Lemon had made considerable headway. The temporary meeting place was a large open framework of poles, roofed with sun-whitened palm boughs. Rough benches had been set up inside, and at the front was Brother Lemon's pulpit, a mahogany box draped with delphinium-coloured velvet. A wide silken banner proclaimed 'Ye Shall Be Saved'.

At the back of the hall, a long table was being guarded by muscular white-robed converts armed with gilt staves. I fancied it must be some sort of communion set-up, but Danso, after a word with one of the men, enlightened me. Those who remained for the entire service would receive free a glass of orange squash and a piece of *kenkey*.

Danso and I stationed ourselves unobtrusively at the back, and watched the crowd pour in. Mainly women, they were. Market woman and fishwife, quail-plump and bawdy, sweet-oiled flesh gleaming brownly, gaudy as melons in trade cloth and headscarf. Young women with sleeping children strapped to their backs by the cover cloth. Old women whose unsmiling eyes had witnessed heaven knows how much death and who now were left with nothing to share their huts and hearts. Silent as sandcrabs, frightened and fascinated, women who sidled in, making themselves slight and unknown, as though apologizing for their presence on earth. Crones and destitutes, shrunken skins scarcely covering their insistent bones, dried dugs hanging loose and shrivelled.

Seven boys, splendidly uniformed in white and scarlet, turbanned in gold, fidgeted and tittered their way into the hall, each one carrying his fife or drum. Danso began to laugh.

'Did you wonder how he trained a band so quickly, Will? They're all from other churches. I'll bet that cost him a good few shillings. He said he wasn't going to do things on the cheap.'

I was glad Danso was amused. He had been sullen and tense all evening, and had changed his mind a dozen times about coming.

The band began to whistle and boom. The women's voices shrilled in hymn. Slowly, regally, his bright hair gleaming like every crown in Christendom, Brother Lemon entered his temple. Over his orlon suit he wore a garment that resembled an academic gown, except that his was a resplendent peacock-blue, embroidered with stars, seven in number. He was followed by seven mites or sprites, somebody's offspring, each carrying a large brass candlestick complete with lighted taper. These were placed at intervals across the platform, and each attendant stood wide-eyed behind his charge, like small bedazzled genii.

Brother Lemon raised both arms. Silence. He began to speak, pausing from time to time in order that his two interpreters might translate into Ga and Twi. Although most of his listeners could not understand the words of Brother Lemon himself, they could scarcely fail to perceive his compulsive fire.

In the flickering flarelight of torches and tapers, the smoky light of the sweat-stinking dark, Brother Lemon seemed to stretch tall as a shadow, tall as the pale horseman at night when children cry in their sleep.

Beside me, Danso sat quietly, never stirring. His face was blank and his eyes were shuttered.

The sun would become black as sackcloth of hair, and the moon would become as blood. In Brother Lemon's voice the seven trumpets sounded, and the fire and hail were cast upon earth. The bitter star fell upon the fountains of waters; the locusts of hell emerged with wings like the sound of chariots. And for the unbelieving and idolatrous — plague and flagellation and sorrow.

The women moaned and chanted. The evening was hot and dank, and the wind from the sea did not reach here.

'Do you think they really do believe, though?' I whispered to Danso.

'If you repeat something often enough, someone will believe you. The same people go to the fetish priest, this man's brother.'

But I looked at Brother Lemon's face. 'He believes what he says.'

'A wizard always believes in his own powers,' Danso said.

Now Brother Lemon's voice softened. The thunders and trumpets of impending doom died, and there was hope. He told them how they could join the ranks of saints and angels, how the serpent could be quelled for evermore. He told them of the New Jerusalem, with its walls of crysolyte and beryl and jacinth, with its twelve gates each of a single pearl. The women shouted and swayed. Tears like the rains of spring moistened their parched and praising faces. I felt uneasy, but I did not know why.

'My people,' Danso remarked, 'drink dreams like palm wine.'

'What is the harm in that?'

'Oh, nothing. But if you dream too long, nothing else matters. Listen — he is telling them that life on earth doesn't matter. So the guinea worm stays in the flesh. The children still fall into the pit latrines and die with excrement in their mouths. And women sit for all eternity, breaking building-stones with hammers for two shillings a day.'

Brother Lemon was calling them up to the front. Come up, come up, all ye who would be saved. In front of the golden candlesticks of brass the women jostled and shoved, hands outstretched. Half in a trance, a woman walked stiffly to the evangel's throne, her voice keening and beseeching. She fell, forehead in the red dust.

'Look at that one,' I said with open curiosity. 'See?'

Danso did not reply. I glanced at him. He sat with his head bowed, and his hands were slowly clenching and unclenching, as though cheated of some throat.

We walked back silently through the humming streets.

'My mother,' Danso said suddenly, 'will not see a doctor. She has a lot of pain. So what can I do?'

'What's the matter with her?'

'A malignant growth. She believes everything will be all right in a very short time. Everything will be solved. A few months, maybe, a year at most——'

'I don't see——'

Danso looked at me.

'She was the woman who fell down,' he said, 'who fell down there at his feet.'

Danso's deep-set eyes were fathomless and dark as sea; life could drown there.

The next morning Brother Lemon phoned and asked me to accompany him to the African market-place. He seemed disturbed, so I agreed, although without enthusiasm.

'Where are the ju-ju stalls?' he enquired, when we arrived.

'Whatever for?'

'I've heard a very bad thing,' he said grimly, 'and I want to see if it's true.'

So I led him past the stalls piled with green peppers and tomatoes and groundnuts, past the tailors whirring on their treadle sewing machines, past trader women in wide hats of woven rushes, and babies creeping like lost toads through the centipede-legged crowd. In we went, into the recesses of a labyrinthian shelter, always shadowed and cool, where the stalls carried the fetish priests' stock-in-trade, the raw materials of magic. Dried roots, parrot beak, snail shell, chunks of sulphur and bluestone, cowrie shells and strings of bells.

Brother Lemon's face was strained, skin stretched luminous over sharp bones. I only realized then how thin he had grown. He searched and searched, and finally he found what he had hoped not to find. At a little stall in a corner, the sort of place you would never find again once you were outside the maze, a young girl sat. She was selling crudely carved wooden figures, male and female, of the type used to kill by sorcery. I liked the look of the girl. She wasn't more than seventeen, and her eyes were almond and daylight. She was laughing, although she sold death. I half expected Brother Lemon to speak to her, but he did not. He turned away.

'All right,' he said. 'We can go now.'

'You know her?'

'She joined my congregation,' he said heavily. 'Last week, she came up to the front and was saved. Or so I thought.'

'This is her livelihood, after all,' I said inadequately. 'Anyway, they can't all be a complete success.'

'I wonder how many are,' Brother Lemon said. 'I wonder if any are.'

I almost told him of one real success he had had. How could I? The night before I could see only Danso's point of view, yet now, looking at the evangelist's face, I came close to betraying Danso. But I stopped myself in time. And the thought of last night's performance made me suddenly angry.

'What do you expect?' I burst out. 'Even Paul nearly got torn to pieces by the Ephesians defending their goddess. And who knows — maybe Diana was better for them than Jehovah. She was theirs, anyway.'

Brother Lemon gazed at me as though he could hardly believe I had spoken the words. A thought of the design contract flitted through my mind, but when you've gone so far, you can't go back.

'How do you think they interpret your golden candlesticks and gates of pearl?' I went on. 'The ones who go because they've tried everywhere else? As ju-ju, Mr. Lemon, just a new kind of ju-ju. That's all.'

All at once I was sorrier than I could possibly say. Why the devil had I spoken? He couldn't comprehend, and if he ever did, he would be finished and done for.

'That's — not true——' he stammered. 'That's — why, that's an awful thing to say.'

And it was. It was.

This city had assimilated many gods. A priest of whatever faith would not have had to stay here very long in order to realize that the competition was stiff. I heard indirectly that Brother Lemon's conversions, after the initial success of novelty, were tailing off. The Homowo festival was absorbing the energies of the Ga people as they paid homage to the ancient gods of the coast. A touring faith-healer from Rhodesia was drawing large crowds. The Baptists staged a parade. The Roman Catholics celebrated a saint's day, and the Methodists parried with a picnic. A new god arrived from the northern deserts and its priests were claiming for it marvellous powers in overcoming sterility. The oratory of a visiting *imam* from Nigeria was boosting the local strength of Islam. Allah has ninety-nine names, say the Muslims. But in this city, He must have had nine hundred and ninety-nine, at the very least. I remembered Brother Lemon's brave estimate — a thousand souls within six months. He was really having to scrabble for them now.

I drove over to the meeting place one evening to take some building plans. The service was over, and I found Brother Lemon, still in his blue and starred robe, frantically looking for one of his pseudo-golden candlesticks which had disappeared. He was enraged, positive that someone had stolen it.

'Those candlesticks were specially made for my mission, and each member of the home congregation contributed towards them. It's certainly going to look bad if I have to write back and tell them one's missing——'

But the candlestick had not been stolen. Brother Lemon came into my office the following day to tell me. He stumbled over the words as though they were a matter of personal shame to him.

'It was one of my converts. He — borrowed it. He told me his wife was barren. He said he wanted the candlestick so he could touch her belly with it. He said he'd tried plenty of other — fetishes, but none had worked. So he thought this one might work.'

He avoided my eyes.

'I guess you were right,' he said.

'You shouldn't take it so hard,' I said awkwardly. 'After all, you can't expect miracles.'

He looked at me, bewildered.

His discoveries were by no means at an end. The most notable of all occurred the night I went over to his bungalow for dinner and found him standing bleak and fearful under the flame tree, surrounded by half a dozen shouting and gesticulating ancients who shivered with years and anger. Gaunt as pariah dogs, bleached tatters fluttering like wind-worn prayer flags, a delegation of mendicants — come to wring from the next world the certain mercy they had not found in this?

'What's going on?' I asked.

Brother Lemon looked unaccountably relieved to see me.

'There seems to have been some misunderstanding,' he said. 'Maybe you can make sense of what they say.'

The old men turned milky eyes to me, and I realized with a start that every last one of them was blind. Their leader spoke pidgin.

'Dis man' — waving in Brother Lemon's direction — 'he say, meka we come heah, he go find we some shade place, he go dash me plenty plenty chop, he mek all t'ing fine too much, he mek we eye come strong. We wait long time, den he say "go, you". We no savvy dis palavah. I beg you, mastah, you tell him we wait long time.'

'I never promised anything,' Brother Lemon said help-lessly. 'They must be crazy.'

Screeched protestations from the throng. They pressed around him, groping and grotesque beside his ivory height and his eyes. The tale emerged, bit by bit. Somehow, they had received the impression that the evangelist intended to throw a feast for them, at which, in the traditional African manner, a sheep would be throat-slit and sacrificed, then roasted and eaten. Palm wine would flow freely. Brother Lemon, furthermore, would restore the use of their eyes.

Brother Lemon's voice was unsteady.

'How could they? How could they think——'

'Who's your Ga interpreter?' I asked.

Brother Lemon looked startled.

'Oh no. He wouldn't say things I hadn't said. He's young, but he's a good boy. It's not just a job to him, you know. He's really interested. He'd never——'

'All the same, I think it would be wise to send for him.'

The interpreter seemed all right, although perhaps not in quite the way Brother Lemon meant. This was his first job, and he was performing it with all possible enthusiasm. But his English vocabulary and his knowledge of funda-mentalist doctrine were both strictly limited. He had not put words into Brother Lemon's mouth. He had only trans-lated them in his own way, and the listening beggars had completed the transformation of text by hearing what they wanted to hear.

In a welter of words in two tongues, the interpreter and Brother Lemon sorted out the mess. The ancients still clung to him, though, claw hands plucking at his suit. He pulled away from them, almost in desperation, and finally they left. They did not know why they were being sent away, but they were not really surprised, for hope to them must always have been suspect. Brother Lemon did not see old men trailing eyeless out of his compound and back to the begging streets. I think he saw something quite different — a procession of souls, all of whom would have to be saved again.

The text that caused the confusion was from chapter seven of Revelation. 'They shall hunger no more, neither thirst any more; neither shall the sun light on them, nor any heat. For the Lamb which is in the midst of the throne shall feed them, and shall lead them unto living fountains of waters, and God shall wipe away all tears from their eyes.'

I thought I would not see Brother Lemon for a while, but a few days later he was at my office once more. Danso was in the back, working out some colour schemes for a new school I was doing, and I hoped he would not come into the main office. Brother Lemon came right to the point.

'The municipal authorities have given me my building site, Mr. Kettridge.'

'Good. That's fine.'

'No, it's not fine,' Brother Lemon said. 'That's just what it's not.'

'What's the matter? Where is it?'

'Right in the middle of shantytown.'

'Well?'

'It's all right for the mission, perhaps, but they won't give me a separate site for my house.'

'I wasn't aware that you wanted a separate site.'

'I didn't think there would be any need for one,' he said. 'I certainly didn't imagine they'd put me there. You know what that place is like.'

He made a gesture of appeal.

'It isn't that I mind Africans, Mr. Kettridge. Honest to goodness, it isn't that at all. But shantytown — the people

73

live so close together, and it smells so bad, and at night the drums and that lewd dancing they do, and the idolatry. I can't — I don't want to be reminded every minute——'

He broke off and we were silent. Then he sighed.

'They'd always be asking,' he said, 'for things I can't give. It's not my business, anyway. It's not up to me. I won't be kept from my work.'

I made no comment. The turquoise eyes once more glowed with proselytizing zeal. He towered; his voice cymballed forth.

'Maybe you think I was discouraged recently. Well, I was. But I'm not going to let it get me down. I tell you straight, Mr. Kettridge, I intend to salvage those souls, as many as I can, if I have to give my very life to do it.'

And seeing his resilient radiance, I could well believe it. But I drew him back to the matter at hand.

'It would be a lot easier if you accepted this site, Mr. Lemon. Do you think, perhaps, a wall——'

'I can't,' he said. 'I — I'm sorry, but I just can't. I thought if you'd speak to the authorities. You're an Englishman——'

I told him I had no influence in high places. I explained gently that this country was no longer a colony. But Brother Lemon only regarded me mournfully, as though he thought I had betrayed him.

When he had gone, I turned and there was Danso, lean as a leopard, draped in the doorway.

'Yes,' he said, 'I heard. At least he's a step further than the slavers. They didn't admit we had souls.'

'It's not that simple, Danso——'

'I didn't say it was simple,' Danso corrected. 'It must be quite a procedure — to tear the soul out of a living body, and throw the inconvenient flesh away like fruit rind.'

'He doesn't want to live in that area,' I tried ineffectually to explain, 'because in some way the people there are a threat to him, to everything he is——'

'Good,' Danso said. 'That makes it even.'

I saw neither Danso nor Brother Lemon for several weeks. The plans for the mission were still in abeyance, and for the moment I almost forgot about them. Then one evening Danso ambled in, carrying a large wrapped canvas.

'What's this?' I asked.

He grinned. 'My church picture. The one I have done for Brother Lemon.'

I reached out, but Danso pulled it away.

'No, Will. I want Brother Lemon to be here. You ask him to come over.'

'Not without seeing the picture,' I said. 'How do I know what monstrosity you've painted?'

'No — I swear it — you don't need to worry.'

I was not entirely convinced, but I phoned Brother Lemon. Somewhat reluctantly he agreed, and within twenty minutes we heard the Buick scrunching on the gravel drive.

He looked worn out. His unsuccessful haggling with the municipal authorities seemed to have exhausted him. He had been briefly ill with malaria despite his up-to-date preventive drugs. I couldn't help remembering how he had looked that first morning at the airport, confidently stepping onto the alien soil of his chosen Thessalonica, to take up his ordained role.

'Here you are, Mr. Lemon,' Danso said. 'I painted a whole lot of stars and candlesticks and other junk in the first version, then I threw it away and did this one instead.'

He unwrapped the painting and set it up against a wall. It was a picture of the Nazarene. Danso had not portrayed any emaciated mauve-veined ever sorrowful Jesus. This man had the body of a fisherman or a carpenter. He was well built. He had strong wrists and arms. His eyes were capable of laughter. Danso had shown Him with a group of beggars, sore-fouled, their mouths twisted in perpetual leers of pain.

Danso was looking at me questioningly.

'It's the best you've done yet,' I said.

He nodded and turned to Brother Lemon. The evangelist's eyes were fixed on the picture. He did not seem able to look away. For a moment I thought he had caught the essential feeling of the thing, but then he blinked and withdrew his gaze. His tall frame sagged as though he had been struck and — yes — hurt. The old gods he could fight. He could grapple with and overcome every obstacle, even his own pity. But this was a threat he had never anticipated. He spoke in a low voice.

'Do many — do all of you — see Him like that?'

He didn't wait for an answer. He did not look at Danso or myself as he left the house. We heard the orchid Buick pull away.

Danso and I did not talk much. We drank beer and looked at the picture.

'I have to tell you one thing, Danso,' I said at last. 'The fact that you've shown Him as an African doesn't seem so very important one way or another.'

Danso set down his glass and ran one finger lightly over the painting.

'Perhaps not,' he admitted reluctantly. 'But could anyone be shown as everything? How to get past the paint, Will?'

'I don't know.'

Danso laughed and began slouching out to the kitchen to get another beer.

'We will invent new colours, man,' he cried. 'But for this we may need a little time.'

I was paid for the work I had done, but the mission was never built. Brother Lemon did not obtain another site, and in a few months, his health — as they say — broke down. He returned whence he had come, and I have not heard anything about the Angel of Philadelphia Mission from that day to this.

Somewhere, perhaps, he is still preaching, heaven and hell pouring from his apocalyptic eyes, and around his head that aureole, hair the colour of light. Whenever Danso mentions him, however, it is always as the magician, the pedlar who bought souls cheap, and sold dear his cabbalistic word. But I can no longer think of Brother Lemon as either Paul or Elymas, apostle or sorcerer.

I bought Danso's picture. Sometimes, when I am able to see through black and white, until they merge and cease to be separate or apart, I look at those damaged creatures clustering so despairingly hopeful around the Son of Man, and it seems to me that Brother Lemon, after all, is one of them.

# The Tomorrow-Tamer

THE dust rose like clouds of red locusts around the small stampeding hooves of taggle-furred goats and the frantic wings of chickens with all their feathers awry. Behind them the children darted, their bodies velvety with dust, like a flash and tumble of brown butterflies in the sun.

The young man laughed aloud to see them, and began to lope after them. Past the palms where the tapsters got wine, and the sacred grove that belonged to Owura, god of the river. Past the shrine where Nana Ayensu poured libation to the dead and guardian grandsires. Past the thicket of ghosts, where the graves were, where every leaf and flower had fed on someone's kin, and the wind was the thin whisper-speech of ancestral spirits. Past the deserted huts, clay walls runnelled by rain, where rats and demons dwelt in unholy brotherhood. Past the old men drowsing in doorways, dreaming of women, perhaps, or death. Past the good huts with their brown baked walls strong against any threatening night-thing, the slithering snake carrying in its secret sac the end of life, or red-eyed Sasabonsam, huge and hairy, older than time and always hungry.

The young man stopped where the children stopped, outside Danquah's. The shop was mud and wattle, like the huts, but it bore a painted sign, green and orange. Only Danquah could read it, but he was always telling people what it said. *Hail Mary Chop-Bar & General Merchant.*

Danquah had gone to a mission school once, long ago. He was not really of the village, but he had lived here for many years.

Danquah was unloading a case of beer, delivered yesterday by a lorry named *God Helps Those*, which journeyed fortnightly over the bush trail into Owurasu. He placed each bottle in precisely the right place on the shelf, and stood off to admire the effect. He was the only one who could afford to drink bottled beer, except for funerals, maybe, when people made a show, but he liked to see the bright labels in a row and the bottle-tops winking a gilt promise of forgetfulness. Danquah regarded Owurasu as a mudhole. But he had inherited the shop, and as no one in the village had the money to buy it and no one outside had the inclination, he was fixed here for ever.

He turned when the children flocked in. He was annoyed at them, because he happened to have taken his shirt off and was also without the old newspaper which he habitually carried.

The children chuckled surreptitiously, hands over mouths, for the fat on Danquah's chest made him look as though the breasts of a young girl had been stuck incongruously on his scarred and ageing body.

'A man cannot even go about his work,' Danquah grumbled, 'without a whole pack of forest monkeys gibbering in his doorway. Well, what is it?'

The children bubbled their news, like a pot of soup boiling over, fragments cast here and there, a froth of confusion.

Attah the ferryman — away, away downriver (half a mile) — had told them, and he got the word from a clerk who got it from the mouth of a government man. A bridge was going to be built, and it was not to be at Atware, where the ferry was, but — where do you think? At Owurasu!

79

This very place. And it was to be the biggest bridge any man had ever seen — big, really big, and high — look, like this (as high as a five-year-old's arms).

'A bridge, eh?' Danquah looked reflectively at his shelves, stacked with jars of mauve and yellow sweets, bottles of jaundice bitters, a perfume called *Bint el Sudan*, the newly-arranged beer, two small battery torches which the village boys eyed with envy but could not afford. What would the strangers' needs be? From the past, isolated images floated slowly to the surface of his mind, like weed shreds in the sluggish river. Highland Queen whisky. De Reszke cigarettes. Chivers marmalade. He turned to the young man.

'Remember, a year ago, when those men from the coast came here, and walked all around with sticks, and dug holes near the river? Everyone said they were lunatics, but I said something would come of it, didn't I? No one listened to me, of course. Do you think it's true, this news?'

The boy grinned and shrugged. Danquah felt irritated at himself, that he had asked. An elder would not have asked a boy's opinion. In any event, the young man clearly had no opinion.

'How do I know?' the boy said. 'I will ask my father, who will ask Nana Ayensu.'

'I will ask Nana Ayensu myself,' Danquah snapped, resenting the implication that the boy's father had greater access to the chief than he did, although in fact this was the case.

The young man's broad blank face suddenly frowned, as though the news had at last found a response in him, an excitement over an unknown thing.

'Strangers would come here to live?'

'Of course, idiot,' Danquah muttered. 'Do you think a bridge builds itself?'

Danquah put on his pink rayon shirt and his metal-rimmed spectacles so he could think better. But his face remained impassive. The boy chewed thoughtfully on a twig, hoisted his sagging loincloth, gazed at a shelf piled with patterned tradecloth and long yellow slabs of soap. He watched the sugar ants trailing in amber procession across the termite-riddled counter and down again to the packed-earth floor.

Only the children did not hesitate to show their agitation. Shrilling like cicadas, they swarmed and swirled off and away, bearing their tidings to all the world.

Danquah maintained a surly silence. The young man was not surprised, for the villagers regarded Danquah as a harmless madman. The storekeeper had no kin here, and if he had relatives elsewhere, he never mentioned them. He was not son or father, nephew or uncle. He lived by himself in the back of his shop. He cooked his own meals and sat alone on his stoep in the evenings, wearing food-smirched trousers and yellow shoes. He drank the costly beer and held aloft his ragged newspaper, bellowing the printed words to the toads that slept always in clusters in the corners, or crying sadly and drunkenly, while the village boys peered and tittered without pity.

The young man walked home, his bare feet making light crescent prints in the dust. He was about seventeen, and his name was Kofi. He was no one in particular, no one you would notice.

Outside the hut, one of his sisters was pounding dried cassava into *kokonte* meal, raising the big wooden pestle and bringing it down with an unvaried rhythm into the mortar. She glanced up.

'I saw Akua today, and she asked me something.' Her voice was a teasing singsong.

Kofi pretended to frown. 'What is that to me?'

'Don't you want to know?'

He knew she would soon tell him. He yawned and stretched, languidly, then squatted on his heels and closed his eyes, miming sleep. He thought of Akua as she had looked this morning, early, coming back from the river with the water jar on her head, and walking carefully, because the vessel was heavy, but managing also to sway her plump buttocks a little more than was absolutely necessary.

'She wants to know if you are a boy or a man,' his sister said.

His thighs itched and he could feel the slow full sweetness of his amiable lust. He jumped to his feet and leapt over the mortar, clumsy-graceful as a young goat. He sang softly, so his mother inside the hut would not hear.

> *Do you ask a question,*
> *Akua, Akua?*
> *In a grove dwells an oracle,*
> *Oh Akua——*
> *Come to the grove when the village sleeps——'*

The pestle thudded with his sister's laughter. He leaned close to her.

'Don't speak of it, will you?'

She promised, and he sat cross-legged on the ground, and drummed on the earth with his outspread hands, and sang in the cool heat of the late afternoon. Then he remembered the important news, and put on a solemn face, and went in the hut to see his father.

His father was drinking palm wine sorrowfully. The younger children were crawling about like little lizards, and Kofi's mother was pulling out yams and red peppers and groundnuts and pieces of fish from bowls and pots stacked in a corner. She said 'Ha — ei——' or 'True, true——' to

82

everything the old man said, but she was not really listening — her mind was on the evening meal.

Kofi dutifully went to greet his grandmother. She was brittle and small and fleshless as the empty shell of a tortoise. She rarely spoke, and then only to recite in her tenuous bird voice her genealogy, or to complain of chill. Being blind, she liked to run her fingers over the faces of her grandchildren. Kofi smiled so that she could touch his smile. She murmured to him, but it was the name of one of his dead brothers.

'And when I think of the distance we walked,' Kofi's father was saying, 'to clear the new patch for the cocoyam, and now it turns out to be no good, and the yams are half the size they should be, and I ask myself why I should be afflicted in this way, because I have no enemies, unless you want to count Donkor, and he went away ten years ago, so it couldn't be him, and if it is a question of libation, who has been more generous than I, always making sure the gods drank before the planting——'

He went on in this vein for some time, and Kofi waited. Finally his father looked up.

'The government men will build a bridge at Owurasu,' Kofi said. 'So I heard.'

His father snorted.

'Nana Ayensu told me this morning. He heard it from Attah, but he did not believe it. Everyone knows the ferryman's tongue has diarrhoea. Garrulity is an affliction of the soul.'

'It is not true, then?'

'How could it be true? We have always used the Atware ferry. There will be no bridge.'

Kofi got out his adze and machete and went outside to sharpen them. Tomorrow he and his father would begin clearing the fallow patch beside the big baobab tree, for the second planting of cassava. Kofi could clear quickly with his machete, slicing through underbrush and greenfeather ferns. But he took no pride in the fact, for every young man did the same.

He was sorry that there would be no bridge. Who knows what excitement might have come to Owurasu? But he knew nothing of such things. Perhaps it was better this way.

A week later, three white men and a clerk arrived, followed by a lorry full of tents and supplies, several cooks, a mechanic and four carpenters.

'Oh, my lord,' groaned Gerald Wain, the Contractor's Superintendent, climbing out of the Land-Rover and stretching his travel-stiffened limbs, 'is this the place? Eighteen months — it doesn't bear thinking about.'

The silence in the village broke into turbulence. The women who had been filling the water vessels at the river began to squeal and shriek. They giggled and wailed, not knowing which was called for. They milled together, clambered up the clay bank, hitched up their long cloths and surged down the path that led back to the village, leaving the unfilled vessels behind.

The young men were returning from the farms, running all together, shouting hoarsely. The men of Owurasu, the fathers and elders, had gathered outside the chief's dwelling and were waiting for Nana Ayensu to appear.

At the *Hail Mary* Danquah found two fly-specked pink paper roses and set them in an empty jam jar on his counter. He whipped out an assortment of bottles — gin, a powerful red liquid known as Steel wine, the beer with their gleaming tops, and several sweet purple Doko-Doko which the villagers could afford only when the cocoa crop was sold. Then he opened wide his door. In the centre of the village, under

the sacred fire tree, Nana Ayensu and the elders met the
new arrivals. The leader of the white men was not young,
and he had a skin red as fresh-bled meat. Red was the
favoured colour of witches and priests of witchcraft, as everyone knew, so many remarks were passed, especially when
some of the children, creeping close, claimed to have seen
through the sweat-drenched shirt a chest and belly hairy
as the Sasabonsam's. The other two white men were
young and pale. They smoked many cigarettes and threw
them away still burning, and the children scrambled for
them.

Badu, the clerk-interpreter, was an African, but to the
people of Owurasu he was just as strange as the white men,
and even less to be trusted, for he was a coast man. He wore
white clothes and pointed shoes and a hat like an infant
umbrella. The fact that he could speak their language did
not make the villagers any less suspicious.

'The stranger is like a child,' Nana Ayensu said, 'but the
voice of an enemy is like the tail of a scorpion — it carries
a sting.'

The clerk, a small man, slight and nervous as a duiker,
sidled up to weighty Opoku, the chief's spokesman, and
attempted to look him in the eye. But when the clerk began
to speak his eyes flickered away to the gnarled branches of
the old tree.

'The wise men from the coast,' Badu bawled in a voice
larger than himself, 'the government men who are greater
than any chief — they have said that a bridge is to be built
here, an honour for your small village. Workmen will be
brought in for the skilled jobs, but we will need local men
as well. The bungalows and labourers' quarters will be
started at once, so we can use your young men in that work.
Our tents will be over there on the hill. Those who want
to work can apply to me. They will be paid for what they

do. See to it that they are there tomorrow morning early. In this job we waste no time.'

The men of Owurasu stood mutely with expressionless faces. As for the women, they felt only shame for the clerk's mother, whoever she might be, that she had taught her son so few manners.

Badu, brushing the dust from his white sleeves, caught their soft deploring voices and looked defiant. These people were bush — they knew nothing of the world of streets and shops. But because they had once thrown their spears all along the coast, they still scorned his people, calling them cowards and eaters of fish-heads. He felt, as well, a dismal sense of embarrassment at the backwardness of rural communities, now painfully exposed to the engineers' eyes. He turned abruptly away and spoke in rapid stuttering English to the Superintendent.

With a swoosh and a rattle, the strangers drove off towards the river, scattering goats and chickens and children from the path, and filling the staring villagers' nostrils with dust. Then — pandemonium. What was happening? What was expected of them? No one knew. Everyone shouted at once. The women and girls fluttered and chattered like parrots startled into flame-winged flight. But the faces of the men were sombre.

Kofi came as close as he dared to the place where Nana Ayensu and the elders stood. Kofi's father was speaking. He was a small and wiry man. He plucked at his yellow and black cloth, twirling one end of it across his shoulder, pulling it down, flinging it back again. His body twitched in anger.

'Can they order us about like slaves? We have men who have not forgotten their grandfathers were warriors——'

Nana Ayensu merely flapped a desolate hand. 'Compose yourself, Kobla. Remember that those of our spirit are meant to model their behaviour on that of the river. We are supposed to be calm.'

Nana Ayensu was a portly man, well-fleshed. His bearing was dignified, especially when he wore his best *kente* cloth, as he did now, having hastily donned it upon being informed of the strangers' approach. He was, however, sweating a great deal — the little rivers formed under the gold and leather amulets of his headband, and trickled down his forehead and nose.

'Calm,' he repeated, like an incantation. 'But what do they intend to do with our young men? Will there be the big machines? I saw them once, when I visited my sister in the city. They are very large, and they feed on earth, opening their jaws — thus. Jaws that consume earth could consume a man. If harm comes to our young men, it is upon my head. But he said they would be paid, and Owurasu is not rich——'

Okomfo Ofori was leaning on his thornwood stick, waiting his turn to speak. He was older than the others. The wrinkled skin of his face was hard and cracked, as though he had been sun-dried like an animal hide. He had lived a long time in the forest and on the river. He was the priest of the river, and there was nothing he did not know. Watching him covertly, Kofi felt afraid.

'We do not know whether Owura will suffer his river to be disturbed,' Okomfo Ofori said. 'If he will not, then I think the fish will die from the river, and the oil palms will wither, and the yams will shrink and dwindle in the planting places, and plague will come, and river-blindness will come, and the snake will inhabit our huts because the people are dead, and the strangler vine will cover our dwelling places. For our life comes from the river, and if the god's hand is turned against us, what will avail the hands of men?'

Kofi, remembering that he had casually, without thought, wished the bridge to come, felt weak with fear. He wanted to hide himself, but who can hide from his own fear and from the eyes of a god?

That night, Kofi's father told him they were to go to the sacred grove beside the river. Without a word or question, the boy shook off sleep and followed his father.

The grove was quiet. The only sounds were the clicking of palm boughs and the deep low voice of Owura the river. Others were there — Kofi never knew who — young men and old, his friends and his uncles, all now changed, distorted, grown ghostly and unknown in the grey moonlight.

'Here is wine from our hands,' Okomfo Ofori said. 'God of the river, come and accept this wine and drink.'

The palm wine was poured into the river. It made a faint far-off splash, then the river's voice continued unchanged, like muted drums. The priest lifted up a black earthen vessel, an ordinary pot fashioned from river clay, such as the women use for cooking, but not the same, for this one was consecrated. Into the pot he put fresh river water, and leaves he had gathered from the thicket of ghosts, and eggs, and the blood and intestines of a fowl whose neck he wrung, and white seeds, and a red bead and a cowrie shell. He stirred the contents, and he stared for a long time, for this was the vessel wherein the god could make himself known to his priest. And no one moved.

Then — and the night was all clarity and all madness — the priest was possessed of his god, Owura the river. Kofi could never afterwards remember exactly what had happened. He remembered a priest writhing like a snake with its back broken, and the clothing trance-torn, and the god's voice low and deep. Finally, dizzied with sleeplessness and fear, he seemed to see the faces and trees blurred into a single tree face, and his mind became as light and empty as an overturned water vessel, everything spilled out, drained, gone.

Back at the hut, Kofi's father told him the outcome. Libation would be poured to the ancestors and to the god of the river, as propitiation for the disturbance of the waters. Also, one young man had been selected to go to the bridge work. In order that the village could discover what the bridgemen would do to the sons of Owurasu, one young man had been chosen to go, as a man will be sent to test the footing around a swamp.

Kofi was to be that young man.

He was put to work clearing a space for the bridgemen's dwellings. He knew his machete and so he worked well despite his apprehension, swinging the blade slowly, bending low from the waist and keeping his legs straight. The heat of the sun poured and filtered down the leaves and bushes, through the fronds and hairy trunks of the oil palms. The knotted grasses and the heavy clots of moss were warm and moist to the feet, and even the ferns, snapping easily under the blade, smelled of heat and damp. Kofi wore only his loincloth, but the sweat ran down his sides and thighs, making his skin glossy. He worked with his eyes half closed. The blade lifted and fell. Towards mid-day, when the river had not risen to drown him, he ventured to sing.

> '*We are listening, we are listening.*
> *Vine, do not harm us, for we ask your pardon.*
> *We are listening, River, for the drums.*
> *Thorn, do not tear us, for we ask your pardon.*
> *River, give the word to Crocodile.*
> *The crocodile, he drums in the river.*
> *Send us good word, for we ask your pardon.*'

Before he left at nightfall, he took the gourd bottle he had brought with him and sprinkled the palm oil on the ground where his machete had cleared.

'Take this oil,' he said to the earth, 'and apply it to your sores.'

Kofi returned home whole, day after day, and finally Nana Ayensu gave permission for other young men to go, as many as could be spared from the farming and fishing.

Six bungalows, servants' quarters, latrines and a long line of labourers' huts began to take shape. The young men of Owurasu were paid for their work. The village had never seen so much cash money before. The white men rarely showed their faces in the village, and the villagers rarely ventured into the strangers' camp, half a mile upriver. The two settlements were as separate as the river fish from the forest birds. They existed beside one another, but there was no communication between them. Even the village young men, working on the bungalows, had nothing to do with the Europeans, whose orders filtered down to them through Badu or the head carpenter. The bridgemen's cooks came to the village market to buy fruit and eggs, but they paid good prices and although they were haughty they did not bother anyone. The carpenters and drivers came to Danquah's in the evening, but there were not many of them and the villagers soon took them for granted. The village grew calm once more in the prevailing atmosphere of prosperity.

In the *Hail Mary Chop-Bar* the young men of Owurasu began to swagger. Some of them now kept for themselves a portion of the money they earned. Danquah, bustling around his shop, pulled out a box of new shirts and showed them off. They were splendid; they shimmered and shone. Entranced, the young men stared. A bottle of beer, Danquah urged. Would the young men have another bottle of beer while they considered the new shirts? They drank, and pondered, and touched the glittering cloth.

Kofi was looked up to now by the other young men. Some of them called him the chief of the young men. He did not admit it, but he did not deny, either. He stretched to his full height, yawned luxuriously, drank his beer in mighty gulps, laughed a little, felt strength flooding through his muscles, walked a trifle crookedly across the room to Danquah, who, smiling, was holding up a blue shirt imprinted with great golden trees. Kofi reached out and grabbed the shirt.

When he left the *Hail Mary* that night, Kofi found Akua waiting for him in the shadows. He remembered another purchase he had made. He drew it out and handed it to her, a green bottle with a picture of flowers. Akua seized it.

'For me? Scent?'

He nodded. She unstopped it, sniffed, laughed, grasped his arm.

'Oh, it is fine, a wonder. Kofi — when will you build the new hut?'

'Soon,' he promised. 'Soon.'

It was all settled between their two families. He did not know why he hesitated. When the hut was built, and the gifts given and received, his life would move in the known way. He would plant his crops and his children. Some of his crops would be spoiled by worm or weather; some of his children would die. He would grow old, and the young men would respect him. That was the way close to him as his own veins. But now his head was spinning from the beer, and his mouth was bitter as lime rind. He took Akua by the hand and they walked down the empty path together, slowly, in the dark, not speaking.

The next week the big machines came rolling and roaring into Owurasu. Lorries brought gangs of skilled labourers, more Europeans and more cooks. The tractor drivers laughed curses at the gaping villagers and pretended to run them down until they shrieked and fled in humiliation like girls or mice.

Gong-gong beat in Owurasu that night, and the drums did not stop their rumble until dawn. The village was in an uproar. What would the machines do? Who were these men? So many and so alien. Low-born coast men, northern desert men with their tribal marks burned in long gashes onto their cheeks and foreheads, crazy shouting city men with no shame. What would become of the village? No one knew.

Nana Ayensu visited the shrine where the carved and blackened state stools of dead chiefs were kept and where the ancestral spirits resided.

'Grandsires, we greet you. Stand behind us with a good standing. Protect us from the evils we know and from the evils we do not know. We are addressing you, and you will understand.'

Danquah sat at the counter of the *Hail Mary* with a hurricane lamp at his elbow. He was laboriously scrawling a letter to his cousin in the city, asking him to arrange for four cases of gin and ten of beer, together with fifty cartons of cigarettes, to be sent on the next mammy-lorry to Owurasu.

Okomfo Ofori scattered sacred *summe* leaves to drive away spirits of evil, and looked again into his consecrated vessel. But this time he could see only the weeping faces of his father and his mother, half a century dead.

When morning came, the big machines began to uproot the coconut palms in the holy grove beside the river. The village boys, who had been clearing the coarse grass from the river bank, one by one laid down their machetes and watched in horrified fascination as the bulldozers assaulted the slender trees. Everyone had thought of the river's being invaded by strangers. But it had never occurred to anyone that Owura's grove would be destroyed.

Kofi watched and listened. Under the noise of the engines he could hear the moaning of Owura's brown waters. Now would come the time of tribulation; the plague and the river-blindness would strike now. The bulldozer rammed another tree, and it toppled, its trunk snapping like a broken spine. Kofi felt as though his own bones were being broken, his own body assaulted, his heart invaded by the massive blade. Then he saw someone approaching from the village.

Okomfo Ofori was the river's priest, and there was nothing he did not know. Except this day, this death. Kofi stared, shocked. The old priest was running like a child, and his face was wet with his tears.

At the work site, the Superintendent listened wearily while the old man struggled to put his anguish into words.

'What's he saying, Badu? If it isn't one damn thing, it's another — what's the trouble now?'

'He says the grove belongs to the gods,' Badu explained.

'All right,' Wain sighed. 'Ask him how much he wants. It's a racket, if you ask me. Will ten pounds do it? It can be entered under Local Labour.'

The village boys looked towards Kofi, who stood unmoving, his machete dangling uselessly from his hand.

'What does it mean? What will happen?'

He heard their questioning voices and saw the question in their eyes. Then he turned upon them in a kind of fury.

'Why do you ask me? I know nothing, nothing, nothing!'

He dropped his machete and ran, not knowing where he was going, not seeing the paths he took.

His mother was a woman vast as mountains. Her blue

cloth, faded and tinged with a sediment of brown from many washings in river water, tugged and pulled around her heavy breasts and hips. She reached out a hand to the head of her crouched son.

So the grove was lost, and although the pleas were made to gods and grandsires, the village felt lost, too, depleted and vulnerable. But the retribution did not come. Owura did not rise. Nothing happened. Nothing at all.

In the days following, Kofi did not go to the bridge work. He built the new hut, and when the gifts were given and taken, Akua made a groundnut stew and half the villagers were invited to share this first meal. Kofi, drinking palm wine and eating the food as though he could never get enough, was drawn into his new wife's smile and lapped around with laughter.

After a week, the young men of Owurasu went back to work for the bridgemen.

The approaches were cleared and the steamy river air was filled with the chunking of the pile-driver and the whirr of the concrete-mixer, as the piers and anchor blocks went in.

To the villagers, the river bank no longer seemed bald without the grove. Kofi could scarcely remember how the palms had looked when they lived there. Gradually he forgot that he had been afraid of the machines. Even the Europeans no longer looked strange. At first he had found it difficult to tell them apart, but now he recognized each.

Akua bought a new cloth and an iron cooking-pot. On one memorable day, Kofi came home from the *Hail Mary* with a pocket torch. It was green and handsome, with silver on its end and silver on the place one touched to make the light come on. Kofi flicked the switch and in the tiny bulb a faint glow appeared. Akua clapped her hands in pleasure.

'Such a thing. It is yours, Kofi?'

'Mine. I paid for it.'

The glow trembled, for the battery was almost worn out from the village boys' handling. Kofi turned it off hastily. Danquah had forgotten to tell him and so he did not know that the power could be replaced.

At the bridge, Kofi's work had changed. Now he helped in the pouring of concrete as the blocks were made. He unloaded steel. He carried tools. He was everywhere. Sweat poured from him. His muscles grew tough as liana vines. He talked with the ironworkers, some of whom spoke his tongue. They were brash, easy-laughing, rough-spoken men, men of the city. Their leader was a man by the name of Emmanuel, a man with a mighty chest, hugely strong. Emmanuel wore a green felt hat enlivened with the white and lightly dancing feathers of the egrets that rode the cattle on the grasslands of the coast. He spoke often to Kofi, telling of the places he had been, the things he had seen.

'The money goes, but who cares? That's an ironworker's life — to make money and spend it. Someday I will have a car — you'll see. Ahh — it'll be blue, like the sea, with silver all over it. Buick — Jaguar — you don't know those names. Learn them, hear me? I'm telling them to you. Wait until you see me on the high steel. Then you'll know what an ironworker does. Listen — I'll tell you something — only men like me can be ironworkers, did you know that? Why? Because I know I won't fall. If you think you might fall, then you do. But not me. I'll never fall, I tell you that.'

Kofi listened, his mouth open, not understanding what Emmanuel was talking about, but understanding the power of the man, the fearlessness. More and more Kofi was drawn to the company of the bridgeman in the evenings at the *Hail Mary*. Akua would click her tongue disapprovingly.

'Kofi — why do you go there so much?'

'I am going,' he would reply, not looking into her eyes. 'It is not for you to say.'

He still went each evening to see his father and his mother. His father was morose, despite the money, and had taken to quoting proverbs extensively.

'Man is not a palm-nut that he should be self-centred. At the word of the elder, the young bends the knee. If you live in an evil town, the shame is yours.'

He would continue interminably, and Kofi would feel uneasy, not certain why his father was offended, not knowing where his own offence lay. But after he had returned to his own hut and had filled himself with bean soup and *kokonte*, he would feel better and would be off again to the *Hail Mary*.

One evening Kofi's father sent the women and younger children away and began to speak with his son. The old man frowned, trying to weave into some pattern the vast and spreading spider-web of his anxieties.

'The things which are growing from the river — we did not know the bridge would be like this, a defiance. And these madmen who go about our village — how many girls are pregnant by them already? And what will the children be like? Children of no known spirit——'

Kofi said nothing at all. He listened silently, and then he turned and walked out of the hut. It was only when he was halfway to the *Hail Mary* that he realized he had forgotten to greet or say farewell to the grandmother who sat, blind and small, in the darkened hut, repeating in her far-off voice the names of the dead.

At the *Hail Mary*, Kofi went over to Emmanuel, who was drinking beer and talking with Danquah. Danquah no longer complained about the village. These days he said that he had always known something wonderful would happen here; he had prayed and now his prayers had been answered. Emmanuel nodded and laughed, shrugging his shoulders rhythmically to the highlife music bellowed by the gramophone, a recent investment of Danquah's. Kofi put one hand on Emmanuel's arm, touching the crimson sheen of the ironworker's shirt.

'I am one of the bridgemen,' he said. 'Say it is true.'

Emmanuel clapped him on the shoulder.

'Sure,' he said. 'You are a bridgeman, bush boy. Why not?'

He winked at Danquah, who stifled a guffaw. But Kofi did not notice.

The dry *harmattan* wind came down from the northern deserts and across the forest country, parching the lips and throats of fishermen who cast their moon-shaped nets into the Owura river, and villagers bent double as they worked with their hoes in the patches of yam and cassava, and labourers on the sun-hot metal of the bridge.

More than a year had passed, and the bridge had assumed its shape. The towers were completed, and the main cables sang in the scorching wind.

Kofi, now a mechanic's helper, scurried up and down the catwalks. He wore only a loincloth and he had a rag tied around his forehead as slight insulation against the fiery sun. He had picked up from the mechanics and ironworkers some of the highlife songs, and now as he worked he sang of the silk-clad women of the city.

Badu, immaculate in white shirt and white drill trousers, called to him.

'Hey, you, Kofi!'

Kofi trotted over to him.

'The bridge will be completed soon,' Badu said. 'Do you want to stay on as a painter? We will not need so many men. But you have worked well. Shall I put your name down?'

'Of course,' Kofi said promptly. 'Am I not a bridgeman?'

Badu gave him a quizzical glance.

'What will you do when the bridge is finished? What will you do when we leave?'

Kofi looked at him blankly.

'You will be leaving? Emmanuel, he will be leaving?'

'Naturally,' Badu said. 'Did you think we would stay for ever?'

Kofi did not reply. He merely walked away. But Badu, watching him go, felt uneasily that something somewhere was disjointed, but he could not exactly put his finger on it.

To the people of Owurasu, the bridge was now different. It had grown and emerged and was an entity. And so another anxiety arose. Where the elders had once been concerned only over the unseemly disturbance of Owura's waters and grove, now they wondered how the forest and river would feel about the presence of this new being.

The forest was alive, and everywhere spirit acted upon spirit, not axe upon wood, nor herb upon wound, nor man upon steel. But what sort of spirit dwelt in the bridge? They did not know. Was it of beneficent or malicious intent? If a being existed, and you did not know whether it meant you good or ill, nor what it required of you, how could you possibly have peace of mind?

A series of calamities enforced the villagers' apprehension. Two of the pirogues drifted away and were found, rock-battered and waterlogged, some distance downriver. A young child fell prey to the crocodile that dwelt under the river bank. Worst of all, three of the best fishermen, who worked downstream near the rapids where the waterflies flourished, developed river-blindness.

When the council of elders met, Kofi was told to attend. He was not surprised, for he had now been the spokesman of the village youth for some time. Nana Ayensu spoke.

'The bridge is beside us, and we live beside this bridge, but we do not know it. How are we to discover its nature?'

Danquah, who was there by reason of his wealth, flatly stated that the bridge had brought good fortune to the village. Business was brisk; money flowed. He could not see why anyone should be worried.

Kofi's father leapt to his feet, quavering with rage. The bridge might have brought good fortune to Danquah, but it had brought ill fortune to everyone else.

'What of my son, spending all his time in the company of strangers? What of Inkumsah's child, buried in the river mud until his limbs rot soft enough for the crocodile to consume? What of——'

'Kobla, Kobla, be calm,' Nana Ayensu soothed. 'Remember the river.'

'The river itself will not be calm,' Kofi's father cried. 'You will see — Owura will not suffer this thing to remain.'

Okomfo Ofori and Opoku the linguist were nodding their heads. They agreed with Kobla. Kofi looked from face to face, the wise and wizened faces of his father, his uncles, his chief and his priest.

'Something is dwelling in it — something strong as Owura himself.'

Silence. All of them were staring at him. Only then did Kofi realize the enormity of his utterance. He was terrified at what he had done. He could not look up. The strength was drained from his body. And yet — the belief swelled and grew and put forth the leaf. The being within the bridge was powerful, perhaps as powerful as Owura, and he, Kofi, was a man of the bridge. He knew then what was meant to happen. The other bridgemen might go, might desert, might falter, but he would not falter. He would tend the bridge as long as he lived. He would be its priest.

When the paint began to appear on the bridge, the people of Owurasu gathered in little groups on the river bank and watched. The men shook their heads and lifted their shoulders questioningly. The women chirped like starlings.

'What's the matter with them?' Gerald Wain asked. 'Don't they like the aluminium paint?'

'They like it,' Badu replied. 'They think it is real silver.'

'What next?' the Superintendent said. 'I hope they don't start chipping it off.'

But the villagers were not primarily concerned with monetary value. The bridge was being covered with silver, like the thin-beaten silver leaf on a great queen's chair. Silver was the colour of queen mothers, the moon's daughters, the king-makers. The villagers wondered, and pondered meanings, and watched the bridge grow moon-bright in the kingly sun.

Kofi, who had been shunned at home ever since his insolence, himself brightened and shone with every brushful of paint he splashed and slapped on the metal. He painted like one possessed, as though the task of garbing the bridge lay with him alone.

In the *Hail Mary* he questioned Emmanuel.

'Where will you go, when you go from here?'

'Back to the city. First I'll have a good time. Everything a man does in the city, I'll do it — hear me? Then I'll look around for another job.'

Kofi was amazed. 'You do not know where you will go?'

'I'll find out,' Emmanuel said easily. 'What about you, bush boy?'

'I will tend the bridge,' Kofi said in a low voice.

Emmanuel's laughter boomed. 'Do you think it needs looking after? Do you think it would fall down tomorrow if no one was here?'

That was not what Kofi had meant. But he did not perceive the difference in their outlooks. He heard only one thing — the bridge did not need a priest. Emmanuel must be wrong. But if he were not? Kofi thought once again of the bridgemen, coming together for a while and then separating once more, going away to look for other places, somewhere. The thought could not be borne. He clicked it off like the little light of the green and silver torch.

He could return to his father's farm. That would please Akua and his mother. His father would welcome another pair of hands at the planting. He thought of his machete and adze. They would need a lot of sharpening. He stood up indecisively, looking from the counter to the door and back again. In his pocket the silver shillings clashed softly as he moved. He pulled them out and held them in his hand, staring at the last of the thin bright discs. Then he grasped Emmanuel's arm, clutching it tightly.

'What will I do? What will I do now?'

Emmanuel looked at him in astonishment.

'Why ask me?'


The towers were painted from small platforms run up on pulleys, and the cables were painted from the catwalks. Then the day came for painting the cross-members at the top of the towers. It was not a job which many men would have wanted, for one had to leave the safety of the catwalk and crawl gingerly out onto the steel beam.

Kofi at once volunteered. He swung himself lightly over

the catwalk and onto the exposed steel. He straddled the beam, two hundred feet above the river, and began to paint.

On either side of the brown waters lay the forest, green and dense, heavy-hanging, sultry and still at mid-day. The palms rose above the tangle of underbrush and fern, and the great buttressed hardwoods towered above the palms. Through and around it all, the lianas twisted and twined. Poinsettia and jungle lily blood-flecked the greens with their scarlet.

Kofi listened to the steely twanging of the cables. The sound, high and sweet as bees or bells, clear as rain, seemed to grow louder and louder, obscuring the bird-voiced forest, surpassing even the deep-throated roar of Owura the river.

Squinting, Kofi could make out other villages, huts like small calabashes in the sun. Then he saw something else. At a distance a straight red-gold streak pierced like a needle through the forest. It was the new road. He had heard about it but he had not seen it before and had not believed it was really there. Now he saw that it would emerge soon here and would string both village and bridge as a single bead on its giant thread.

Emmanuel would ride along there in a mammy-lorry, shouting his songs. At some other village, some other bridge, Emmanuel would find his brothers waiting for him, and he would greet them and be with them again.

Then Kofi knew what to do. He was no longer the bridge's priest, but now the thought could be borne. He was fearless, fearless as Emmanuel. He knew the work of the bridge. In the far places, men would recognize him as a bridgeman. The power of it went with him and in him. Exultant, he wanted to shout aloud his own name and his praises. There was nothing he could not do. Slowly, deliberately, he pulled himself up until he was standing there on the steel, high above the forest and the river. He was above even the bridge itself. And above him, there was only the sky.

Then he did something that Emmanuel would never have done on the high steel — he looked up. The brightness of the bridge seemed strangely to pale in the sunfire that filled his eyes. For an instant he looked straight into the sun. Then, blinded, he swayed and his foot slipped on the silver paint. He pitched forward, missing the bridge entirely, and arched into the river like a thrown spear.

The bridgeworkers' shouted alarm, as they saw him, was each man's cry of terror for himself, who might have been the one to fall. The pirogues went out, and the men of the village dragged the river. But Kofi's body was not found.

'What could have possessed the idiot?' the Superintendent cried, in anger and anguish, for it was the only fatal accident on the job.

'He did not believe the bridge would hurt him, perhaps,' Badu said.

'Did he think it was alive?' Wain said despairingly. 'Won't they ever learn?'

But looking up now, and hearing the metallic humming of the cables, it seemed to him that the damn thing almost was alive. He was beginning to have delusions; it was time he went on leave.

As for the people of Owurasu, they were not surprised. They understood perfectly well what had happened. The bridge, clearly, had sacrificed its priest in order to appease the river. The people felt they knew the bridge now. Kofi had been the first to recognize the shrine, but he had been wrong about one thing. The bridge was not as powerful as Owura. The river had been acknowledged as elder. The queenly bridge had paid its homage and was a part of Owurasu at last.

The boy's father quoted, stoically and yet with pride,

the proverb — 'A priest cannot look upon his god and live.' Kofi's mother and his widow mourned him, and were not much consoled by the praises they heard of him. But even they, as they listened, felt a certain awe and wondered if this was indeed the Kofi they had known.

Many tales were woven around his name, but they ended always in the same way, always the same.

'The fish is netted and eaten; the antelope is hunted and fed upon; the python is slain and cast into the cooking-pot. But — oh, my children, my sons — a man consumed by the gods lives forever.'

# The Rain Child

I RECALL the sky that day — overcast, the flat undistinguished grey nearly forgotten by us here during the months of azure which we come to regard as rights rather than privileges. As always when the rain hovers, the air was like syrup, thick and heavily still, over-sweet with flowering vines and the occasional ripe paw-paw that had fallen and now lay yellow and fermented, a winery for ants.

I was annoyed at having to stay in my office so late. Annoyed, too, that I found the oppressive humidity just before the rains a little more trying each year. I have always believed myself particularly well-suited to this climate. Miss Povey, of course, when I was idiotic enough to complain one day about the heat, hinted that the change of life might be more to blame than the weather.

'Of course, I remember how bothersome you found the heat one season,' I parried. 'Some years ago, as I recollect.'

We work well together and even respect one another. Why must we make such petty stabs? Sitting depressed at my desk, I was at least thankful that when a breeze quickened we would receive it here. Blessings upon the founders of half a century ago who built Eburaso Girls' School at the top of the hill, for at the bottom the villagers would be steaming like crabs in a soup pot.

My leg hurt more than it had in a long time, and I badly wanted a cup of tea. Typical of Miss Povey, I thought, that she should leave yet another parental interview to me.

Twenty-seven years here, to my twenty-two, and she still felt acutely uncomfortable with African parents, all of whom in her eyes were equally unenlightened. The fact that one father might be an illiterate cocoa farmer, while the next would possibly be a barrister from the city — such distinctions made no earthly difference to Hilda Povey. She was positive that parents would fail to comprehend the importance of sending their little girls to school with the proper clothing, and she harped upon this subject in a thoroughly tedious manner, as though the essence of education lay in the possession of six pairs of cotton knickers. Malice refreshed me for a moment. Then, as always, it began to chill. Were we still women, in actuality, who could bear only grudges, make venom for milk? I exaggerated for a while in this lamentably oratorical style, dramatizing the trivial for lack of anything great. Hilda, in point of fact, was an excellent headmistress. Like a budgerigar she darted and fussed through her days, but underneath the twittering there was a strong disciplined mind and a heart more pious than mine. Even in giving credit to her, however, I chose words churlishly — why had I not thought 'devout' instead of 'pious', with its undertones of self-righteousness? What could she possibly have said in my favour if she had been asked? That I taught English competently, even sometimes with love? That my irascibility was mainly reserved for my colleagues? The young ones in Primary did not find me terrifying, once they grew used to the sight of the lady in stout white drill skirt and drab lilac smock faded from purple, her greying hair arranged in what others might call a *chignon* but for me could only be termed a 'bun', a lady of somewhat uncertain gait, clumping heavily into the classroom with her ebony cane. They felt free to laugh, my forest children, reticent and stiff in unaccustomed dresses, as we began the alien speech. 'What are we doing, class?' And, as I sat down clumsily on the straight chair, to show them, they made their murmured and mirthful response — 'We ah siddeen.' The older girls in Middle School also seemed to accept me readily enough. Since Miss Harvey left us to marry that fool of a government geologist, I have had the senior girls for English literature and composition. Once when we were taking *Daffodils*, Kwaale came to class with her arms full of wild orchids for me. How absurd Wordsworth seemed here then. I spoke instead about Akan poetry, and read them the drum prelude *Anyaneanyane* in their own tongue as well as the translation. Miss Povey, hearing of it, took decided umbrage. Well. Perhaps she would not have found much to say in my favour after all.

I fidgeted and perspired, beginning to wonder if Dr. Quansah would show up that day at all. Then, without my having heard his car or footsteps, he stood there at my office door, his daughter Ruth beside him.

'Miss——' He consulted a letter which he held in his hand. 'Miss Violet Nedden?'

'Yes.' I limped over to meet him. I was, stupidly, embarrassed that he had spoken my full name. Violet, applied to me, is of course quite ludicrous and I detest it. I felt as well the old need to explain my infirmity, but I refrained for the usual reasons. I do not know why it should matter to me to have people realize I was not always like this, but it does. In the pre-sulpha days when I first came here, I developed a tropical sore which festered badly; this is the result. But if I mention it to Africans, they tend to become faintly apologetic, as though it were somehow their fault that I bear the mark of Africa upon myself in much the same way as any ulcerated beggar of the streets.

Dr. Quansah, perhaps to my relief, did not seem much at ease either. Awkwardly, he transferred Miss Povey's typewritten instructions to his left hand in order to shake hands with me. A man in his middle fifties, I judged him to be. Thickly built, with hands which seemed too immense to be a doctor's. He was well dressed, in a beige linen suit of good cut, and there was about his eyes a certain calm which his voice and gestures lacked.

His daughter resembled him, the same strong coarse features, the same skin shade, rather a lighter brown than is usual here. At fifteen she was more plump and childish in figure than most of our girls her age. Her frock was pretty and expensive, a blue cotton with white daisies on it, but as she was so stocky it looked too old for her.

'I don't know if Miss Povey told you,' Dr. Quansah began, 'but Ruth has never before attended school in this — in her own country.'

I must have shown my surprise, for he hastened on. 'She was born in England and has lived all her life there. I went there as a young man, you see, to study medicine, and when I graduated I had the opportunity to stay on and do malaria research. Ultimately my wife joined me in London. She — she died in England. Ruth has been in boarding schools since she was six. I have always meant to return here, of course. I had not really intended to stay away so long, but I was very interested in malaria research, and it was an opportunity that comes only once. Perhaps I have even been able to accomplish a certain amount. Now the government here is financing a research station, and I am to be in charge of it. You may have heard of it — it is only twenty miles from here.'

I could see that he had had to tell me so I should not think it odd for an African to live away from his own country for so many years. Like my impulse to explain my leg. We are all so anxious that people should not think us different. See, we say, I am not peculiar — wait until I tell you how it was with me.

'Well,' I said slowly, 'I do hope Ruth will like it here at Eburaso.'

My feeling of apprehension was so marked, I remember, that I attempted exorcism by finding sensible reasons. It was only the season, I thought, the inevitable tension before the rains, and perhaps the season of regrets in myself as well. But I was not convinced.

'I, too, hope very much she will like it here,' Dr. Quansah said. He did not sound overly confident.

'I'm sure I shall,' Ruth said suddenly, excitedly, her round face beaming. 'I think it's great fun, Miss Nedden, coming to Africa like this.'

Her father and I exchanged quick and almost fearful glances. She had spoken, of course, as any English schoolgirl might speak, going abroad.

I do not know how long Ruth Quansah kept her sense of adventure. Possibly it lasted the first day, certainly not longer. I watched her as carefully as I could, but there was not much I could do.

I had no difficulty in picking her out from a group of girls, although she wore the same light green uniform. She walked differently, carried herself differently. She had none of their easy languor. She strode along with brisk intensity, and in consequence perspired a great deal. At meals she ate virtually nothing. I asked her if she had no appetite, and she looked at me reproachfully.

'I'm starving,' she said flatly. 'But I can't eat this food, Miss Nedden. I'm sorry, but I just can't. That awful mashed stuff, sort of greyish yellow, like some funny kind of potatoes — it makes me sick.'

'I'm afraid you'll have to get used to cassava,' I said, restraining a smile, for she looked so serious and so offended. 'African food is served to the girls here, naturally. Personally I'm very fond of it, groundnut stew and such. Soon you won't find it strange.'

She gave me such a hostile glance that I wondered uneasily what we would do if she really determined to starve herself. Thank heaven she could afford to lose a few pounds.

Our girls fetched their own washing water in buckets from our wells. The evening trek for water was a time of singing, of shouted gossip, of laughter, just as it was each morning for their mothers in the villages, taking the water vessels to the river. The walk was not an easy one for me, but one evening I stumbled rather irritably and unwillingly down the stony path to the wells.

Ruth was there, standing apart from the others. Each of the girls in turn filled a bucket, hoisted it up onto her head and sauntered off, still chattering and waving, without spilling a drop. Ruth was left alone to fill her bucket. Then, carrying it with both her hands clutched around the handle, she began to struggle back along the path. Perhaps foolishly, I smiled. It was done only in encouragement, but she mistook my meaning.

'I expect it looks very funny,' she burst out. 'I expect they all think so, too.'

Before I could speak she had swung the full bucket and thrown it from her as hard as she could. The water struck at the ground, turning the dust to ochre mud, and the bucket rattled and rolled, dislodging pebbles along its way. The laughter among the feathery *niim* trees further up the path suddenly stopped, as a dozen pairs of hidden eyes peered. Looking bewildered, as though she were surprised and shocked by what she had done, Ruth sat down, her sturdy legs rigid in front of her, her child's soft face creased in tears.

'I didn't know it would be like this, here,' she said at last. 'I didn't know at all.'

In the evenings the senior girls were allowed to change from their school uniforms to African cloth, and they usually did so, for they were very concerned with their appearances and they rightly believed that the dark-printed lengths of mammy-cloth were more becoming to them than their short school frocks. Twice a week it was my responsibility to hobble over and make the evening rounds of the residence. Ruth, I noticed, changed into one of her English frocks, a different one each time, it appeared. Tact had never been my greatest strength, but I tried to suggest that it might be better if she would wear cloth like the rest.

'Your father would be glad to buy one for you, I'm sure.'

'I've got one — it was my mother's,' Ruth replied. She frowned. 'I don't know how to put it on properly. They — they'd only laugh if I asked them. And anyway——'

Her face took on that defiance which is really a betrayal of uncertainty.

'I don't like those cloths,' she said clearly. 'They look like fancy-dress costumes to me. I'd feel frightfully silly in one. I suppose the people here haven't got anything better to wear.'

In class she had no restraint. She was clever, and she knew more about English literature and composition than the other girls, for she had been taught always in English, whereas for the first six years of their schooling they had received most of their instruction in their own language. But she would talk interminably, if allowed, and she rushed to answer my questions before anyone else had a chance. Abenaa, Mary Ansah, Yaa, Kwaale and all the rest would regard her with eyes which she possibly took to be full of awe for her erudition. I knew something of those bland brown eyes, however, and I believed them to contain only scorn for one who would so blatantly show off. But I was wrong. The afternoon Kwaale came to see me, I learned

111

that in those first few weeks the other girls had believed, quite simply, that Ruth was insane.

The junior teachers live in residence in the main building, but Miss Povey and I have our own bungalows, hers on one side of the grounds, mine on the other. A small grove of bamboo partially shields my house, and although Yindo the garden boy deplores my taste, I keep the great spiny clumps of prickly pear that grow beside my door. Hilda Povey grows zinnia and nasturtiums, and spends hours trying to coax an exiled rosebush into bloom, but I will have no English flowers. My garden burns magnificently with jungle lily and poinsettia, which Yindo gently uproots from the forest and puts in here.

The rains had broken and the air was cool and lightened. The downpour began predictably each evening around dusk, so I was still able to have my tea outside. I was exceedingly fond of my garden chair. I discovered it years ago at Jillaram's Silk Palace, a tatty little Indian shop in the side streets of the city which I seldom visited. The chair was rattan with a high fan-shaped back like a throne or a peacock's tail, enamelled in Chinese red and decorated extravagantly with gilt. I had never seen anything so splendidly garish, so I bought it. The red had since been subdued by sun and the gilt was flaking, but I still sat enthroned in it each afternoon, my ebony sceptre by my side.

I did not hear Kwaale until she greeted me. She was wearing her good cloth, an orange one patterned with small black stars that wavered in their firmament as she moved. Kwaale had never been unaware of her womanhood. Even as a child she walked with that same slow grace. We did not need to hope that she would go on and take teacher training or anything of that sort. She would marry when she left school, and I believed that would be the right thing for her to do. But sometimes it saddened me to think of what life would probably be for her, bearing too many children in too short a span of years, mourning the inevitable deaths of some of them, working bent double at the planting and hoeing until her slim straightness was warped. All at once I felt ashamed in the presence of this young queen, who had only an inheritance of poverty to return to, ashamed of my comfort and my heaviness, ashamed of my decrepit scarlet throne and trivial game.

'Did you want to see me, Kwaale?' I spoke brusquely.

'Yes.' She sat down on the stool at my feet. At first they had thought Ruth demented, she said, but now they had changed their minds. They had seen how well she did on her test papers. She was sane, they had decided, but this was so much the worse for her, for now she could be held responsible for what she did.

'What does she do, Kwaale?'

'She will not speak with us, nor eat with us. She pretends not to eat at all. But we have seen her. She has money, you know, from her father. The big palm grove — she goes there, and eats chocolate and biscuits. By herself. Not one to anyone else. Such a thing.'

Kwaale was genuinely shocked. Where these girls came from, sharing was not done as a matter of moral principle, but as a necessary condition of life.

'If one alone eats the honey,' Kwaale said primly in Twi, 'it plagues his stomach.'

It was, of course, a proverb. Kwaale was full of them. Her father was a village elder in Eburaso, and although he did precious little work, he was a highly respected man. He spoke continuously in proverbs and dispensed his wisdom freely. He was a charming person, but it was his wife, with the cassava and peppers and medicinal herbs she sold in the market, who had made it possible for some of their children to obtain an education.

'That is not all,' Kwaale went on. 'There is much worse. She becomes angry, even at the young ones. Yesterday Ayesha spoke to her, and she hit the child on the face. Ayesha — if it had been one of the others, even——'

Ayesha, my youngest one, who had had to bear so much. Tears of rage must have come to my eyes, for Kwaale glanced at me, then lowered her head with that courtesy of the heart which forbids the observing of another's pain. I struggled with myself to be fair to Ruth. I called to mind the bleakness of her face as she trudged up the path with the water bucket.

'She is lonely, Kwaale, and does not quite know what to do. Try to be patient with her.'

Kwaale sighed. 'It is not easy——'

Then her resentment gained command. 'The stranger is like passing water in the drain,' she said fiercely.

Another of her father's proverbs. I looked at her in dismay.

'There is a different saying on that subject,' I said dryly, at last. 'We had it in chapel not so long ago — don't you remember? From Exodus. "Thou shalt not oppress a stranger, for ye know the heart of a stranger, seeing ye were strangers in the land of Egypt".'

But Kwaale's eyes remained implacable. She had never been a stranger in the land of Egypt.

When Kwaale had gone, I sat unmoving for a while in my ridiculous rattan throne. Then I saw Ayesha walking along the path, so I called to her. We spoke together in Twi, Ayesha and I. She had begun to learn English, but she found it difficult and I tried not to press her beyond her present limits. She did not even speak her own language very well, if it was actually her own language — no one knew for certain. She was tiny for her age, approximately six. In her school dress she looked like one of those stick figures I used to draw as a child — billowing garments, straight lines for limbs, and the same disproportionately large eyes.

'Come here, Ayesha.'

Obediently she came. Then, after the first moment of watchful survey which she still found necessary to observe, she scrambled onto my lap. I was careful — we were all careful here — not to establish bonds of too-great affection. As Miss Povey was fond of reminding us, these were not our children. But with Ayesha, the rule was sometimes hard to remember. I touched her face lightly with my hand.

'Did an older girl strike you, little one?'

She nodded wordlessly. She did not look angry or upset. She made no bid for sympathy because she had no sense of having been unfairly treated. A slap was not a very great injury to Ayesha.

'Why?' I asked gently. 'Do you know why she did that thing?'

She shook her head. Then she lifted her eyes to mine.

'Where is the monkey today?'

She wanted to ignore the slap, to forget it. Forgetfulness is her protection. Sometimes I wondered, though, how much could be truly forgotten and what happened to it when it was entombed.

'The monkey is in my house,' I said. 'Do you want to see her?'

'Yes.' So we walked inside and brought her out into the garden, my small and regal Ankyeo who was named, perhaps frivolously, after a great queen mother of this country. I did not know what species of monkey Ankyeo was. She was delicate-boned as a bird, and her fur was silver. She picked with her doll fingers at a pink hibiscus blossom, and Ayesha laughed. I wanted to make Ankyeo perform all her tricks, in order to hear again that rare laughter. But I knew I must not try to go too fast. After a while Ayesha tired of watching the monkey and sat cross-legged beside my chair, the old look of passivity on her face. We would have to move indoors before the rain started, but for the moment I left her as she was.

Ruth did not approach silently, as Kwaale and Ayesha had done, but with a loud crunching of shoes on the gravel path. When she saw Ayesha she stopped.

'I suppose you know.'

'Yes. But it was not Ayesha who told me.'

'Who, then?'

Of course I would not tell her. Her face grew sullen.

'Whoever it was, I think it was rotten of her to tell——'

'It did not appear that way to the girl in question. She was protecting the others from you, and that is a higher good in her eyes than any individual honour in not tattling.'

'Protecting — from me?' There was desolation in her voice, and I relented.

'They will change, Ruth, once they see they can trust you. Why did you hit Ayesha?'

'It was a stupid thing to do,' Ruth said in a voice almost inaudible with shame, 'and I felt awful about it, and I'm terribly sorry. But she — she kept asking me something, you see, over and over again, in a sort of whining voice, and I — I just couldn't stand it any more.'

'What did she ask you?'

'How should I know?' Ruth said. 'I don't speak Twi.'

I stared at her. 'Not — any? I thought you might be a little rusty, but I never imagined — my dear child, it's your own language, after all.'

'My father has always spoken English to me,' she said. 'My mother spoke in Twi, I suppose, but she died when I was under a year old.'

'Why on earth didn't you tell the girls?'

'I don't know. I don't know why I didn't——'

I noticed then how much thinner she had grown and how her expression had altered. She no longer looked like a child. Her eyes were implacable as Kwaale's.

'They don't know anything outside this place,' she said. 'I don't care if I can't understand what they're saying to each other. I'm not interested, anyway.'

Then her glance went to Ayesha once more.

'But why were they so angry — about her? I know it was mean, and I said I was sorry. But the way they all looked——'

'Ayesha was found by the police in Lagos,' I said reluctantly. 'She was sent back to this country because one of the constables recognized her speech as Twi. We heard about her and offered to have her here. There are many like her, I'm afraid, who are not found or heard about. She must have been stolen, you see, or sold when she was very young. She has not been able to tell us much. But the Nigerian police traced her back to several slave-dealers. When they discovered her she was being used as a child prostitute. She was very injured when she came to us here.'

Ruth put her head down on her hands. She sat without speaking. Then her shoulders, hunched and still, began to tremble.

'You didn't know,' I said. 'There's no point in reproaching yourself now.'

She looked up at me with a kind of naive horror, the look of someone who recognizes for the first time the existence of cruelty.

'Things like that really happen here?'

I sighed. 'Not just here. Evil does not select one place for its province.'

But I could see that she did not believe me. The wind was beginning to rise, so we went indoors. Ayesha carried the stool, Ruth lifted my red throne, and I limped after them, feeling exhausted and not at all convinced just then that God was in His heaven. What a mercy for me that the church in whose mission school I had spent much of my adult life did not possess the means of scrutinizing too precisely the souls of its faithful servants.

We had barely got inside the bungalow when Ayesha missed the monkey. She flew outside to look for it, but no amount of searching revealed Ankyeo. Certain the monkey was gone forever, Ayesha threw herself down on the damp ground. While the wind moaned and screeched, the child, who never wept for herself, wept for a lost monkey and would not be comforted. I did not dare kneel beside her. My leg was too unreliable, and I knew I would not be able to get up again. I stood there, lumpish and helpless, while Ruth in the doorway shivered in her thin and daisied dress.

Then, like a veritable angel of the Lord, Yindo appeared, carrying Ankyeo. Immediately I experienced a resurrection of faith, while at the same time thinking how frail and fickle my belief must be, to be so influenced by a child and a silver-furred monkey.

Yindo grinned and knelt beside Ayesha. He was no more than sixteen, a tall thin-wristed boy, a Dagomba from the northern desert. He had come here when he was twelve, one of the scores of young who were herded down each year to work the cocoa farms because their own arid land had no place for them. He was one of our best garden boys, but he could not speak to anyone around here except in hesitant pidgin English, for no one here knew his language. His speech lack never bothered him with Ayesha. The two communicated in some fashion without words. He put the monkey in her arms and she held Ankyeo closely. Then she made a slight and courtly bow to Yindo. He laughed and shook his head. Drawing from his pocket a small charm, he showed it to her. It was the dried head of a chameleon, with blue glass beads and a puff of unwholesome-looking fur tied around it. Ayesha understood at once that it was this object which had enabled Yindo to find the monkey. She made another and deeper obeisance and from her own pocket drew the only thing she had to offer, a toffee wrapped in silver foil which I had given her at least two weeks ago. Yindo took it, touched it to his talisman, and put both carefully away.

Ruth had not missed the significance of the ritual. Her eyes were dilated with curiosity and contempt.

'He believes in it, doesn't he?' she said. 'He actually believes in it.'

'Don't be so quick to condemn the things you don't comprehend,' I said sharply.

'I think it's horrible.' She sounded frightened. 'He's just a savage, isn't he, just a——'

'Stop it, Ruth. That's quite enough.'

'I hate it here!' she cried. 'I wish I were back at home.'

'Child,' I said, 'this is your home.'

She did not reply, but the denial in her face made me marvel at my own hypocrisy.

Each Friday Dr. Quansah drove over to see Ruth, and usually on these afternoons he would call in at my bungalow for a few minutes to discuss her progress. At first our conversations were completely false, each of us politely telling the other that Ruth was getting on reasonably well. Then one day he dropped the pretence.

'She is very unhappy, isn't she? Please — don't think I am blaming you, Miss Nedden. Myself, rather. It is too different. What should I have done, all those years ago?'

'Don't be offended, Dr. Quansah, but why wasn't she taught her own language?'

He waited a long moment before replying. He studied the clear amber tea in his cup.

'I was brought up in a small village,' he said at last. 'English came hard to me. When I went to Secondary School I experienced great difficulty at first in understanding even the gist of the lectures. I was determined that the same thing would not happen to Ruth. I suppose I imagined she would pick up her own language easily, once she returned here, as though the knowledge of one's family tongue was inherited. Of course, if her mother had lived——'

He set down the teacup and knotted his huge hands together in an unexpressed anguish that was painful to see.

'Both of them uprooted,' he said. 'It was my fault, I guess, and yet——'

He fell silent. Finally, his need to speak was greater than his reluctance to reveal himself.

'You see, my wife hated England, always. I knew, although she never spoke of it. Such women don't. She was a quiet woman, gentle and — obedient. My parents had chosen her and I had married her when I was a very young man, before I first left this country. Our differences were not so great, then, but later in those years in London — she was like a plant, expected to grow where the soil is not suitable for it. My friends and associates — the places I went for dinner — she did not accompany me. I never asked her to entertain those people in our house. I could not — you see that?'

I nodded and he continued in the same low voice with its burden of self-reproach.

'She was illiterate,' he said. 'She did not know anything of my life, as it became. She did not want to know. She refused to learn. I was — impatient with her. I know that. But——'

He turned away so I would not see his face.

'Have you any idea what it is like,' he cried, 'to need someone to talk to, and not to have even one person?'

'Yes,' I said. 'I have a thorough knowledge of that.'

He looked at me in surprise, and when he saw that I did know, he seemed oddly relieved, as though, having exchanged vulnerabilities, we were neither of us endangered. My ebony cane slipped to the ground just then, and Dr. Quansah stooped and picked it up, automatically and casually, hardly noticing it, and I was startled at myself, for I had felt no awkwardness in the moment either.

'When she became ill,' he went on, 'I do not think she really cared whether she lived or not. And now, Ruth — you know, when she was born, my wife called her by an African name which means "child of the rain". My wife missed the sun so very much. The rain, too, may have stood for her own tears. She had not wanted to bear her child so far from home.'

Unexpectedly, he smiled, the dark features of his face relaxing, becoming less blunt and plain.

'Why did you leave your country and come here, Miss Nedden? For the church? Or for the sake of the Africans?'

I leaned back in my mock throne and re-arranged, a shade ironically, the folds of my lilac smock.

'I thought so, once,' I replied. 'But now I don't know. I think I may have come here mainly for myself, after all, hoping to find a place where my light could shine forth. Not a very palatable admission, perhaps.'

'At least you did not take others along on your pilgrimage.'

'No. I took no one. No one at all.'

We sat without speaking, then, until the tea grew cold and the dusk gathered.

It was through me that Ruth met David Mackie. He was an intent, lemon-haired boy of fifteen. He had been ill and was therefore out from England, staying with his mother while he recuperated. Mrs. Mackie was a widow. Her husband had managed an oil palm plantation for an African owner, and when he died Clare Mackie had stayed on and managed the place herself. I am sure she made a better job of it than her husband had, for she was one of those frighteningly efficient women, under whose piercing eye, one felt, even the oil palms would not dare to slacken their efforts. She was slender and quick, and she contrived to look dashing and yet not unfeminine in her corded jodhpurs and open-necked shirt, which she wore with a silk paisley scarf at the throat. David was more like his father, thoughtful and rather withdrawn, and maybe that is why I had agreed to help him occasionally with his studies, which he was then taking by correspondence.

The Mackies' big whitewashed bungalow, perched on its cement pillars and fringed around with languid casuarina trees, was only a short distance from the school, on the opposite side of the hill to the village. Ruth came to my bungalow one Sunday afternoon, when I had promised to go to the Mackies', and as she appeared bored and despondent, I suggested she come along with me.

After I had finished the lesson, Ruth and David talked together amicably enough while Mrs. Mackie complained about the inadequacies of local labour and I sat fanning myself with a palm leaf and feeling grateful that fate had not made me one of Clare Mackie's employees.

'Would you like to see my animals?' I heard David ask Ruth, his voice still rather formal and yet pleased, too, to have a potential admirer for his treasures.

'Oh yes.' She was eager; she understood people who collected animals. 'What have you got?'

'A baby crocodile,' he said proudly, 'and a cutting-grass — that's a bush rat, you know, and several snakes, nonpoisonous ones, and a lot of assorted toads. I shan't be able to keep the croc long, of course. They're too tricky to deal with. I had a duiker, too, but it died.'

Off they went, and Mrs. Mackie shrugged.

'He's mad about animals. I think they're disgusting. But he's got to have something to occupy his time, poor dear.'

When the two returned from their inspection of David's private zoo, we drove back to the school in the Mackies' bone-shaking jeep. I thought no more about the visit until late the next week, when I realized that I had not seen Ruth after classes for some days. I asked her, and she looked at me guilelessly, certain I would be as pleased as she was herself.

'I've been helping David with his animals,' she explained enthusiastically. 'You know, Miss Nedden, he wants to be an animal collector when he's through school. Not a hobby — he wants to work at it always. To collect live specimens, you see, for places like Whipsnade and Regent's Park Zoo. He's lent me a whole lot of books about it. It's awfully interesting, really it is.'

I did not know what to say. I could not summon up the sternness to deny her the first friendship she had made here. But of course it was not 'here', really. She was drawn to David because he spoke in the ways she knew, and of things which made sense to her. So she continued to see him. She borrowed several of my books to lend to him. They were both fond of poetry. I worried, of course, but not for what might be thought the obvious reasons. Both Ruth and David needed companionship, but neither was ready for anything more. I did not have the fears Miss Povey would have harboured if she had known. I was anxious for another reason. Ruth's friendship with David isolated her more than ever from the other girls. She made even less effort to get along with them now, for David was sufficient company.

Only once was I alarmed about her actual safety, the time when Ruth told me she and David had found an old fishing pirogue and had gone on the river in it.

'The river——' I was appalled. 'Ruth, don't you know there are crocodiles there?'

'Of course.' She had no awareness of having done anything dangerous. 'That's why we went. We hoped to catch another baby croc, you see. But we had no luck.'

'You had phenomenal luck,' I snapped. 'Don't you ever do that again. Not ever.'

'Well, all right,' she said regretfully. 'But it was great fun.'

The sense of adventure had returned to her, and all at once I realized why. David was showing Africa to her as she wanted to be shown it — from the outside.

I felt I should tell Dr. Quansah, but when I finally did he was so upset that I was sorry I had mentioned it.

'It is not a good thing,' he kept saying. 'The fact that this is a boy does not concern me half so much, to be frank with you, as the fact that he is a European.'

'I would not have expected such illogicalities from you, Dr. Quansah.' I was annoyed, and perhaps guilty as well, for I had permitted the situation.

Dr. Quansah looked thoughtfully at me.

'I do not think it is that. Yes — maybe you are right. I don't know. But I do not want my daughter to be hurt by any — stupidity. I know that.'

'David's mother is employed as manager by an African owner.'

'Yes,' Dr. Quansah said, and his voice contained a bitterness I had not heard in it before, 'but what does she say about him, in private?'

I had no reply to that, for what he implied was perfectly true. He saw from my face that he had not been mistaken.

'I have been away a long time, Miss Nedden,' he said, 'but not long enough to forget some of the things that were said to me by Europeans when I was young.'

I should not have blurted out my immediate thought, but I did.

'You have been able to talk to me——'

'Yes.' He smiled self-mockingly. 'I wonder if you know how much that has surprised me?'

Why should I have found it difficult then, to look at him, at the face whose composure I knew concealed such aloneness? I took refuge, as so often, in the adoption of an abrupt tone.

'Why should it be surprising? You liked people in England. You had friends there.'

'I am not consistent, I know. But the English at home are not the same as the English abroad — you must have realized that. You are not typical, Miss Nedden. I still find most Europeans here as difficult to deal with as I ever did. And yet — I seem to have lost touch with my own people, too. The young laboratory technicians at the station — they do not trust me, and I find myself getting so very impatient with them, losing my temper because they have not comprehended what I wanted them to do, and——'

He broke off. 'I really should not bother you with all this.'

'Oh, but you're not.' The words came out with an unthinking swiftness which mortified me later when I recalled it. 'I haven't so many people I can talk with, either, you know.'

'You told me as much, once,' Dr. Quansah said gently. 'I had not forgotten.'

Pride has so often been my demon, the tempting conviction that one is able to see the straight path and to point it out to others. I was proud of my cleverness when I persuaded Kwaale to begin teaching Ruth Quansah the language of her people. Each afternoon they had lessons, and I assisted only when necessary to clarify some point of grammar. Ruth, once she started, became quite interested. Despite what she had said, she was curious to know what the other girls talked about together. As for Kwaale, it soothed her rancour to be asked to instruct, and it gave her an opportunity to learn something about Ruth, to see her as she was and not as Kwaale's imagination had distorted her. Gradually the two became, if not friends, at least reasonably peaceful acquaintances. Ruth continued to see David, but as her afternoons were absorbed by the language lessons, she no longer went to the Mackies' house quite so often.

Then came the Odwira. Ruth asked if she might go down to the village with Kwaale, and as most of the girls would be going, I agreed. Miss Povey would have liked to keep the girls away from the local festivals, which she regarded as dangerously heathen, but this quarantine had never proved practicable. At the time of the Odwira the girls simply disappeared, permission or not, like migrating birds.

Late that afternoon I saw the school lorry setting off for Eburaso, so I decided to go along. We swerved perilously down the mountain road, and reached the village just in time to see the end of the procession, as the chief, carried in palanquin under his saffron umbrella, returned from the river after the rituals there. The palm-wine libations had been poured, the souls of the populace cleansed. Now the Eburasahene would offer the new yams to the ancestors, and then the celebrations would begin. Drumming and dancing would go on all night, and the next morning Miss Povey, if she were wise, would not ask too many questions.

The mud and thatch shanties of the village were empty of inhabitants and the one street was full. Shouting, singing, wildly excited, they sweated and thronged. Everyone who owned a good cloth was wearing it, and the women fortunate enough to possess gold earrings or bangles were flaunting them before the covetous eyes of those whose bracelets and beads were only coloured glass. For safety I remained in the parked lorry, fearing my unsteady leg in such a mob.

I spotted Kwaale and Ruth. Kwaale's usual air of tranquillity had vanished. She was all sun-coloured cloth and whirling brown arms. I had never seen anyone with such a violence of beauty as she possessed, like surf or volcano, a spendthrift splendour. Then, out of the street's turbulence of voices I heard the low shout of a young man near her.

'Fire a gun at me.'

I knew what was about to happen, for the custom was a very old one. Kwaale threw back her head and laughed. Her hands flicked at her cloth and for an instant she stood there naked except for the white beads around her hips, and her *amoanse*, the red cloth between her legs. Still laughing, she knotted her cloth back on again, and the young man put an arm around her shoulders and drew her close to him.

Ruth, tidy and separate in her frock with its pastel flowers, stared as though unable to believe what she had seen. Slowly she turned and it was then that she saw me. She began to force her way through the crowd of villagers. Instantly Kwaale dropped the young man's hand and went after her. Ruth stood beside the lorry, her eyes appealing to me.

'You saw — you saw what she——'

Kwaale's hand was clawing at her shoulder then, spinning her around roughly.

'What are you telling her? It is not for you to say!'

Kwaale thought I would be bound to disapprove. I could have explained the custom to Ruth, as it had been explained to me many years ago by Kwaale's father. I could have told her it used to be 'Shoot an arrow', for Mother Nyame created the sun with fire, and arrows of the same fire were shot into the veins of mankind and became life-blood. I could have said that the custom was a reminder that women are the source of life. But I did not, for I was by no means sure that either Kwaale or the young man knew the roots of the tradition or that they cared. Something was permitted at festival time — why should they care about anything other than the beat of their own blood?

'Wait, Ruth, you don't understand——'

'I understand what she is,' Ruth said distinctly. 'She's nothing but a——'

Kwaale turned upon her viciously.

'Talk, you! Talk and talk. What else could you do? No man here would want you as his wife — you're too ugly.'

Ruth drew away, shocked and uncertain. But Kwaale had not finished.

'Why don't you go? Take all your money and go! Why don't you?'

I should have spoken then, tried to explain one to the other. I think I did, after a paralysed moment, but it was too late. Ruth, twisting away, struggled around the clusters of people and disappeared among the trees on the path that led back to the mountain top.

The driver had trouble in moving the lorry through the jammed streets. By the time we got onto the hill road Ruth was not there. When we reached the school I got out and limped over to the Primary girls who were playing outside the main building. I asked if they had seen her, and they twirled and fluttered around me like green and brown leaves, each trying to outdo the others in impressing me with their display of English.

'Miss Neddeen, I seein' she. Wit' my eye I seein' she. She going deah——'

The way they pointed was the road to the Mackies' house.

I did not especially want the lorry to go roaring into the Mackies' compound as though the errand were urgent or critical, so when we sighted the casuarina trees I had the driver stop. I walked slowly past David's menagerie, where the cutting-grass scratched in its cage and the snakes lay in bright apathetic coils. Some sense of propriety made me hesitate before I had quite reached the house. Ruth and David were on the verandah, and I could hear their voices. I suppose it was shameful of me to listen, but it would have been worse to appear at that moment.

'If it was up to me——' David's voice was strained and tight with embarrassment. 'But you know what she's like.'

'What did she say, David? What did she say?' Ruth's voice, desperate with her need to know, her fear of knowing.

'Oh, well — nothing much.'

'Tell me!'

Then David, faltering, ashamed, tactless.

'Only that African girls mature awfully young, and she somehow got the daft notion that — look here, Ruth, I'm sorry, but when she gets an idea there's nothing anyone can do. I know it's a lot of rot. I know you're not the ordinary kind of African. You're almost — almost like a — like us.'

It was his best, I suppose. It was not his fault that it was not good enough. She cried out, then, and although the casuarina boughs hid the two from my sight, I could imagine their faces well enough, and David's astounded look at the hurt in her eyes.

'Almost——' she said. Then, with a fury I would not have believed possible, 'No, I'm not! I'm not like you at all. I won't be!'

'Listen, Ruth——'

But she had thrust off his hand and had gone. She passed close to the place where I stood but she did not see me. Once again I watched her running. Running and running, into the forest where I could not follow.

I was frantic lest Miss Povey should find out and notify Dr. Quansah before we could find Ruth. I had Ayesha go all through the school and grounds, for she could move more rapidly and unobtrusively than I. I waited, stumping up and down my garden, finally forcing myself to sit down and assume at least the appearance of calm. At last Ayesha returned. Only tiredness showed in her face, and my heart contracted.

'You did not find her, little one?'

She shook her head. 'She is not here. She is gone.'

Gone. Had she remained in the forest, then, with its thorns and strangular vines, its ferned depths that could hide death, its green silences? Or had she run as far as the river, dark and smooth as oil, deceptively smooth, with its saurian kings who fed of whatever flesh they could find? I dared not think.

I did something then that I had never before permitted myself to do. I picked up Ayesha and held the child tightly, not for her consoling but for my own. She reached out and touched a finger to my face.

'You are crying. For her?'

Then Ayesha sighed a little, resignedly.

'Come then,' she said. 'I will show you where she is.'

Had I known her so slightly all along, my small Ayesha whose childhood lay beaten and lost somewhere in the shanties and brothels of Takoradi or Kumasi, the airless upper rooms of palm-wine bars in Lagos or Kaduna? Without a word I rose and followed her.

We did not have far to go. The gardeners' quarters were

at the back of the school grounds, surrounded by *niim* trees and a few banana palms. In the last hut of the row, Yindo sat cross-legged on the packed-earth floor. Beside him on a dirty and torn grass mat Ruth Quansah lay, face down, her head buried in her arms.

Ayesha pointed. Why had she wanted to conceal it? To this day I do not really know, nor what the hut recalled to her, nor what she felt, for her face bore no more expression than a pencilled stick-child's, and her eyes were as dull as they had been when she first came to us here.

Ruth heard my cane and my dragged foot. I know she did. But she did not stir.

'Madam——' Yindo's voice was nearly incoherent with terror. 'I beg you. You no give me sack. I Dagomba man, madam. No got bruddah dis place. I beg you, mek I no go lose dis job——'

I tried to calm him with meaningless sounds of reassurance. Then I asked him to tell me. He spoke in a harsh whisper, his face averted.

'She come dis place like she crez'. She say — do so.' He gestured unmistakably. 'I — I try, but I can no do so for she. I too fear.'

He held out his hands then in an appeal both desperate and hopeless. He was a desert man. He expected no mercy here, far from the dwellings of his tribe.

Ruth still had not moved. I do not think she had even heard Yindo's words. At last she lifted her head, but she did not speak. She scanned slowly the mud walls, the tin basin for washing, the upturned box that served as table, the old hurricane lamp, and in a niche the grey and grinning head of the dead chameleon, around it the blue beads like naive eyes shining and beside it the offering of a toffee wrapped in grimy silver paper.

I stood there in the hut doorway, leaning on my ebony

cane to support my cumbersome body, looking at the three of them but finding nothing simple enough to say. What words, after all, could possibly have been given to the outcast children?

I told Dr. Quansah. I did not spare him anything, nor myself either. I imagined he would be angry at my negligence, my blundering, but he was not.

'You should not blame yourself in this way,' he said. 'I do not want that. It is — really, I think it is a question of time, after all.'

'Undoubtedly. But in the meantime?'

'I don't know.' He passed a hand across his forehead. 'I seem to become tired so much more than I used to. Solutions do not come readily any more. Even for a father like myself, who relies so much on schools, it is still not such an easy thing, to bring up a child without a mother.'

I leaned back in my scarlet chair. The old rattan received my head, and my absurdly jagged breath eased.

'No,' I said. 'I'm sure it can't be easy.'

We were silent for a moment. Then with some effort Dr. Quansah began to speak, almost apologetically.

'Coming back to this country after so long away — you know, I think that is the last new thing I shall be able to do in my life. Does that seem wrong? When one grows older, one is aware of so many difficulties. Often they appear to outweigh all else.'

My hands fumbled for my cane, the ebony that was grown and carved here. I found and held it, and it both reassured and mocked me.

'Perhaps,' I said deliberately. 'But Ruth——'

'I am taking her away. She wants to go. What else can I do? There is a school in the town where a cousin of mine lives.'

'Yes. I see. You cannot do anything else, of course.'
He rose. 'Goodbye,' he said, 'and——'
But he did not finish the sentence. We shook hands, and
he left.

At Eburaso School we go on as before. Miss Povey and
I still snipe back and forth, knowing in our hearts that we
rely upon our differences and would miss them if they were
not there. I still teach my alien speech to the young ones,
who continue to impart to it a kind of garbled charm. I
grow heavier and I fancy my lameness is more pronounced,
although Kwaale assures me this is not the case. In few
enough years I will have reached retirement age.

Sitting in my garden and looking at the sun on the prickly
pear and the poinsettia, I think of that island of grey rain
where I must go as a stranger, when the time comes, while
others must remain as strangers here.

# Godman's Master

THE sky cracked open like a broken bowl that held a sea-full. The moment the rain began, the thick heat vanished. Humans and animals would shudder in the unaccustomed cool until the returning sun made the drenched foliage steam. Hours passed, and the dense rain went on, soaking the palms down to their fibrous roots, turning the forest moss spongy and saturated, causing the great ferns to droop like bedraggled peacocks. The water coursed down the flanks of the hardwood trees, and in high and sighing branches the ravens and scarlet-winged parrots huddled, their bold voices overcome by the wind's even more raucous voice. In the grey-green baobab trees, the egrets wrapped their cloak-wings around themselves like flocks of sorcerers, white as mist. The wild bees and dancing gnats and tribes of flies all disappeared as though they had never been. The children of Ananse, the Father of Spiders, from the giant hairy banana spiders down to diminutive crimson jewel spiders, all crept back into the deep and hidden womb of their mother the forest.

Moses Adu knew he was driving too fast, but he wanted to cover as much of the journey as possible before nightfall. The spiral road through the hills was bad enough in the grey light of the day rain; in the dark it could be dangerous. He braked around a corner, blinking his eyes and trying to stare away the rain which slanted down on the windscreen and seemed almost to be flowing across his own glasses.

The windscreen wipers were not working properly. Moses wondered uneasily if he had been cheated on the price of the old Hillman. He did not know much about cars. He had bought this one two weeks ago, the day he arrived back in Africa. He could not really afford a car yet, but he had not wanted to ride a mammy-lorry, like any labourer or bushboy, when he went to see his parents after four years away at university in England. The car might not be much good, but it had been worth the money, Moses decided. The visit had gone well. His father, who was a government clerk, had been almost inarticulate with the new pride of having a pharmacist son. His mother, of course, had been upset that Moses would not stay with them longer, but even she had been placated when he told of the job that was waiting for him in the coast city.

Night was coming on, when Moses saw a village ahead. He slowed the car. The huts and shanties came into focus, red mudbrick, glossed with the wet, the walls partially eaten away by years of rains like this, rains that would lick and spit until finally the dwellings melted and crumbled like huts of sugar.

No movement at all in the village, no sign of inhabitants. Only the hypnotic persistency of the rain. Then — and Moses' nerves jolted with shock — a quick frightened darting of some live thing onto the road directly in front of the wheels. Moses braked hard; the car slithered on the rain-greasy road. There was a thud as the car hit the creature and came to a stop.

For a moment Moses could not look. He had hit a child — he could think of nothing but that. Finally he opened the door. When he saw that the dead thing was not a child but a goat, his relief was so great he could barely climb back in the car and light a cigarette.

Within ten seconds, the car was surrounded by a dozen

villagers. Although they spoke in Twi, which was Moses'
mother-tongue, the fact that they all shouted at once made
it difficult to follow any one of them. The gist, however, was
plain. The goat would have to be paid for.

Moses was willing to pay for the goat, but he refused to
pay the sum demanded by the throng.

'Too much,' he said firmly. 'You know it's too much for
that miserable creature.'

The goat's owner, a loose-limbed man with the unsmiling
face and shrewd eyes of a peasant-farmer who knows he
will never be anything but poor, began to shake both fists
at Moses.

'As the proverb says, the stranger has large eyes, but they
see nothing in the village. The goat was pregnant — look
there, do I have to slit her belly? I have lost two goats.'

'I am willing to pay for one,' Moses said irritably, 'but
not two. I'm not a fool, and I'm not a rich man, either.'

Laughter, bitter as woodsmoke.

'He says he is not a rich man, Kobla. Look at his clothes —
see? Did you notice his shoes when he stepped outside a
moment ago? Here — look, if you stick your head in this
window, you can see them. Not rich — ei! They say a
crab cannot walk straight ahead nor a city man tell the
truth——'

Moses knew it was no use. He was, of course, a wealthy
man to them. He would not stand outside in the pelting
rain as they did. They had only their skins to get soaked,
and the loincloths bound around bony hips. The silver
rain streaked down them, making their bodies glisten as
though with oil and their muscles contract and clench
against the chill. Moses felt ashamed, keeping them standing there, hunched and shaking, like dogs without shelter.

'Do you have to stand there and drown?' he said brusquely. 'If there is a place to go, I will come with you.'

The village had one chop-bar, they told him. Moses struggled into his trench-coat and followed them. The chop-bar was clay and wattle, like the other dwellings, but it had a roof of corrugated iron. Inside, a kerosene lamp burned, feebly pushing away the shadows from the narrow room. Low wooden benches were placed haphazardly around the clay floor, and under one bench a hen sat ruffling grimy white feathers and glaring with malevolent ebony eyes. The air reeked of smoke and the red palm oil used in cooking. On a wooden counter stood an old marmalade jar full of pink and dusty paper roses.

'They sell beer here,' one of the village young men told Moses shyly. 'And palm wine.'

An old man, the boy's father, perhaps, or his uncle, turned on him and told him with furious pride to hold his tongue, for they were not beggars. So Moses bought half a dozen bottles of beer, as the villagers had confidently expected he would.

Back to the question of the goat. When Moses enquired if there were any police in the village, they shook their heads. No, they said, the gods had spared them that kind of outsider, although sometimes a constable arrived from somewhere on his bicycle; but whatever he asked about, they never told him anything, so he soon went away again.

'A chief, then?'

Yes, they all agreed. That was the thing to do, the very thing. The matter should be taken before the chief, who would decide whether the stranger owed for one goat or two.

'Fine,' Moses said. 'Let us go and see him now.'

Their chief would be delighted to see him, the villagers said. Nana Owosu was well known for the graciousness with which he received strangers. Further, he had a fine house — made of stone, it was, and every man in the village had helped to build it — a house worth seeing. There was, however, one small difficulty. Nana Owosu was away at the moment, visiting his daughter at Tafo. He would, they said hopefully, almost certainly be back within a week.

Moses managed a semblance of calm.

'Look here — I will give you three pounds for the she-goat, and two bottles of palm wine for the unborn one. How is that?'

No, they chorused gravely, it would not do at all. That was not the sum they had in mind. The goat's owner was a poor man, greatly afflicted — he had no children, think of the shame of it — and here was a rich stranger, trying to cheat him on the best goat in his herd, and what an insult to offer only two bottles of palm wine for what might have been another fine animal.

'I am not trying to cheat you,' Moses said helplessly. 'But if we cannot settle it——'

The solution appeared to strike all of them at the same moment, as though they possessed not individual minds but a corporate mind, all nerves and ganglia mysteriously inter-connected.

'Of course,' they said, with obvious relief. 'Why did we not think of it before? We will take him to the oracle.'

Moses grinned in embarrassment. 'Oracle? Some sort of *suman*, a fetish?'

'No, no,' they said. 'An oracle. His priest also possesses powerful *suman*, but the oracle is an *obosom*, a god. He will tell us what to do. He cannot be wrong, you see. He lives in a box in the house of his priest.'

Moses had never encountered an oracle or the priest of an oracle. A box? He wondered what the trick would be. Ventriloquism? Should he go and see? He wanted to go, and yet he felt a repugnance about taking part in such a game even as onlooker. He was not an especially religious man, but he did, after all, belong to a family that had been Christian for three generations. As a pharmacist, too, one who was pledged to fight with sulpha and nivaquine the ancient darkness of fetish and necromancy, could he consult an oracle, even if it were done only to appease the complex simplicity of the village men? Moses turned his face away from the villagers, in case their illiterate eyes should be able to read him.

A god-in-the-box. Like the up-jumping jacks, the toy men, the hawk-nosed clown men who stayed still until you pressed the spring, then leapt and bowed, grimacing in paint, frightening children too young to know wood from flesh.

'It is not far to the dwelling of the oracle,' the goat's owner was saying. 'You will come with us?'

And Moses, surprised at himself, nodded abruptly and got to his feet.

The house of the oracle's priest was not mudbrick. Made of cement blocks, it had been whitewashed and the corrugated roof painted green. A wealthy house, for this village. But the yard was untended. The coarse grass grew hiphigh, and around the stoep and lintel the moonflower vines hung like great green clotted spider-webs, the clustered blossoms torn and shredded by rain.

Moses shivered in the wet wind, and found himself imagining how humiliated he would be if by any chance he were to experience fear in this place.

There was no answer to their knock and no light visible within the house. Moses' glasses were blurred by rain, so the carved door and the blown moonflowers and the crouched villagers all looked to him as though they existed in some deep pool, and he, peering and straining, could see them only vaguely through the shifting waters. He took off his glasses and put his face close to the blank window. And saw, looking out at him, not two eyes but one. One gleaming amber eye.

Moses drew back, startled and then irritated. The tricks had begun already. Just then the door was opened by a girl child. She seemed not to notice the familiar men of the village. Her wide alarmed eyes were fixed on Moses, sombre and stocky in his good beige trench-coat. He laughed and bent down to her.

'Do not be afraid, little queen mother.'

But she turned and fled. He could hear her voice shrilling from the back of the house.

'A stranger is here! A strange man — one we have not seen before.'

And a man's voice, harsh.

'I know. I know. Hush, foolish one.'

The man appeared in the open doorway. The single eye was explained, for in one empty socket the skin hung loose and scarred. Otherwise, he was a handsome man. His cheekbones were high and prominent, his features well-shaped. He wore a headband of leather, bound with amulets and charms. His bracelets, too, were fetish-pieces — cords, knotted with lumps of *nufa* medicine, links of iron chain, snippets of red cloth, and the bones of small animals. His cloth, draped around him in the traditional style, was yellow velvet, brown-patterned to resemble a leopard's pad-marks.

'I am Faru,' he said in an expressionless voice. 'Why have they brought you to me?'

The villagers explained, and after the oracle's fee had been discussed at length and finally agreed upon, the priest led them inside, still looking dubiously at Moses.

The oracle's room was lighted with a kerosene lamp of white china sprinkled with enamelled violets. On a wall hung an old *afona*, a sword, with a double-bulbed handle and a broad cutlass blade that was now thick with rust. On the same wall was a string of Muslim prayer beads, red and black, and nearby an ebony cross, with its Saviour dying in a gilt agony. On the bare unswept floor stood two figures, male and female, crudely carved in a pale wood and smeared with cockerel's blood and the hard dried yolk of sacrificial eggs.

Moses, looking at the conglomeration of symbols, felt queasy and apprehensive. He remembered hearing once about the fetish grove at Elmina, where a crucifix and baptismal bowl were said to be used in the rites of the god Nana Ntona, who had centuries before been Saint Anthony when the Portuguese built a chapel there. Moses had found a sour amusement in that transformation — history's barb, however slight, against the slavers. But this assimilation was different. The presence of the crucifix bothered him, here in this foetid room with the eye of Faru the priest winking goldenly.

Against the far wall stood a long table, containing at one end a *kuduo*, an ornate jar with twisted handles, cast in brass a long time ago and now encrusted with dirt and verdigris. In the centre of the table rested a mahogany box, perhaps two and a half feet long, in appearance not unlike a child's coffin. The lid of the box was tightly shut.

The villagers squatted on their haunches, looking around the room with nervous reverence. Moses stubbornly remained standing, ignoring the chair that the oracle's priest pointed out to him.

In a deep resonant voice, Faru addressed the oracle, explaining the predicament. A moment's silence. The villagers leaned forward expectantly, and even Moses breathed softly and slowly as he listened. Then from the box came a sound.

A tiny cough, as though a butterfly had cleared its throat. The voice that followed was small and tenuous, entirely different in pitch and emphasis from the voice of Faru.

'Listen while I speak.' The voice quivered, stopped to cough, then resumed. 'The stranger is a good man. Some men would have run away and refused to pay at all, and what could you do about it, Kobla Oware? You must take what the stranger has offered you and be satisfied. If you do so, and if you give my priest twenty shillings and also three bottles of palm wine so he may pour libation to me, then your good heart will be remembered. Your wife will at last conceive and you will be mocked at no more.'

Moses had heard ventriloquism in England, but never a performance like this one. The oracle's priest was facing them squarely. His mouth was clamped shut and his jaw rigid, not a flicker of movement. He was — it had to be admitted — a master.

Kobla Oware, the childless one, sat perfectly still. Not wanting to see the look of tremulous exultation that changed and lightened the villager's dour face, Moses looked away and as he did so he found himself staring straight into the tiger eye of the priest. Moses glared angrily, but the priest's gaze never faltered. Then, as Moses handed Kobla Oware the money for the dead goat, he could feel the ravenous eye slipping away from himself, losing interest, coming to rest on the notes in the villager's hand.

Faru joked and laughed with the village men as he led them out of the room. Moses, who had just deposited his share of the oracle's fee in the brass *kuduo*, was about to follow when something stopped him.

The box coughed once more, a gentle apologetic sound.

Moses swung around, feeling both foolish and terrified.

'Who — what is it?' he whispered.

There was a flutter of movement inside the box.

'I beg you, I beg you, I beg you,' the small voice gasped, 'let me free!'

Hardly knowing what he was doing, or why, but moved by the urgency of the voice, Moses stepped quickly over to the box and began wrenching at the lid.

'Hurry, hurry, before he gets back,' the voice pleaded. 'The latch is on the other side, stupid.'

Moses found the latch, fumbled at it and finally raised the lid. He forced himself to look inside. There lay the man-forsaken little god.

The creature's face was old, as old as Africa, as old as all earth. But it was not the leathery oldness of health. The skin of this face was pouched and puffy; it had a look of unpleasant softness, like skin soaked too long in water. The eyes were so sorrowfully wise they seemed not to own the ludicrously stunted body, palpitating with panic under its tangle of rags.

Moses could not move a muscle. He could only look and look. The creature, now struggling weakly to rise from the straw-lined box, was certainly a man, but it seemed impossible that he possessed the same component parts as other humans. Everything about him must surely be different — his liver a frail mauve like a wild orchid, his heart as green and trembling as a blade of grass.

'Quick, quick,' the little creature squeaked. 'Open that window and put me outside. You go out the door. I will meet you on the road. Oh, hurry!'

There was no time to think. Moses could hear the priest's heavy voice, still talking with the villagers. He opened the window and thrust the oracle outside into the darkness. Then he walked rapidly out of the room.

Moses never knew how the creature managed to scuttle across the road and past the villagers without being noticed. But when he himself had finally reached the car, his heart thundering, the oracle was there before him. They climbed in, and Moses, despite the rain and the treacherous road drove away from the village as though he were being pursued by demons who rode the black wind.

When they were at a safe distance, Moses slowed the car. Immediately, the little man, who was still shaking like a withered moonflower in a storm, began to babble his gratitude.

'Oh, I bless your name, I bless it! He kept me there — oh a long time, I cannot remember how long. I will bless your name every day of my life. There were holes in the box but I had to breathe very small and small and small. Oh you would not believe how foul the air was — it has ruined my lungs; lately I cough all the time. I heard the servant child say it was a stranger coming, someone not of the village. Not many strangers come. The last was a Dagomba man — Faru knew his language, a little, but I did not. I was afraid you might be the same — a different tongue — but then I heard you speak, and I knew you would save me. Oh, I bless your name.'

'Who are you?' Moses asked.

'I am Godman Pira,' the ex-oracle replied. 'One of the *pirafo*, you know, a dwarf. Can I help it? Does that make me any less a man? I am different, maybe, but I am as much a man as any of them. Do you think so? Do I seem that way to you? To one who has lived in a box for so long it is sometimes hard to tell——'

'You are a man,' Moses said gruffly. 'Of course you are.'

He wished he could look at the creature without feeling a slight shock of revulsion. Perhaps it was the humidity in the box that had given the waterlogged appearance to the creases of the face.

'I want to be a man,' Godman Pira said. 'I have always

belonged to some priest, you see. Before this one, it was another, and before him, another. Always the same thing. It is a very hard life, to be an oracle. Some of the *pirafo* used to be court jesters to the kings of Ashanti. But not any more. No one wants to laugh any more, perhaps.'

'Why did you never reveal yourself to one of the villagers?' Moses asked. 'Why did you not tell them you were human?'

'It would have been no use,' Godman said. 'They would not have known what to do. They are afraid of Faru, and anyway, they would not have believed I was a person like themselves. If I am an oracle, they know how to act with me. They pour libation, and ask questions, and I stay in my box and they do not have to approach me very closely. But if I am a man, what are they to do with me? It would only have confused them. They are good people, but they do not like to look at things they have not seen before.'

Moses remembered the owner of the goat.

'Godman, why did you tell Kobla Oware his wife would conceive?'

The little man laughed softly.

'Easy,' he boasted. 'It is not so difficult to astound people by prophesying. She has conceived already, but Kobla does not know it yet. We had information, you see. Two of the village crones. Faru was the clever one. The things I could tell you——'

He chortled again, hugging his short arms around himself.

'I wouldn't have thought,' Moses said stiffly, 'that you would find much in Faru to admire.'

'Oh, I didn't!' Godman cried. 'I hated him. You cannot know how much I hated him. Every day I used to pray to the real gods that his bowels would be knotted and closed until he died of putrefaction.'

145

Then the little man began to tremble once more.

'How angry he will be when he finds the box empty!
Maybe he will follow me and find me and take me back.
Or else he will kill me. You will not let him? You will keep
him away? Say you will keep him away!'

'I do not think he will dare to follow,' Moses said. 'And
if he did, how could he find you in the city?'

'He sees through walls,' Godman quavered. 'His eye
sees everywhere. So he used to say.'

'You don't really believe that, do you?'

'I don't know——' Godman hesitated. 'Now that I am
with you it seems — oh, it is hard for me to know. Do you
think all he said might have been lies? I thought so sometimes, but when you are in a box, you are not sure what you
think. Sometimes it seems that you are only dreaming you
are awake, when all the time you sleep and sleep——'

'He lied to you,' Moses said firmly. 'You do not need to
be afraid of him any longer.'

'Do you really think so? Tell me once more, then I will
believe it. He might not bother to follow me. He knew
I was growing ill, and he thought I would die soon. I would
have died, too, if I had stayed there. Perhaps he will journey
and find another dwarf — it would pay him better. Yes,
I think that is what he will do. But — oh, what if he does
seek me out? You will not let him take me back?'

'There are police in the city,' Moses said reassuringly.
'I will go to them, if you like, and explain about Faru.
Perhaps they——'

'Oh, I have just remembered!' Godman cried. 'If there
are police where we are going, I think Faru will not approach
that place. He was once put in a prison, a long time ago,
and he would never allow himself to be put there again.
He is like a leopard, you know — he could not endure a
cage.'

146

'Yet he kept you in one.'

'He did not think that was the same thing,' Godman said simply. 'And after all, he did buy me.'

'But,' Moses protested, 'don't you realize? A man cannot buy another man. A law forbids it. Why, that is as bad as the slavers, in the old days. People are not allowed to do that sort of thing now.'

'Really?' Godman said. 'There — you see? I am learning so much from you already. Soon I will know everything about how to live as a man.'

'What — what are you planning to do, once we reach the city?'

'I do not mind,' Godman said promptly. 'You are clever. You will think of something.'

'I mean — where will you go?'

Godman Pira settled himself more comfortably on the seat of the car.

'Wherever you are going,' he said. 'I will go with you, wherever you go.'

Moses looked at him, appalled.

Moses often thought afterwards that he ought never to have allowed Godman to know where he lived. But when they reached the city, the little man seemed on the point of collapse with exhaustion and the excitement of his escape. Moses had previously rented two frugally furnished rooms; they were not large, but neither was Godman, so Moses reluctantly granted him shelter, telling him emphatically that he must leave as soon as he was rested. The next evening, however, Godman was still there. Moses tried to reason with him.

'You will have to find some kind of work. That is what men do — they work. You cannot stay here. It is impossible.'

The little man coughed and shivered, and his sickly damp-looking face took on an expression of calculated pathos.

'What could I do?' he asked, lowering purplish-lidded eyes but managing to watch Moses' face all the time. 'Alone, what could I do? I know only how to be an oracle. I swear it — I will be no trouble to you. I will eat no more than the bird that picks at the teeth of the crocodile. I do not take up much room. I will be so quiet you will forget I am here — yes, as quiet as the little lizards who never waken you when they run across your walls at night. And I will help — I will wash your clothes, and if you get another broom, not that monstrous thing there, I will sweep your house for you. Oh, you will see how well I will work——'

Moses snorted. 'You? Sweep the house? You haven't the strength.'

'There, you see,' Godman twittered, waving his hands, 'you have said it yourself. What work could I do in this city where everything is so big? If you turn me out, I will die. Oh, the pity — to be freed only to die like a mouse——'

'But, Godman, you're not my responsibility. I have work to do, troubles, worries.'

'You brought me here,' Godman said sulkily.

'You asked me to bring you!' Moses cried.

'I did not know it would be like this,' Godman said miserably. 'So many people, and the noise, and those high buildings——'

He turned to Moses and held out both his hands.

'Oh, I am so frightened in this unknown place. How shall I know what to do, unless you are with me, to tell me what to do?'

'All right, all right,' Moses said grudgingly. 'A week, then, until you are more accustomed to the city. Perhaps

you will be stronger by then, too. But whether you are or
not, you must go. Do you understand?'

'Oh yes!' Godman said gaily. 'I understand. When I
am with you, I understand everything.'

At the end of the week, the scene was enacted all over
again. And once more Godman stayed.

Only a child is agile enough to be small. Inside the house,
Godman managed fairly well, but on the street his stump-
legs stumbled with his fear. At first he could not be persuaded
to go out alone at all, and when finally he ventured out
timidly, he refused to go more than a few blocks away. The
cars and bicycles, the jostling market women with their
huge wheel-like head trays, the quick children whose voices
could so easily turn to jeering, the high and heavy shops
white-blazing in the sun, the streets close and tangled as
vines, streets where anyone might easily lose the way and
where a very small man might conceivably never find it
again — all these, and the eyes of the city's curiosity, were
terrifying enough to Godman, but they were not all.

'I know Faru will never find me in this place, he said
gravely to Moses one evening. 'I know it very well. But —
somehow, I know it so much better when you are with
me.'

So for the most part the dwarf remained indoors, waiting
all day for Moses to return from work. Despite the promise
of silence, after the restricted years Godman's loquaciousness
knew no bounds. The moment Moses arrived home, the
voice began to chirp and never ceased until Godman went
to sleep. Moses would try to read and would angrily tell
Godman to keep quiet. But concentration would still be
impossible, because Godman in abject apology would
squeeze and fold himself together until he seemed no bigger
than an embryo and would maintain a silence so plainly
sorrowful that Moses would finally throw down his book

in disgust and tell the little man he might speak. Immediately, Godman would jump up, put on the tea-kettle, and come marching back, wearing a chaplet of leaves and carrying in his hand a lime stuck on a twig.

'Omanhene, great chief, see — I am your soul-bearer, and here is my staff. '

And Moses would laugh despite himself, and be annoyed at his laughter. When Moses stripped himself to bathe, Godman would be there, perched like a great-eyed owl on the dresser that held the wash basin, admiring with gentle clucking exclamations the immensity of Moses' parts compared with his own, until Moses, embarrassed, and annoyed at his embarrassment, would order him out of the room. And always Godman would go, humbly, never knowing what his offence had been but never questioning that Moses was right.

A hundred times Moses was on the point of telling the little man he must leave. But where could he go? What would he be able to do, by himself, in this city of giants? Moses could imagine Godman squashed like a cockroach under the heedless tramping feet of the markets and streets.

Gradually, the dwarf's health improved. He would never be anything but fragile, but the exhausting cough disappeared and he seemed to find breathing less a burden than it had been. His skin, mercifully, lost some of its crinkled sogginess. Moses no longer found him repulsive to look at, but whether this change was due to an actual improvement in Godman's appearance or merely to an acceptance born of familiarity, Moses did not know. He brought home bottles of codliver oil and samples of vitamin pills for the ex-oracle. He was not prompted by sentiment or any real concern. But a pharmacist could not allow an obvious case of malnutrition and vitamin deficiency to remain untreated in his house. Besides, as Godman grew stronger, he was able to earn his board by doing some of the household tasks. Moses prided himself upon being a practical man.

And yet, one night when Godman went out to buy cigarettes for Moses from a trader woman who had a stall across the road, and did not return, Moses set out to look for him. He finally found him near a cluster of roadside stalls some distance away, crouched in a gutter, unable to fend off the stick-thrusting urchins who were tormenting him. The trader woman near the house had closed her stall, and he had not wanted to return without the cigarettes. Moses slapped and swore at the boys, who seemed stunned at his sudden and furious descent upon them. Then he picked up Godman and carried him home like a child.

In the months that followed, Godman became quite adept at cooking. He often spent most of the day preparing some favourite food for Moses — groundnut stew, soup with snails, ripe plantain cakes.

'I like to see you eat,' he said once, as Moses took another helping. 'What an appetite you've got! No wonder you are such a strong man. Now, I'll tell you how I learned to make this dish. The big woman upstairs — you know, the big big one, wears an orange cloth patterned with little insects, they look like dung beetles to me, just the thing for her, her breath stinks, no wonder, she's always eating sweets, what can you expect — well, she showed me. She put her charcoal burner on the stoep outside our window and she saw me watching her, so she offered to show me just how she made the soup. The cocoyam leaves must not be boiled too long, that's the thing. And when you take the snails out of their shells, you wash them in water with lime juice. Clever, eh?'

'Very clever,' Moses said, with his mouth full. 'If you

learned man's work half as well as you learn women's, you would be a great success.'

Godman looked offended. 'The white men have men for their cooks, and you are more important than any white man. Of course, if you do not want me to make soup for you——'

'I was joking,' Moses said hastily. 'I'm sorry. The soup is fine. I have never tasted better.'

And Godman, mollified, sang to himself in an unmusical croak as he cleared away the dishes.

Moses bought several pieces of tradecloth for the dwarf, to replace his flimsy rags. When Godman saw them, he seized one and draped it around himself at once. Then he rushed around the room to the dresser, scrambled up, and stood for a long time, silent, looking into the mirror, awed by his own splendour.

'Oh, I am a chief, a king. See there, the fishes on the cloth, that blue one, he with the tail like a palm leaf —oh, and the red of his eyes! The greatest of all fish, isn't he? And the snail, see, just like the ones I put in the soup. Oh, did any person ever see such a fine cloth as this?'

Moses turned away, feeling a sense of sadness and shame at how little this richness had cost him.

That same week, Moses first met Mercy Ansah. Mercy was a teacher in a primary school. She was pretty and intelligent; her family was reasonably well off, but not so rich that Moses need feel the girl was out of his reach. He began to take her out frequently, and several times he went to her home for dinner. He wondered if it would be proper to invite her to his place. He had no family here, but Godman would prepare the meal.

Godman. Moses felt sick. Could he say to Mercy Ansah —'There is a certain dwarf, formerly an oracle, who shares my dwelling——'? Mercy would think he was insane. The situation had gone far enough. However helpless, Godman would have to go.

But if Godman went, Moses would have to go back to preparing his own unappetizing meals. Either that or buy his food in some grimy chop-bar. All at once Moses saw that he was wondering not how the dwarf would manage alone, but how he himself would manage without Godman.

Moses was so distressed by the realization that he refused to think about it. He invited Mercy for dinner, and he explained nothing. Mercy, far from being repelled by the dwarf, seemed to find him interesting. Perhaps she regarded Godman only as a curiosity — Moses could not tell. But she praised the little man's cooking, and when Godman had left the room, she spoke of him again.

'You are quite lucky, Moses, to have such a good servant.'

Moses blinked. Of course. That was why Godman's presence had not seemed strange to her. She had simply assumed Godman was his servant.

'Yes,' he said slowly, 'perhaps I am lucky.'

'Do you pay regular wages for such a small man?' Mercy laughed.

Moses did not reply.

When he returned after taking Mercy Ansah home, Moses found Godman still awake and waiting for him.

'What a fine woman she is! What a splendid choice! Is her father rich? You will marry her? She has a good heart — in her voice and her eyes, it was plain. She is gentle. You must marry a gentle woman, not one of those shrewish ones who nag and yelp. What a pair you will make! And oh, my master, what children you will have!'

Moses sat down tiredly.

'Godman, listen to me. I cannot afford to have a servant,

and anyway, I do not want one. Somehow I had not seen until tonight — it happened so gradually — the work you do——'

'Do I not work well? Are you displeased with me? The groundnut stew — oh, I prepared it carefully, carefully, I swear it——'

'Yes, yes, it was a fine stew,' Moses said impatiently. 'Only — you do not know some things about living as a man. A man — a man has to work and be paid for it. I cannot pay you, Godman.'

'Sometimes you speak so strangely. It grieves me when I do not know what you mean. Pay? You do pay me. You protect me. What could I do alone? Without you, I am nameless, a toad that the boys stone. Oh, I bless your strength — have I not said so? Where is there a man like my master?'

'Stop it!' Moses shouted. 'You must not call me that. You are not my servant.'

'I have called you master before, many times,' Godman said reproachfully, 'and you never became angry. Why are you so angry now?'

Moses stared. 'Before? You said it before? And I did not even——'

'Anyway, what does it matter?' Godman continued. 'It is all foolishness, this talk. Why should I not call you master? You are my master — and more——'

Then he capered like a dusty night-moth.

'Oh, I see it now!' he cried. 'Of course you are angry. I am stupid, stupid! My head is the head of an earthworm, small and blind. Every servant says "master" and what does he mean by it? Nothing. But for me, it was not that. Did you not know — can you not have realized what I meant?'

'What are you trying to say? Say it.'

'You are my priest,' Godman said. 'What else?'

Moses could not speak. Godman's priest, the soul-master, he who owned a man. Had Godman only moved from the simple bondage of the amber-eyed Faru to another bondage? And as for Moses himself — what became of a deliverer who had led with such assurance out of the old and obvious night, only to falter into a subtler darkness, where new-carved idols bore the known face, his own? Horrified, Moses wondered how much he had come to depend on Godman's praise.

'Godman, try — try to understand. That is a word you must not speak. Not to me. Never, never to me.'

Godman looked puzzled.

'You saved me,' he said. 'You cannot deny that you saved me. I would have died if I had stayed there much longer. You lifted the lid of the box and let me out. It was no other man. You were the one. Who else, then, should protect me? Who else should I serve? Who else's name should I forever bless? You freed me. I am yours.'

Moses put his head down onto his hands.

'There is more to freedom,' he said, 'than not living in a box.'

Godman fixed ancient eyes upon Moses.

'You would not think so if you had ever lived in a box.'

Moses raised his head and forced himself to look at the dwarf. He and Godman were bound together with a cord more delicate, more difficult to see, than any spun by the children of Ananse. Yet it was a cord which could strangle.

'You have been here too long,' Moses said dully. 'The time has come for you to go.'

The little man, seeing from Moses' face that he was in earnest, began to moan and mourn, hugging his arms around

155

himself and swaying to and fro in an anguish that was both ridiculous and terrible.

'Why, why, why? What have I done? How have I offended you? Why do you forsake me? Oh, I did not know you had such a sickness in your heart. And I am not ready to go — I am not ready yet — I will die, certainly——'

Moses felt a saving anger.

'No one is ever ready,' he said. 'And you will not die.'

But later, after the arguments and the explanations he knew to be useless, when at last he locked his door and turned off his lamp and could hear only the sound of his own breathing, Moses no longer felt certain. All that night he lay awake in case there should be a faint rustling at his door. But none came.

In the next few weeks, Moses worried a good deal and asked himself unanswerable questions and sometimes saw in dreams the oracle as he had appeared in that first glimpse — a fragment of damp and flaccid skin, a twist of rag on the festering straw. Then Moses would waken, sweating and listening, and would smoke one cigarette after another until he was able to push the picture from his mind. But after a while he thought of Godman less and less, and finally he thought of him scarcely at all.

One evening, about a year later, when he returned after work to the whitewashed bungalow that was his home now, his wife Mercy handed him that day's newspaper.

'Look, Moses——'

It was a large advertisement for a travelling troupe of jugglers, snake-charmers and sleight-of-hand magicians. In one corner was a photograph of a very small man, a man not three feet tall, a toy-sized man dressed in an embroidered robe and a turban. Moses read the words under the picture.

*Half god*                  *Half man*
### SEE REAL LIVE ORACLE
*Hundreds of years old*
*Smallest man alive*
*— Foretells future —*

Moses put down the paper. 'An oracle — it was the only thing he knew how to be. Half man — did you see? A halfman.'

'Moses — don't blame yourself.'

Moses turned on her. 'Who else? I should have known no one would hire him for any proper work.'

'He really couldn't have stayed,' Mercy said primly. 'It was all very well when you were a single man. But I could not have stood it for long — to have him running around the house like a weird child, wrinkled and old——'

'That is not why I made him go,' Moses snapped. 'It was — something else.'

'I know,' Mercy said at once. 'Yes, I know. You told me.'

It was true that he had told her. But she did not know. No one knew, least of all Godman himself.

'I thought I was doing what had to be done,' Moses said. 'But now — I wonder who owns him this time?'

'Will you go there?' Mercy asked.

'No,' Moses said fiercely. 'I don't want to see him.'

But of course he did go. The show was in a great grey flapping tent at the edge of town. Moses pushed and elbowed his way through the crowd that waited to be admitted, shouting young men and their gay-talking girls. Inside the tent was a long stage, and there sat Godman, flamboyant as a canna lily in scarlet turban and green robe. When the little man saw Moses, he jumped down and ran towards him.

'Mister Adu! It is my old friend! I never thought to see your face again. Here — come and sit down behind this curtain. We can talk until the people come in.'

'How are you, Godman?' Moses asked uncertainly. 'Do they treat you well?'

'Oh yes. They give me money, you know, and the food is plentiful. Moving around all the time, I find it is hard on my lungs — different air in each place, so the lungs have trouble sometimes. My old cough comes back in the rainy season. But I cannot really complain. Do you like my robe? I have four, all different colours, and a silk turban to go with each.'

'You are still an oracle,' Moses said tonelessly. 'You have not changed much.'

The little man looked at him in surprise.

'What did you expect?' he said haughtily. 'Did you think I would turn into a giant? Lucky for me I am alive at all, after the way you treated me. Oh, I don't hold it against you now, but you must admit it was cruel, almost as cruel as Faru, whose eye still burns at me when I sleep. I stayed under the *niim* tree outside your house that night — you never knew I was there. I could not move my legs. They were dead with fear, two pillars of stone. But in the morning I crawled away, and oh, the things that have happened since that day — it would take me a year and more than a year to tell you. For I ate cat, and slept cold, and trapped cutting-grass, and shrivelled in the sun like a seed. And I drank palm wine with a blind beggar, and pimped for a painted girl, and sang like a bird with a mission band for the white man's god. And I rode a blue mammy-lorry with a laughing driver who feared the night voices, and I walked the forest with a leper who taught me to speak pidgin, and I caught a parrot and tamed it and put into its mouth the words "money sweet" and we begged together until I tired of it and sold it to an old woman who had no daughters. And — the rest I forget.'

'You are the same,' Moses said, bewildered. 'And yet — you are not quite the same.'

A tall, heavily built man slouched past, arranging his black and turquoise cloth casually over one shoulder. Godman called out to him in pidgin.

'Hey, you Kwaku! Meka you ready?'

'I ready one-time. Go 'long, man. I coming.'

Moses peered questioningly at Godman.

'Who's that?' he asked sharply. 'Not another——? Not your——?'

'That one?' Godman said offhandedly. 'Oh, that is only Kwaku. We do the oracle part together. These young men who pay to see us — they do not believe, you know, but we make them laugh. They like me — you would be surprised. It is not such an easy thing, to find where the laughter is hidden, like gold in the rock. One has to be skilled for this work. The *pirafo* used to be fine jesters, and now, perhaps, again.'

He touched Moses lightly on the hand, and Moses, looking at the man, began to comprehend.

'You have done well,' Moses said. 'At first I did not see it, but now I see it.'

Godman shrugged.

'I have known the worst and the worst and the worst,' he said, 'and yet I live. I fear and fear, and yet I live.'

'No man,' Moses said gently, 'can do otherwise.'

The band began to assemble. Two boys with the wide faces of coast fishermen, but now wearing pink striped shirts and fancy sombreros, grinned as they clambered onto the stage with their battered cornets. A lanky desert man, his ancient past burned onto his face in the long gashes that told his tribe, began to plink at a flower-painted guitar. The drummer set up the kettle drum and the bass drum, new and shiny, beside the graceful thonged drums and the carved wood drums born of the forest longer ago than anyone could tell. Shuffling feet, scraping chairs, as the crowd came in.

And Godman Pira waved to Moses and hopped up to take his place with the other performers on the broad and grimy stage.

# A Fetish for Love

'**D**IS my wife, madam,' Sunday said, standing to attention quite unnecessarily. 'She name Love.'

Had the African woman been pocked as a sprig
of coral, or ancient as a prophetess, Constance would still
have been delighted with the name. But Love was young
and had an agreeable appearance, so the name was even
more of a treasure.

Surely Sunday would be less difficult now. He was a great
deal older than Love, and the disparity seemed sad, but
Constance did not want to consider even the possibility of
more problems. Sunday, virtually major-domo in this
house for the six years Brooke had lived here as a bachelor,
had not taken easily to the presence of Brooke's wife. He
was polite, always, but he was not friendly. Constance was
friendly, and she saw no reason why other people should not
be the same. Another thing — Sunday resented the slightest
criticism. He constantly carped at Ofei, the steward-boy,
but when Constance mentioned (quite quietly, suppressing
her horror and indignation) that the kitchen store-room was
a-flutter with the amber wings of cockroaches, Sunday
marched in angrily and saturated everything with D.D.T.
spray, ruining an entire case of expensive imported potatoes.
Sunday's wife had never lived here with him on the coast.
She had stayed in her up-country village, where he used to
visit her occasionally on week-ends, cadging a lift with a
lorry-driver he knew. When he suggested bringing his wife

here, Constance had agreed at once. Of course. Why had they not thought of it sooner? He would be happier and therefore more reasonable.

Constance held out her hand, and the girl took it, but very lightly, touching only the fingertips.

'I greet madam.' The voice was a hushed whisper, only a shade removed from silence.

Sunday was strapping on his cook's apron once more. His ageing but still-handsome face now yielded a warm astonishing smile.

'She too fear, madam. Nevah she stay for Eur'pean house befoah dis time. She stay for bush. But I teach she, madam. She savvy some small pidgin.'

Small pidgin. No wonder she was so shy. Had 'pidgin', through some semantic maze, come from 'pigeon'? Love herself was like some small pigeon, soft and plump, fine-feathered in cloth of a blue delicate as sky, printed with yellowing green leaves like ripe limes. She stood perfectly still, but uncertainly, as though her heart might any moment rise in panic and she herself fly away, as noiselessly as she had come.

'I'm glad you're here, Love,' Constance said, enunciating distinctly. 'I do hope you'll be happy with us.'

Love looked at her blankly. Sunday translated, an angry spitting out of words in his own tongue, ending with an admonition in pidgin — 't'ank madam'.

'I t'ank madam,' Love said obediently.

Now a little parrot. Constance smiled at her own slight sense of irritation. Love would learn.

'She'll do the baby's wash, Sunday?'

'Yes, madam. I tell you so. She do all. You got some cloth for wash now?'

'She can start with the bucket of nappies. It's in the bathroom.'

'One-time, madam,' Sunday said. 'I bring now.'

The girl waited, not understanding, the brown face expressionless as a bird's. Sunday started out of the kitchen, his gaunt body bent forward in his hurry. He paused beside his wife and muttered to her. She nodded, and now the composure in her face seemed a genuine calm, not merely a bulwark against fear. Constance felt reassured and hopeful.

That evening she told Brooke about the arrival.

'It was worth all the arrangements, to get her here. He'll be more settled. Probably he'll work better, too.'

'He worked all right before, I thought,' Brooke said.

'You didn't know. You weren't here all day. He was — well, not exactly sullen, but——'

'That's his nature, Con. You can't change it. But if he wants her here, there's no reason why she shouldn't be.'

'Wait till you see her. You'll understand what I mean. She's simply lovely. I hope you don't agree too heartily.'

'Don't be daft,' Brooke said, and Constance, laughing, sat down on a hassock beside his chair and leaned her head against his arm, for she could not truthfully imagine Brooke wanting anyone else. They had been married for a year and a half, and now they had Small Thomas, who was sleeping at the moment, pink and milky under his mosquito net, and Constance, who had taught too long at a girls' school in England, still felt surprise at this wealth so unexpectedly acquired. Brooke continued to read the airmail edition of *The Times*, but he put a hand out and touched her hair.

'She did Small Thomas's washing today,' Constance continued, 'and it was perfect.'

The baby's name now almost seemed to be Small as well as Thomas, because that was the way Sunday referred to him, so Constance and Brooke had picked up the expression as well. The Africans had a knack with names. Constance was fascinated by the titles painted on the jaunty and jouncing lorries, themselves descriptively termed 'mammy-wagons'. Tiger Boy, King Kong, One-time Boy, Bless You, Freedom Man. The names of people were no less appealing. Imagine anyone called Sunday. When Constance had asked him about it, he said it was because his name was Kwesi, and she had sensed some mystery, rich and strange, until Brooke matter-of-factly told her Kwesi was the name given to the Sunday-born. Long ago Sunday had worked for some burning missionary, to whom African names meant darkness and damnation, so he had placatingly changed his name for the job's sake. Now Constance wondered about Love.

'How do you suppose she got the name, Brooke? At a mission school? I'll wager anything you like that it's from Saint Paul to the Corinthians. "Now abideth these three — Faith, Hope and——" Did you know that some churches substitute Love? Probably if she'd gone to a different one she'd have been called Charity, which would have been so cold, in comparison, wouldn't it?'

'Her village isn't far from Eburaso,' Brooke said absently, leafing through the paper to find the financial page. 'I expect someone in her family worked for Opie, Grange & Love, that's all. Big ironmongers. Sell mainly those black iron cooking-pots the Africans use.'

'How dramatic you are.'

'Mm?' He looked up then, and smiled. 'Sorry. Only——'

'What is it, Brooke?'

He put an arm around her.

'Be careful,' he said.

Constance had to admit after a few weeks that Love was something of a disappointment. Sunday remained unchanged, neither happier nor unhappier than before. Love herself was an enigma. She worked so quietly and moved so unobtrusively one hardly knew she was there. The features of her face seemed to denote a gentleness, yet she was no more friendly than Sunday. Her understanding of English had improved, and now she appeared to grasp nearly everything Constance said to her. But she replied only with a laconic 'Yes, madam' or 'No, madam'. Even to Sunday, Love spoke very little. When he shouted at her from the kitchen doorway, she would nod wordlessly and fetch wood for the stove. She worked with an easy physical grace, yet stolidly, with a phlegmatic quality that troubled Constance.

Sunday was a Christian who, unlike Brooke and Constance, went regularly to church. He would set off, dressed in his best khaki trousers and jacket, swinging his ebony cane with its mighty brass handle the size of a door-knob, shouting his haughty greeting to neighbouring cooks and stewards languidly enjoying a sabbath laziness in their own compounds. A few paces behind her husband Love would walk, softly splendid in her cloth of limes and sky.

'Does she want to go with him?' Constance peered thoughtfully out the window. 'Does she not want to? Impossible to tell. Does she mind walking behind him in that way? I certainly would.'

'You're not her,' Brooke said. 'Think we should take Small Thomas to the beach this morning, Con?'

On weekdays, while the bungalow was being cleaned by Ofei, Constance would put the baby in his pram and take him to the open front stoep. She would not leave him alone. Sometimes puff-adders were killed in the garden, and a scorpion was occasionally discovered on the bungalow's ochre walls, veiled by the moonflower vines. Constance stayed beside Small Thomas, talked to him, scrutinized his face to see if he had yet mastered the art of smiling. When he slept, sometimes Constance would read. More frequently, she merely meditated in the opium sunshine watching the hibiscus petals sleazily disarrayed like garish satin petticoats in the slight wind, or the mud-wasps hovering like miniature helicopters, or the sleek grey lizard perched on his grey and camouflaging rock, waiting to flick his lariat tongue around the incautious flies.

Since Love's arrival, Constance had a new occupation in the mornings. Concealed by the stoep pillar, she watched Love work. She was not trying to check on the girl's efficiency. She wanted, quite simply, to see Love's face when the girl believed herself to be alone.

Today Love was wearing her oldest cloth, a shabby salmon-pink, faded and hideously patterned in what appeared to be the keys for some giant prison door. Her bare broad feet, her least attractive feature, squelched in the damp earth of the garden as she carried the bucket to the flat stone beside the outdoor tap. She squatted and began to rub soap on Small Thomas's soiled clothing. Her arms moved rhythmically, and soon her body swayed and bent to the same beat. Then she began to sing. Her song was neither gay nor sad. It was a voice chanting, repetitive as rain, and that was all. Her face was no different from the one she always wore.

Love finished the washing and put the wet white pile in an enormous basin which she hoisted onto her head. She sauntered effortlessly over to the clothes-line as though the headpan had been weightless as a leaf. When everything was pegged on the line she returned, dumped the wash water, rinsed and cleaned the buckets. The soap frothed around her feet.

'Love!'

The girl's head came up. 'Madam?'

'Would you stay with Small Thomas for a few minutes? I'm going next door. I shan't be long.'

With the unhurried calm which Constance had come to expect of her, Love walked over to the stoep and sat down beside the pram. Constance fussed a little over the baby, needlessly rearranging the coverlets. Then she walked briskly away, knowing her sense of momentary freedom was not a betrayal of her child, yet feeling it must be so.

When Constance returned, the garden boy was chopping with his machete at the coarse grass in the uncultivated half-acre at the side of the house. Constance had told Love she could use this land for a tomato patch, which was the thing Love seemed to want above all else. The garden boy was nasally intoning a highlife tune. The girl on the stoep sat with her back to Constance and did not hear her approach.

Love had Small Thomas in her arms. She was not crooning to him, or speaking. She made no sound at all. She was not even rocking him to and fro, as Constance herself might have done to stop his crying. Love was only holding him, lightly, almost loosely, and looking at him.

Startled at her own intensity, Constance felt she must see Love's face. She had to see it, to know what it contained now, this moment. She turned and walked around the other side of the bungalow, and when she approached again she walked with particular care so that her shoes would not scuff betrayingly against stones. Then, hardly knowing what to expect, she looked at Love.

Nothing. Nothing to be seen. Perhaps a warning pebble had been dislodged after all, for everything had changed back, like the metamorphosis in a child's fairy tale — when the spell is broken, all things return to their own forms and no one can believe it was ever otherwise. Small Thomas was in his pram, dozing. Love sat beside the pram, her cloth in neat folds around her.

Constance felt cheated and at the same time disgusted at

herself. She examined the baby's pram and turned crossly to Love.

'You picked him up, Love, didn't you?'

Love looked at her without blinking.

'No, madam,' she said evenly. 'I no do so.'

'You did!' Constance cried. 'I——'

But of course she could not say why she knew. She lifted the baby and took him indoors. Did she imagine it or had she seen on Love's bland mouth, just then, the merest trace of a smiling malice?

Hunter & Peacock, Exporters-Importers, had offices in town close to the Club, so Brooke did not come home for lunch. Alone, Constance munched a slab of omelette. As Sunday brought the sweet, a blancmange of alarming solidity, she turned to look at him through the serving hatch. He was pushing the blancmange gingerly with one finger to a more properly central place on the plate. Everything must present a correct appearance. He disapproved entirely of Ofei, who sometimes forgetfully served plates from the wrong side. Sunday prided himself upon his precise knowledge, and he vehemently resisted any attempt to alter or abandon tradition. Constance, to save money, had tried to have fewer courses served at dinner, but it had not worked. Clearly, both soup and fish were necessary to Sunday's peace of mind.

'That looks good,' Constance said, with an approval she did not feel. Then, casually, 'I meant to ask you, Sunday — how long have you been married to Love?'

'Four year, madam.'

'That long? She doesn't look old enough——'

His fleeting scowl told her that interest (permissible, even admirable) had once more become curiosity.

'You no savvy, madam. African girl no be same——'

'Oh, of course.' She nodded rapidly, in embarrassment. She wanted to stop, but was compelled on. 'She — you haven't had children?'

'No, madam.' The voice was flat, unstressed.

Now something else occurred to her. Was he polygamous? Plenty of men were, here. She wondered how Love would feel, sharing him, perhaps, with some irascible leather-skinned matron his own age.

'Is Love — is she your only wife, Sunday?'

Ought she, perhaps, not to have asked? But he was used to questions. He had worked in domestic service for twenty-five years.

'Yes, madam,' he said, and his oddly patient voice distressed Constance more than if he had (inexcusably) shouted. 'I got only dis one.'

Now she wanted to make some restitution, to erase somehow her probing.

'I'm so glad you brought her here,' she said impulsively. 'She's awfully nice.'

'Yes, madam,' Sunday said.

Late that afternoon Constance heard him beating Love.

At first, when she heard the roaring out in the compound, she did not think much about it. Sunday was variable. His frequent bouts of irritation with Ofei usually amounted only to frowns and muttered insults. Occasionally, however, his temper would erupt like fireworks in a lightless sky, and he would rant dementedly at Ofei or the garden boy over a triviality which the day or even the hour before would scarcely have ruffled him at all. Usually Constance took no notice. But today, when the sound continued, she began to listen.

Sunday's bitter voice rose and rose until it was as piercing as a vindictive crone's. It dropped, roughened, grew low and hoarse with threat. Then Love's brief voice, as he hit her. Again and again. Afterwards, quiet everywhere, until the first cicadas of evening struck up their monotonous violins.

Constance found Love at the side of the bungalow and knelt beside her. The blood on the girl's face had dried, leaving dark rivers like cooled lava on her skin. She was not crying. Crouching, she had drawn the cover-cloth from her shoulders halfway around her head, as though to make herself invisible this way.

'Let me — at least let me bathe your face, put something on it——'

'I beg you——' Love strained for the words. 'You go, madam. I no need for notheen. I beg you go.'

'I can't leave you here like this. What will you do? You won't stay with him now, after what he——'

Only then did the girl look at her, and Constance saw the slight frown, the puzzled eyes.

'I nevah go, madam.'

'But——'

The girl slipped her cover-cloth back around her shoulders and began to brush her fingers lightly across her face. Her tongue licked away the red crust around her mouth.

'You t'ink my muddah greet me well?' Love said steadily, without inflection. 'Where you t'ink I go, madam?'

Constance knew it was not within her rights to speak to Sunday about the matter, but she took Love as her reason, although she was not certain whether she felt actual sympathy for the girl, who was now placidly hoeing the land the garden boy had cleared, or whether she was moved only by a sense of justice outraged.

Sunday stood to attention. His eyes were wary but his face was still emboldened by the anger that had filled him like rum. But Constance was angry, too, so she faced him without hesitation.

'Why, Sunday? Why did you do that to her?'

'Madam?' As always when a touchy subject was broached, he pretended not to comprehend.

'You know quite well what I mean.'

Sunday did not speak at once. He pulled the edge of his cook's apron through his tightly knotted hands like a handkerchief through a ring. She saw then that the sweat from his forehead was running down into his eyes like tears. He made no move to wipe his face. His hands continued to work the cloth. His features might have been those of a gold-weight figure, long ago cast in bronze and now time-darkened. Then he spoke — not to her, it seemed, but to whatever God or gods dwelt behind his eyes.

'What I do for get dis trouble? What I nevah do, for get dis trouble? Love, she fine for all t'ing, but for dis one t'ing she nevah fine. Dis woman nevah make pickin. She no be propra woman for dis t'ing. Man he no got pickin, what he do? Who care for he? Nevah she make for me one small son——'

The words clotted in his throat. He did not even look at Constance. Perhaps he had forgotten she was there. He turned and walked away, and his hands were over his eyes.

Constance told Brooke that evening.

'I can see that he feels badly, but it's dreadful that he should take it out on her. As though it were something she could help. As usual, she has nothing to say. But how on earth must she feel? I don't know what to do.'

'Con,' Brooke said gently, 'why don't you just do nothing, my dear?'

'Nothing?' Constance cried. 'Brooke, she has nowhere to go. And she certainly can't do anything for herself. She doesn't know. You were right about the name, by the way. She's never been to school in her life. Maybe I should take her to see Guy. He's not a gynaecologist, but he might be able — there might be some quite simple thing that could be put right.'

Brooke shrugged. 'Well, I suppose it can't do any actual harm.'

'But you don't think I should take her? Why not? What is it?'

'I wonder,' Brooke said slowly, 'if Love is really as helpless as you think?'


Guy Bennington was a tiny man with a pallid moustache like stiffly bundled straw. He looked ineffectual, mild as porridge. In fact, however, he worked prodigiously and was in consequence irritable and impatient much of the time.

Constance sat in the chair opposite his desk. Love stood, hesitantly, poised for flight, just inside the doorway. She had not wanted to come, even when Constance explained.

'She bush girl — no savvy doctah palavah,' Sunday had said apologetically. 'She will go. I tell she.'

He had spoken to Love brusquely. She had nodded in her docile way and had followed Constance out to the car. But she had not said a word all the way to the doctor's office.

'You're looking well, Constance,' Guy said. 'How's Thomas?'

'Thriving, thanks. I didn't come about myself. You know our cook—Sunday?'

'Yes.' The doctor looked over at Love. 'That his wife? Not bad. What's the trouble?'

Constance told him. Guy sighed.

'I suppose you haven't any idea how many children here die in the first year of their lives, from malaria and typhoid and such? Or how many grow up in the markets and gutters, like so many cockroaches? Our problem isn't too few babies — it's too many. We can't look after those we've got.'

Constance leaned her elbows on his desk and looked at him intently. 'That's — people. This is a person. It's not the same thing.'

'There must be an answer to that,' Guy said with a grudging smile. 'Perhaps if I weren't so busy I might think of it. All right. Leave her here. I'll examine her and have the usual tests done.'

The African nurse began to speak to Love in her own tongue. Love did not reply. She stood absolutely still, her face blank as water. Only when Constance, turning to go, glanced and smiled, did she see the tremor of fear in Love's eyes.

When Constance returned, the girl was waiting for her on the steps outside.

'You all right, Love?'

'Yes, madam.'

'It wasn't too bad, then? I told you — I know Dr. Bennington well. He's a very good man.'

'A good man, madam.'

Parroting, parroting. Nothing of her own. What did she think? Constance could not tell. She went inside to see Guy Bennington.

'Well?'

'I know you'd like to hear every single detail,' Guy said, 'but I haven't time for that. I've got fifty people waiting to see me, and how I'm going to cope with them, I wish I knew.'

His voice was edgy and abrupt. He handed Constance a prescription slip.

'Here. She can start with this. After a few months, we'll see.'

Constance felt she was being put off. 'But what do you think, Guy? Was there anything definite?'

'You expect everything to be plain as a wart on your

finger. Well, it's not. She can try that stuff or not, as she pleases. I don't give a damn.'

'Of course she will. I only wanted to know——'

'What you wanted was a guarantee,' Guy said tiredly. 'It's what everyone wants. I'm afraid I can't give it. I'm not God, although sometimes I think it would be an advantage if I were. Nothing like a miracle to boost one's reputation.'

Constance had the driver stop at Palm Chemists. The prescription proved to be a thick liquid of an interesting pale green hue. Love's face, as she looked at the medicine, took on a faint animation. Gratified and heartened, Constance allowed her to hold the bottle on the way home.

Now the administering of Love's medicine became a ritual. Each morning Constance would go out to the kitchen, measure a spoonful of the murky green potion, and give it to the girl. Sunday, stern as a recording angel, stood by to ensure that his wife swallowed every drop.

'She no savvy doctah befoah dis time,' he would say, with benevolent condescension, 'but now she savvy small-small, madam.'

Once or twice, opening her mouth like an infant bird, Love giggled. This in itself was progress, Constance felt. For the most part, Love's face was as enclosed as ever, but perhaps she was beginning to relax. That might be important. The elimination of tension. Constance began to speculate — if it was a boy, he could play with Small Thomas. She wondered what they would call him. She would not mind being godmother, if they asked her. But the months went by, and the first bottle was replaced by a second and a third. Constance did not like to question Love directly, and Love did not volunteer any pertinent information.

Love's tomatoes were planted and grew and bore fruit in

what seemed an incredibly short time to Constance. Love gave some of them to Constance, and the rest she sold in the town markets. Each week when Constance went into town to do her shopping, Love accompanied her with tomato-laden baskets. In the car, Constance attempted to talk, but Love only murmured her apathetic 'yes' or 'no' replies. Once, however, she displayed a pair of filigree ear-rings like golden spider-webs.

'How pretty,' Constance said enthusiastically. 'Where did you get them?'

'Sunday, he give for me,' Love said. She lowered her eyes, then glanced at Constance almost slyly. 'Palavah time, he give for me.'

Sunday had given her the earrings after he beat her. Constance, confused and at a loss, tried to decipher a meaning from the girl's face but once again she could find nothing there.

When Constance had finished her shopping that morning, the driver did not head towards the market to pick up Love.

'Madam 'gree we go for Tintown?' he asked casually. 'Love go deah dis time.'

Constance was surprised and a little annoyed, but she agreed. Tintown was one of the outskirts of the city, a collection of mud and wattle huts inhabited by the very poor, a puzzle of narrow convoluted streets roamed by goats and children, a confusion of tin-roof shanties and shops, broken-down tea houses where marijuana was sold, brothels where girls in flowered cloths lolled in dusty doorways.

The driver kept one hand on the horn. Honking like a gander, the car bumped and skidded through the streets of Tintown. The driver drew up outside a decayed hut, leaned out and shouted, then settled down to wait. Constance smoked a cigarette and grew impatient. She started to open the car door. The driver swung around.

'No, madam,' he said warningly. 'You no go deah. Dis one no good for you.'

'Why? What's she doing? Does she have relatives here?'

'No, madam.'

'Well, tell me, then.'

The driver shrugged. 'Woman wey live deah, she sell some power t'ing, plenty different-different t'ing.'

'What on earth do you mean, Kofi?'

'She ju-ju woman,' the driver said.

Constance stared at him. Then, overwhelmed with her anger, she got out of the car and walked inside the hut. The place was partitioned with an old shower-curtain of cracked plastic speckled with grey mould and patterned with ferns and fishes. The outer room was bare — only a wooden chair with one leg missing, and a chipped enamel dish containing a tin spoon and a congealed chunk of *fu-fu*. Constance drew aside the grimy plastic and stepped into the other room.

She blinked away the darkness and soon she could make out a packing-case topped with a piece of orange velveteen which was spotted with oil from a red clay bowl bearing a smokily burning wick. For a long moment she focused her eyes upon the makeshift table before she could summon stamina to look further. On the greasy plush surface lay innumerable oddities — a bundle of dried and darkened roots, a saucer of leaves snipped into shreds, black bowls full of bluestone and raw yellow sulphur, a leather amulet, a pocket mirror cracked across its face, a string of small rusty bells, iron keys, an ivory crucifix daubed with pale clay into which had been set the glittering green and amber splinters from broken beer bottles.

Constance forced her eyes up and away, and saw a woman kneeling, forehead almost touching the earth floor. It was Love.

Nearby, the ju-ju woman squatted. She was enormously fat, puffed out and spreading like a blowfish in some cavern of the sea. Her cloth, black and red, quivered and shook with its burden of flesh. She wore no headscarf and her unbraided and unoiled hair sprouted from her head like a black gigantic dandelion gone to seed. In her huge silver-ringed hands she held a cord dotted with lumps of clay and cowrie shells. Her eyes were almost lost in flesh, but when at last she looked up, the eyes unburied themselves, grew to diamonds, hard and sharp. She did not speak. She gazed for a second, then hawked up phlegm from her throat and spat into the dust at Constance's feet.

'Love——' Constance spoke more loudly than she had intended, and the girl, startled, jerked up her head. Her face took on a defensive look.

'I pay wit' my money, madam. I sell tamantas for market. Dis no be money wey you give for Sunday.'

'Never mind that.' Now Constance was able to infuse her voice with steadiness and confidence. 'We're going home, Love. Come on.'

Love shook her head and spoke almost inaudibly. 'I can no do so.'

For the first time Constance felt frightened, but of what she did not know. She spoke severely, scoldingly.

'Love, get up at once. You're coming back with me. Do you hear?'

The girl, staring up at her, started to obey. She had half risen when the old woman began to speak, crooningly, a slow outpouring of words that washed and waned like tides. Harsh and soothing by turns, the words beat upon Love, and she sank down again until she was crouched on all fours like some small soft-furred animal in a cage it cannot see but knows to be there.

'Love!' Constance cried, astounded at the pain in her

own voice. 'She can't do anything for you. She can't! It won't work. Don't you see?'

Love looked at Constance as though she did not recognize her. The ju-ju woman put one hand on the girl's forehead and began stroking the skin, lightly, insistently. Then she spoke, not gloatingly, not even with emphasis, simply a statement.

'Mek you go, madam. I t'ink she no hear you propra dis time.'

Constance turned without a word and walked away. When she had pushed through the plastic curtain and emerged once more into the daylight, she found her face was wet with tears, but she did not know whether they were for Love or merely for herself, that she had lost.

She had the driver stop at Guy Bennington's office. She wiped her streaked face and walked in. She had not intended to tell him everything, but she did.

'You'll have to see her again,' she finished. 'There must be something else you could try. At least you could explain to her that she mustn't go there. She won't accept it from me, apparently.'

'That's what hurts, isn't it?' Guy said.

Constance began to deny it. Then she remembered how she had felt at the ju-ju woman's hut, and could not reply after all. The whole business had begun with such clarity, but now she was no longer sure of her own reasons.

'I really didn't want to tell you,' Guy continued, 'but I suppose I shall have to, now.'

'What is it?' Constance felt a quick fury, like that of a child who realizes the grown-ups are keeping something from her and yet cannot force them to reveal the violent mysteries of their exclusive world.

'There's nothing wrong with Love,' Guy said bluntly. 'She's as able to have children as you are.'

Constance could not believe it. 'Then why——?'

'The medicine? Quite harmless. A glucose mixture.'

'But,' Constance cried, 'that's no better than the old woman's——'

'Not a bit better,' he admitted. 'But I wasn't actually prescribing for Love. For you, rather.'

'For me!'

'Well, you were determined that something had to be done, weren't you? Now please don't take umbrage, Constance. I haven't time to cope with hysterical women.'

He handed her a cigarette and lit it for her.

'You didn't know what happened to Sunday's two previous wives, Constance?'

'Wives? He told me Love was the only one.'

'There were two before Love. He sent them away. Because they didn't bear him any children.'

'That's——' Constance stammered. 'Why, it's monstrous.'

'Is it? Not to have children is something of a disgrace. Not merely a heartbreak. A deep shame. I don't think he'll send this one away, though. He's getting old. And she — well, she bears his anger. Fortunately, she's able to.'

'How can she? How can she stand it?'

'She may accept the blame as rightfully hers, for all I know. If not — well, she's wise enough not to cast it up to him.'

'It's damned unfair,' Constance said.

Guy met her reproachful eyes. 'Do you think so? To be a cook in a European house — it's not as fashionable as it used to be, you know. Several of his nephews are clerks, and another's studying law. I suspect he may have found it relatively easy to be proud, once, but now not so easy. As for this — there could be any number of causes, and the chances are that I wouldn't be able to help him. I'd rather not risk it. Perhaps he knows it's his burden. Perhaps he won't let himself know. But if he were forced to recognize and admit — could he bear it, do you think?'

Constance remembered the necessary haughtiness of the man, the white apron clenched in his hands, and the way he had covered his eyes.

'I don't know,' she said slowly. 'I — can't know.'

'No more can I.'

It was only then that she wondered how Guy could have learned as much as he had about Sunday's life. Then she realized.

'Why didn't Brooke simply tell me? Why didn't he tell *me*?'

'If he had,' Guy said, 'wouldn't you have wanted to persuade Sunday to consult your ju-ju man?'

Love walked back to the bungalow that day. Neither she nor Constance ever mentioned their encounter in Tintown. The orderly routine of living went on unchanged. Love did Small Thomas's washing, and sometimes she sat beside him while Constance went to a friend's for morning coffee. The medicine bottle was not refilled, and one day Constance, seeing it there with its slimy remnants, threw it out. Sunday never spoke of it. He was accustomed to employers' spasmodic enthusiasms and the inevitable dwindling of their interest.

Occasionally there would be an uproar in the compound, and Constance would hear Sunday shouting his grief, and Love's voice, soon turning to silence. From time to time the girl displayed a gold bracelet or a bright beaded necklace, which Constance dutifully admired. Love's face remained impassive.

One morning, rising earlier than usual to feed a dismally howling Small Thomas, Constance looked out of the bedroom window to the garden and saw Love. The girl was kneeling on the hard earth. She held a carved figure, a child of wood. Her hands cradled it. She broke upon it an egg, and her fingers rubbed the yellow life into the wooden arms, the wooden legs and belly.

Then she lifted her head. The stolid look was gone. In its place, a hopeless and enduring hope burnished the unsuspected face of Love.

# The Pure Diamond Man

'ONE year ago, when I was young,' said Tetteh, 'I was always thinking I am Luck's very boy.'

Daniel smiled. 'Scientifically, you realize, a consistently lucky person is an impossibility. You didn't honestly believe you were an exception?'

Tetteh had not changed in the five years since they last met. If anything, he seemed younger now to Daniel, who had changed so much. Their mother-tongues were different, so they spoke together in English, and Tetteh's speech, as haphazard as ever, made Daniel wonder a little uncomfortably if his own careful precision gave an effect of pomposity.

Tetteh's fingers were tapping in seeming absentmindedness at the empty glass, and finally Daniel relented and ordered another beer. At mid-morning the chop-bar was almost deserted. The proprietor, bulging with beery flesh under his dirty white trousers and green striped pyjama top, was washing glasses in a tin basin enamelled with overblown carnations. Above the bottles of Blood Wine, Iron Wine, orange squash, grenadine and gin on the shelves, corpulent blue flies buzzed lazy and slow, like old drunks without the price of solace. The fat man left his dishwashing and brought the beer, yawning as he placed the tray on the flimsy table with its fancy wrought-iron legs leprous with rust.

'I was believing with strength,' Tetteh admitted. 'Say I found a silver coin in the dust. My thought would be — this coin is quite natural to find, because of this friendly liking which Luck has for me personally. If some man freely gave me some good — like you, Daniel, this moment, a beer to a friend who owns plenty of trouble but no pence — why, then I would return for him thanks in best manner, but saying as well, quietly, *Thank you, Uncle*, for I was Luck's nephew in those happy and bygone days. It was so all my life. When I was a small boy in my village, people always calling me Luck Child, and even many strange stories you could hear then in Gyakrom about me.'

'Tales of your miraculous powers, I suppose.'

'Well, people saying one day I walk out in the bush, and when my eye meets some giant fern, I say "Fern, I greet you, and what have you got for me today?" And at once a large toad with muscled back legs hops out from those branchy weeds and lands in my hands. And when I say "Thank you, Fern, this is a fine present for a man who never in his life was owning a toad", then at once that toad changes into a weighty emerald and its eyes — what else? — gold, of course. I am only telling you what the Gyakrom people saying, Daniel. It is not known who was first starting that story. Maybe my Uncle Luck whispered it into some person's ear, for after that day many young men eagerly hire my Luck to do some little work for them, for reasonable fee (I would take money or palm wine; I was not a difficult boy) until the Reverend Timothy Quarshie of Saint Sebastian Mission in our village unhappily was discovering it and had my father beat me with a bamboo cane.'

'It was a good try, anyway.'

'When I was at mission school,' Tetteh went on, '— do you remember, Daniel, drinking strong brews together, you and I, while hiding behind the latrines, before you go off to England for college and to learn drinking of sherry and other dainty potables which by no means having liveliness enough for healthy African stomachs? — well, in those times my Luck was staying by my side day and night. Father Halloran himself — remember that man's big voice and how his big spectacles all surrounded by copper frames and when he takes them off you see two green spots like mould on his nose? — he was often saying to me, "You are getting through on luck, Tetteh, sheer luck." Why he need to tell me? I was knowing better than he was knowing that thing. If I help my Uncle, in the examinations, just a little — why, if your Luck helps you, then you must help your Luck, too, some time, you agree?'

'You didn't need to help your luck,' Daniel said. 'You didn't need luck, either, if it comes to that. You were smart enough, if you'd only believed it.'

'At all, man. I was in need. Those many years I was being Fortune's boy, even (so I believe then) on that night, one year past, when I stroll chancefully to this same Paradise Chop-Bar.'

Tetteh glanced out the window at the pink and white lettering of the chop-bar sign, the old enamels peeling in shreds or puffed out in tiny bubbles from the heat and damp. Then he teetered back on the spider-shanked chair until it nearly went spinning, rocked forward again, crashed his shining shoes, yellow as jaundice, down on the concrete floor, and slammed on the shivering table his bare brown hairless arms. He tilted to the back of his head a green fedora decorated with three round button-pins — *Freedom & Justice*, *Nothing-with-Man*, and *Amaryllis Light Ale*. He grinned and grimaced, flung open his arms so that the sunflowers on his mauve mammy-cloth shirt seemed to sprout high and wide, concealing his skinniness with their plump golden petals.

'This very place,' he cried, 'which the sign telling us is some proper heavenly dwelling. You are a believer in signs, Daniel? I am believing in all such things.'

He laughed.

184

'Maybe this sign has no special meaning for you, Daniel, now you are a big newspaper man, or for Sam Etroo — you remember him — he is Doctor Samuel Etroo now, and when I meet him in the street I think he has some specks of dust in his eyes, for he is unable to see me. Or Darku, in politics — you must take off your hat, when you see him, and if you are wearing no hat, then take off your head — he does not greatly care what, but you must show respect in proper manner. You are "been-to" men, my friend. What should you be needing with heavenly signs? But I am a boy from Gyakrom, and I am following my Luck and greatly wishing for some divine happenings to provide me with sufficiency of cash. Cash, Daniel — a sweet word. This cash I want for purposes which I now tell you. Namely, to start some small business of mine which will grow quickly and giantly, like some paw-paw tree, making full fruits for me. There, you see — I dash you my dream, free, for nothing, and now I am in your power. So that night when my eye meets that gentle sign PARADISE, pink and white as we are told of angels, I at once sing *Lead, Kindly Luck*. In my pocket this sum — three shillings and fourpence.'

Tetteh paused.

'On that remembered night,' he said, 'I first was setting my eyes upon my pure diamond man.'

The small chop-bar was crowded that evening. Tetteh had to work his way around the drinkers, around the bumping and shuffling boys and their high-heeled girls who had to dance even here. Tetteh paid for one glass of beer and carried it high above his head to avoid spilling any of it. The only vacant chair was at a table beside an open window. With every tweak of breeze, the light curtain lifted and the city scents of night fluttered and spun in — the salt sea, peppery soups, heat, bodies, dust, and peeled oranges the roadside stalls sold. Tetteh sat down and sipped his beer slowly. He did not notice the man sitting beside him at the table, until the other spoke, to himself but aloud.

'Sickening.'

Tetteh turned. The voice was distinctly English. Europeans did not often patronize the chop-bars. The man was young, with yellow hair plastered flat to his scalp with perspiration. His face was long, his hazel eyes large and despondent. He wore a white linen suit, and on the table beside him lay a piece of headgear long fallen from fashion here — a solar topee. Tetteh leaned towards him.

'Excuse me. You are not finding this drink suitable for your delicate stomach?'

'What?' said the stranger. 'Oh, I see. No, you misunderstand. I was referring to the dancers. The way they're dancing, you know, and the music. Calypso. Highlife. Just cheap jazz, really, nothing else.'

The chop-bar proprietor cranked the handle of the gramophone and put on another record.

> *I gev my money to my wife*
> *For mek me chop —*
> *Time I come back from beezniz*
> *My wife run away.*

'So,' Tetteh said, smiling his annoyance, 'highlife is not for you. Then why do you stay?'

The European sighed and ordered another gin.

'You don't see the point, do you? You're like all the rest. Selling your birthright for a mess of gramophone records.'

Tetteh opened wide his eyes and clenched his fists.

'How is that again, please?'

But the stranger only waved a weary hand and drank half his gin-and-tonic at a gulp.

'Don't be offended. And don't for heaven's sake expect me to fight you. You look rather undernourished, I must say, but I don't doubt you could win. I never fought anyone in my life, and I most certainly don't intend to begin now. No — all I meant was that I'm disappointed. Sleazy nylon shirts. Pidgin English — a depravity, if I may say so. This highlife caper. Signs advertising political meetings and anti-malarial pills. All of it so dreary. The Lord knows England is drab enough. I thought it would be different here.'

'What you think to see in this place?' Tetteh enquired unpleasantly. 'Men with big spears and wearing maybe one banana leaf?'

'You may not believe it,' the stranger said, 'but I've read extensively about the structure of tribal society here. Always had a personal interest in this country, owing to my family's finances. Your ancient culture had a weird magnificence about it — witchfinders' dance, festivals of the dead, offerings to the river gods, the medicine man's phenomenal sense of the dramatic. To me, those things constitute the true Africa. What's more, it still exists. But how to discover it? That's the maddening part. I've been in villages, but people clam up so. I found one revolting crone who purported to be a fetish priestess, but she turned out to be only another Bible spinner. Stabbed verses with a meat skewer. Didn't read them, of course — gave them to her clients, to swallow like pills. Universal cure-all. Grotesque — one should be grateful — but hardly African. It's the pure customs which interest me, not these dilutions.'

Tetteh looked at the other man curiously.

'Those old ways — why you like them so greatly?'

'I told you,' the white man said in his gentle voice. 'They have a terrifying splendour.'

'I hear you,' Tetteh said, shrugging, 'but I do not say

your words are staying in my ear. What was bringing you here, anyway?'

'Sorry. Ought to have introduced myself sooner. I'm Philip Hardacre. Ever heard of the Hardacre Mine? Diamonds. My grandfather discovered it and leased the mineral rights, crafty old bastard. Family felt I ought to visit the place, I can't think why.'

Tetteh whistled. 'Diamonds — in your own hands, all those diamonds.'

Hardacre smiled tiredly. 'They ought to belong to you — I suppose that's what you're thinking. Don't fret, your government will find a way of getting them back one of these days. You could have the whole bloody lot as far as I'm concerned. All I ever wanted was to become an anthropologist, but of course the family wouldn't hear of it.'

Tetteh regarded Hardacre thoughtfully and with a new interest. It seemed to him that the white man's linen suit was covered with miniature lights, and the lights were diamonds, and the diamonds pierced at Tetteh's eyes and shone in a blaze of stars.

'Those bush people you mention,' he said offhandedly. 'I am remembering one small village which is known to me, very deep in the bush. No proper road there, and no one entering that place unless with greatest difficulty. In that village of Gyakrom is one old man who owns some very strong ju-ju, or so I heard it. He is priest for some python god, and is calling frequently many pythons out of their forest. You are acquainted with pythons? No poison, but they strangle. Yet for this old man they never strangle. At all.'

Hardacre dropped his bored expression. 'Look here, are you serious?'

'In my life I am never more serious than this moment.'

He would need a few days, Tetteh stipulated, to convince the ju-ju man of Gyakrom, for such practitioners of magic were well known for their reluctance to perform before the eyes of foreigners. With the proper observances to the god, however, the matter could be arranged. Hardacre contributed willingly enough the funds for palm-wine libation, but when it came to Tetteh's fee he showed an unexpected tendency to haggle. Tetteh remained firm.

'Myself, I would not walk even one step for such a thing. If I see this man for you, then you must pay. Fifty pounds — for you this is not such an amount.'

Hardacre yielded at last. The night was balmy and the streets nearly deserted when the two of them ambled out of the now-peaceful Paradise Chop-Bar. Hardacre placed his solar topee on his flat pale hair.

'I'm a bit squiffed. Hope I shan't regret this tomorrow.'

'At all!' cried Tetteh. 'I tell you, it was Luck brought you to me.'

He toasted with an imaginary glass the unseen presence.

'I thank you, Uncle,' he said.

At daybreak, after three hours' sleep, Tetteh boarded a mammy-lorry. He was wearing his best clothes. He would not appear in his village in anything less. His trousers were a little threadbare, but well pressed and still recognizably grey flannel. His nylon shirt shone in electric orange like a neon light. The other passengers, several dozen of them, sat or crouched or perilously clung at the back of the lorry, amid the sacks of sugar and crates of yellow soap. But Tetteh paid the extra and rode beside the driver. The mammy-lorry was green and lustrous as a mango leaf, and it had KING KONG painted on the front and GOD SAVE SOULS on the back.

'The old road, Kofi, into Gyakrom,' Tetteh said, 'what is it like now?'

The driver laughed. 'Gone. It is gone. Fallen into the

river. Grown over with vines and mangrove. What do you care about the old road?'

But Tetteh only smiled and donned his sun-glasses, which he never wore except when he visited Gyakrom, and generously offered the driver a cigarette.

The village faced the river and was surrounded on the other three sides by forest, a heavy green wall of palms and ferns and small thorny bushes, all tangled and matted together like snarled hair or cats' fur full of burrs. The marketplace was still crowded when the lorry pulled up, although it was almost dusk. The driver shouted, and a swarm of small dust-silvered boys ran to help him unload the sugar and soap.

Tetteh, ignoring the market and its people, flew out of the lorry like a locust spreading his orange wings, and made for home. It was a hut like any other, mud plastered over woven sticks and thatched with palm boughs. Tetteh's brother Kwaame was outside. He was a powerfully built man, and although he was two years younger than Tetteh, he always seemed older, for it was he who had stayed home to help with the cocoa farm, and his face already bore an enclosed and habitually worried expression.

'Tetteh!' Kwaame looked up. 'You are in trouble?'

Light-limbed, Tetteh capered and twirled, his shirt glittering in the last frail sunlight. He clapped his hands, whistled like a tree toad, moved his shoulders and narrow hips to a highlife beat.

'No! No trouble. Money. Money, money, money. We are going to be rich.'

Tetteh's mother appeared in the doorway, a large and heavy woman wearing a dark blue cloth patterned with trees that branched fantastically like sea-coral.

'Tetteh! It is really you!' Tears came immediately to her eyes. She spread her arms and gathered Tetteh in like a slip of driftwood to some great shore. Then she held him away at arm's length, scrutinized and scolded him.

'Why do you not come home more often? Your bones show — do you never eat at all in that place, that city? It wounds my heart to see you.'

'I am a boy born to wound his mother's heart,' Tetteh said cheerfully, putting his arm around her waist and leading her into the hut. 'See how thin you are growing with worry.'

Tetteh's father was inside. He scowled and blinked his eyes when he saw his son.

'You! What has made the paramount chief honour us with his presence? I thought you had forgotten where Gyakrom was.'

'Welcome me, papa.'

'All right,' the old man grumbled. 'I welcome you, then. Here — what are you doing with those, Tetteh?'

Tetteh had begun busily collecting an assortment of objects and placing them outside the hut door. Three blue saucepans; a headpan and basin of Japanese manufacture, enamelled with peacocks and gigantic peonies; half a dozen tin spoons; a hurricane lantern; two shaky rush-bottomed chairs which had been purchased cheaply from an impecunious merchant twenty years ago; a gilt-tasselled white satin pillow bearing the elephant and palm insignia of the old Gold Coast Regiment; three china saucers with the cups missing, embellished with Biblical scenes and given to Tetteh's mother in the distant past by some missionary's wife at whose confident knock the gates of heaven had no doubt long since opened wide; Tetteh's baptismal certificate from Saint Sebastian Mission, with a floral border of forget-me-nots; a green glass vase cracked at the bottom; a third of a bottle of De Kuyper's Dutch gin; a box of Blood Purifying Pills; a large alarm clock; and, finally, a small gramophone which lacked a handle and which only Kwaame, who had a mechanical flair, could ingeniously wind with a piece of wire and a twig.

'Are you mad?' Tetteh's father cried. 'Put them down at once. Does my own son rob me?'

'Please, papa, trust me. I am not taking them far. They will be looked after. It is only for a few days. Come here, Kwaame. I need you. You must get the boys busy, all the boys in the village. A python hunt. Two shillings for a dead, five for a living one. You'll do it?'

Kwaame hesitated, then his laughter boomed through the hut. Not so much happened in Gyakrom, and Tetteh had the ability to make life eventful.

'For you, madman, I will do whatever you say, this once. But why?'

Tetteh half-closed his eyes.

'We are going to play a game,' he said. 'It is called Casting Nets For The Diamond Fish. Listen, and I will tell you.'

Tetteh pulled up the rented lorry in front of his father's dwelling. Philip Hardacre climbed out, groaned, cautiously felt his limbs for possible dislocations, and vainly attempted to brush off his white linen suit which was covered with a fine powdering of red dust and a number of black oil smears from the lorry.

'Oh, my Lord,' he said, 'I can hardly move. No wonder the village is isolated. I've never seen such a road in my life. I swear I thought we weren't going to make it, Tetteh.'

Kwaame bounded around the corner of the hut. He appeared to be clad only in a leopard skin, although in fact he wore his loincloth unobtrusively beneath it, for decency. Tetteh recognized the pelt. It had hung in Opoku the Drummer's hut for as long as he could remember, and was in consequence slightly bald in patches, for the fur had been nibbled at by cockroaches throughout the years. On his head Kwaame wore a gazelle skull with one horn missing and small red feathers stuffed into the eye sockets. He brandished his machete, newly-sharpened, within a few inches of Hardacre's face, and the Englishman drew back.

'My word, he doesn't look very friendly.'

'He is a tempered person,' Tetteh agreed, 'but you he will not harm. He is the ju-ju man's helper.'

He grasped Hardacre's elbow and took him inside the dwelling. The room was bare of furniture — not so much as a stool. A pile of calabashes and earthen pots stood beside the door. The hut had been decorated by Kwaame, following Tetteh's instructions. Strings of bush-rat bones and chicken feet were festooned across the room. Large bunches of leaves and grass, dotted with pellets of clay, hung from the thatched roof. Several wooden clubs stood in one corner, with feathers and clusters of cowrie shells tied around them. Hardacre sank down onto a grass mat.

'What's the significance of the leaves, Tetteh?'

'Magical medicine,' Tetteh said sternly. 'Do not touch, please. Special for the gods of this house.'

'Perhaps the old man will be kind enough to elaborate on the question of the household gods,' Hardacre said, 'and their connection with the broader tribal deities. The relationship of gods, of course, mirrors the structure of the extended family group. I wish I didn't have such a rotten headache. What a ghastly ride that was. Good heavens, who's this?'

Tetteh's mother was wearing a skirt of dried palm fibre, a fringe of fresh banana leaves around her full bosom, a shaky-looking headdress of white hen feathers, and an exceedingly surly expression. Tetteh grinned.

'Wife of the ju-ju man. Real bush lady, this one.'

'I have prepared a good groundnut stew,' Tetteh's mother said crossly. 'I worked all morning. I wish now I had rested

193

instead. Your white man probably cares only for drink, anyway.'

'It would be such an advantage if I spoke the language,' Hardacre said regretfully. 'What did she say, Tetteh?'

'She is saying she has ready a great feast for honouring you, man. Look, here is the python priest now.'

Tetteh's father had been persuaded to don the grimy loincloth he wore when he worked in the fields, and to strap a dagger around his chest, but beyond this point he would not go. He dragged himself into the hut with painful slowness, as though suffering from partial paralysis. After a swift and shamefaced glance at Hardacre, he turned to his son.

'Greed is an affliction of the soul. You will have us all in serious trouble one of these days.'

Tetteh politely translated for Hardacre. 'The old man, he is welcoming you to Gyakrom and praying his python god to give full blessings for you.'

Hardacre looked pleased. 'That's decent of him, I must say. When will he perform the rites?'

'First the meal,' Tetteh said, holding out a bowl of palm wine, 'and then the snake-calling.'

After the trip Hardacre was thirsty, and once he had downed the first bowlful he found the palm wine quite palatable.

'My meeting you like that——' he said feelingly, after the fourth bowl had been emptied. 'You were absolutely right, Tetteh — it was a real stroke of luck.'

Tetteh lifted his wine bowl in salute. 'Live long, Uncle, and never leave me.' Then, seeing Hardacre's puzzled expression, he explained. 'Just some words I say when I drink. No meaning for you, man.'

When they had eaten, Tetteh grabbed a small drum and thrust it into his father's arms.

'Drum, papa!'

With a look of disgust, Tetteh's father picked up the curved stick and tapped once. Then he threw it down.

'I cannot.'

Kwaame seized the stick and began to drum, clumsily but with verve. Tetteh tore out to the lorry and came back with a paper bag, from which he took half a dozen crudely-carved fetish figures. Hardacre examined them.

'Intriguing — where did you get them, Tetteh?'

'Secret place,' Tetteh said. 'Perhaps later I will be telling you.'

Tetteh's father frowned. 'I do not like those things here.'

'They are nothing,' Tetteh said in his own tongue. 'Nothing has been done to them. They come straight from the carver. Nothing has been said over them. They are harmless.'

'Still, I do not like it.'

'Papa, it is all right. They sell them like baskets of groundnuts in the city market. Anyone can buy them there.'

'That is what you say.'

'No difficulty, is there?' Hardacre asked anxiously.

'No, no, man,' Tetteh swung into English. 'The old fellow wanting to be sure all things are correct for his snake god, that is all.'

He disappeared again and returned a moment later carrying by the feet a struggling, squawking white chicken. He tethered it and placed it on a stone block, where it lay palpitating and all at once eerily silent.

'A cockerel for the god,' he explained to Hardacre. 'While the young man is drumming magic drummings and saying magic sayings, then the python priest is cutting this same cockerel's throat, and when the blood running down, the god drinking it, you see. Then, if we have luck, the pythons coming out of the bush.'

Tetteh's father was glancing dubiously across the room at the chicken. He shouted for his wife.

'Come here, Akosua! You had better make sure this is the right hen. It would be just like Tetteh to take the young cockerel instead, and we would have no eggs next year.'

'Papa——' Tetteh pleaded. 'Don't you think I know a cockerel from a hen? Anyway, you do not need a cockerel to get eggs, except the eggs for hatching.'

'And a child does not need a father, either, I suppose?' the old man snorted.

'I learned about the eggs at school,' Tetteh said defensively.

'That is the sort of thing they taught you. No wonder you act in such a peculiar fashion.'

Tetteh's mother examined the fowl. 'This is the right one. A hen, the lame old one. See her leg?'

Tetteh threw up his hands. His father merely shrugged. Then Tetteh shook himself, jumped to his feet, snuffed out all but one of the wicks burning dim in vessels of oil, tiptoed across the room to Hardacre and placed wiry fingers on the whiteman's shoulders until he flinched. The light in the hut was feeble and shot through with shadows and shadowy presences. The drum rumbled and Kwaame chanted. Tetteh's father raised his knife. Hardacre breathed rapidly.

But the old man, the squirming fowl underneath his hand, hesitated. The sweat stood out on his forehead, and the wrist of his knife-hand trembled. Tetteh, now sitting cross-legged beside Hardacre, half rose and then sank back again uncertainly.

'What is it, papa? What is wrong?'

'What if they are offended?' Tetteh's father said in a low and distant voice. 'Perhaps it will go badly for all of us here. What if they believe themselves mocked?'

'Who?' Tetteh almost shrieked. 'Who?'

The old man looked blankly at his son. 'Those whose names and powers you have forgotten.'

Then he seemed to recover himself. He coughed a little and blinked his eyes.

'Now I will have to see Bonsu, to set the matter right,' he said plaintively. 'Well, it cannot be helped. Let the false cockerel die, then, for it would have been killed for the cooking-pot tomorrow, anyway.'

The knife came down and the blood spurted. Tetteh, sloughing off his momentary anxiety, danced with a reckless joy. A crackling of dry palm boughs sounded overhead, and from the hut roof three dark writhing coils appeared and began spiralling downward. Tetteh caught Hardacre's arm.

'The pythons from the bush, man. They are here.'

Hardacre leaped out of the way. 'My God, did it actually work?'

At that moment a voice like a judgement roared outside the hut, and the struggling reptiles abruptly disappeared. Tetteh whirled, his startled eyes questioning his brother. But Kwaame stood paralysed, listening to the deep and god-like voice. Like dead butterflies on a pin they all stood fixed in the attitudes they had held when the voice began. Hardacre's arms were outstretched and rigid. The old man's hands were stiff around the reddened knife.

Then a figure appeared in the hut doorway. A grey-haired man, a portly and rather elderly African, clad in a black suit with a high white collar. Released, the people in the hut stirred and breathed. Tetteh's mother, palm leaves rustling, fled into the back room.

'Two boys are on your roof, Kobla,' the Reverend Timothy Quarshie said mildly. 'I shouted at them to get down.'

His glance took in the adorned hut, the block, the bleeding fowl.

'What are you doing here?' he cried. 'What can you be thinking of, Kobla?'

Tetteh's father threw down the knife. 'It was nothing. A jest of this boy's. Yes, I am an old fool. Tell me.'

The Reverend Timothy Quarshie regarded both Tetteh and Hardacre with disapproving eyes.

'You, sir,' he said to Hardacre in English. 'I do not have any idea what you are doing here, but I must tell you I think you are a bad influence on my congregation that I have spent nearly twenty-five years building up. I never thought to see an elder of my church acting so.'

Hardacre stared. 'An elder of your church?'

'Indeed, and a member of my congregation for many years. I myself baptised all his children, including Kwaame and Tetteh here.'

'His children? Tetteh?' Hardacre looked at Tetteh, who groaned and put his hands over his eyes.

'I see.' Hardacre faced the pastor. 'Well, sir, I'm exceedingly sorry, but I was very interested in ancient customs, you see, and I'd hoped to find in Gyakrom the preservation of such observances. Tetteh told me——'

'You are interested in such things?' Quarshie seemed surprised. 'Why did you not go to see Bonsu, then?'

'Who's he?'

'Why, the fetish priest, what else?'

'The — good heavens — do you know him?'

'Of course,' the pastor said, rather irritably. 'Everyone in Gyakrom knows Bonsu. Who knows him better than I? I have been trying to convert him for — let me see — it will be fourteen years this August since I first tried to convert Bonsu. Nearly every evening we have a game of checkers, Bonsu and I. He is certainly the best checker player in Gyakrom, I will say that for him. And, of course, no one makes a bunion cure equal to his.'

'Do you mean to tell me that you, a pastor, buy remedies from a witchdoctor?'

'I am a foot sufferer,' the Reverend Timothy said with dignity. 'Corns and bunions trouble me. Bonsu makes the best foot ointment I have ever discovered. Are you suggesting I should not relieve my feet in this manner?'

Hardacre was spared a reply, for Tetteh's mother now re-appeared, respectably clad in her best cloth, a handsome blue-veined print patterned with golden and great-eyed fish. The pastor turned to greet her. Then his attention was caught by the fetish figures, which Tetteh was unsuccessfully attempting to stow away in the paper bag. The pastor picked one up, looked at it, and threw it down.

'Not even good carving. I have a dozen better than that.'

Hardacre gaped. 'How can you?'

'Quite simple,' Quarshie replied calmly. 'People who join the church give such figures to me, along with amulets, charms, magical bracelets, phylacteries of unchurchly origin, *nufa* medicine, and other assorted pieces of what you would call ju-ju. A certain man brought me such a collection this evening. I have not had time to burn them as yet.'

'You surely don't destroy them?' Hardacre cried in an anguished voice.

'Indubitably,' Quarshie said. 'That is the very thing which I do.'

'Do you think you could see your way clear to selling that lot to me instead? I am speaking as a private collector, but I might ultimately donate the things to a museum.'

The Reverend Timothy Quarshie stood quite still, evidently engaged in some sort of soul struggle.

'Saint Sebastian Mission,' he said finally, 'has a tower — a small one, true, but a real tower. We have never had a bell. I have in my possession many catalogues showing church bells, and I often look through these booklets and

think which bell I would choose if ever any money came by
some miracle into my hands. You would not believe how
many kinds of church bells are made. All sorts — large,
small, brass, bronze, iron, low voices and also tones high
and musically sweet. I sometimes hear them in my dreams
— all those bells, pealing and chiming for evermore.'

He brought his hands together in a clapping gesture that
was half prayerful.

'I will do it! You shall have the *suman*.'

'You couldn't by any chance introduce me to this Bonsu?'

'Nothing would be easier. He does not live very far from
here.'

'I'm sorry to leave like this,' Hardacre said to Tetteh,
'but I'm sure you'll understand. I've settled with you for
the lorry. I don't really think I owe you anything more,
do you?'

'Go,' Tetteh said bitterly. 'But if you look for justice,
man, you will not be finding it in this world.'

Later that night Kwaame came back to the hut after a
brief foray and reported that Bonsu was displaying some sort
of rites in the sacred grove beside the river for the edification
of the stranger. Tetteh rose from his sleeping-mat and went
out into the darkness.

The grove was hushed. The tree toads chirped in muted
chorus and an occasional night bird cried. Tetteh concealed
himself behind a clump of bushes. Soon Bonsu with two
acolytes appeared, followed by Hardacre, stumbling in the
gloom. Bonsu, a bent and bow-legged old man, wore his full
regalia — palm fibre kilt, white tunic, strings of charms
around wrists and ankles. In his hands he carried his *kukuo*,
the earthen pot in which he could see the future. He filled
the pot with river water, into which he poured palm wine.
The two youths handed him eggs, intestines of a fowl, a brass
gold-weight, and he placed these in the *kukuo*. In the murky

light of the wood torches, Tetteh could see Bonsu's gnarled hands as he set the earthen pot with great care on the ground. Hardacre's face now bore an expression of happy fulfilment. Speaking to himself in a furious whisper, Tetteh was not even aware that he spoke aloud.

'How much for that? Twenty pounds? Thirty? That scoundrel Bonsu — if I could only strangle him——'

Behind him, a slight movement and a hand placed gently on his shoulder.

'Fifty pounds,' the Reverend Timothy Quarshie said, with a faint chuckle. 'That was the sum agreed upon.'

Tetteh swung around. 'You! How do you know?'

The pastor settled himself comfortably on his haunches beside Tetteh in the thorny underbrush.

'Yesterday,' he said, 'after all these years, Bonsu finally joined the church. Perhaps he thought I would not continue to play checkers with him otherwise, or perhaps — I don't know. He still believes in the old gods, of course. I cannot ask too much, and maybe it is only a question of names anyway. He will sell herb cures as always, but no more charms or predictions. It was his carvings and *suman* which I sold to Mr. Hardacre. Bonsu has tonight a special permission. Half the money is to go to Saint Sebastian. He is looking into his *kukuo* for the last time.'

'I am ruined,' Tetteh said. 'But do not upset yourselves, you and Bonsu.'

The pastor smiled, deafly absorbed in his own thoughts.

'I am going to let Bonsu choose the bell,' he said. 'I think it is only right that he should.'

Tetteh got to his feet silently.

'Where are you going?' Quarshie asked. 'I was hoping you would stay in Gyakrom.'

'Not me,' Tetteh replied. 'I am going back to the city. I still must follow my Luck, although at this moment he seems to be gone, now that I have lost forever my diamond man.'

The Paradise Chop-Bar was beginning to fill with midday customers as Tetteh finished.

'Did you ever hear what happened to Hardacre?' Daniel asked.

From his pocket Tetteh drew a crumpled letter and handed it over.

'Your friend the Englishman stayed on in Gyakrom for one lengthy month,' the letter began. 'The sickness forced it. Malaria and diarrhoea made him quite uncomfortable and also worried. He seemed grateful for my prayers and even more for my paludrine and aspirin. When he was somewhat recovered, we tried to cheer him the best we could. Opoku kindly drummed for him, and Bonsu offered to get out his *kukuo* for one more time, but Mr. Hardacre said indeed no, the grove was full of mosquitoes at night and he did not think he could survive another fever. We thought he did not have much manners, in the ways he spoke. He complained of the food, saying he grew tired of cassava and yam. It was, of course, unfortunate that he picked up both guinea-worm and roundworm, but to hear him you would think no one had ever before had these little creatures inside them. Bonsu tried several of his worm cures, but they were unhappily not so effective. Oftentimes Mr. Hardacre would wander down to the swamp and stare at it for as much as one hour. Then he would return to tell us what a menace it was for our health, with mosquitoes breeding there in fertile abundance. He also had many rude things to say about no proper drains being in Gyakrom, and what could we expect but all these worms, and so on. We tried to tell him about the Gyakrom Drain And Swamp Committee, newly-formed with your father as the head. Very certainly, something is going to be done — it is just a question for all of us to reach agreement on what we ought to be doing, and when to start, and other problems. But this was not good enough for Mr. Hardacre. Everything must be done this minute. A restless man. He had once been planning, I know, to go north into the desert, where he had heard that some of the Moshi people still live in their ancient ways. But something must have made him change his mind, for when he left he said he would return at once to England and did not mean to travel so very much in future. We have our handsome iron bell, a solemn note yet joyful, and for this we give thanks. I have promised your mother that I will urge you to come home and settle down in a peaceful life. I do urge this, but I fear you have hardened your heart. Yours faithfully, Timothy Quarshie (Rev.).'

Daniel handed back the letter with a laugh.

'Please, no laughter,' Tetteh said. 'I was losing at that time my hopeful wealth, Daniel, and even worse, losing my Luck, for never since has he made appearance. When I think of that clever man Quarshie and that snakely Bonsu——'

He broke off, and a pensive look came into his eyes. 'Daniel — lend me your pen.'

He scribbled for a few minutes on the back of the letter. Then he handed the paper to Daniel. There, in Tetteh's scrawl, appeared these words:

### ARE YOU A FOOT SUFFERER?
### TRY BONSU CORN CURE
Best All-African Remedy
Working like Magic
for corns, bunions,
callouses, tender feet,
sore ankles, etc., etc.

**TETTEH LUCK CO. INC. SOLE DISTRIBUTORS**

'What do you think?' he asked anxiously.

'Good,' Daniel smiled. 'It looks good.'

Tetteh snatched up the paper and began to dash out of the chop-bar. Then he stopped, came back to the table and picked up his glass. Raising it, he drained the last of the beer in a toast to the unseen presence.

'I thank you, Uncle,' Tetteh said gravely, 'and I welcome you back.'

Daniel watched him go, the boy from Gyakrom, rushing away in a burst of sunflowers to seek his fortune in the city streets.

# The Voices of Adamo

IS mother was warmth and coolness. Warmth at daybreak when the children, sleeping like clustered toads in the dank hut corner, wakened hungry and straggled outside to find always that she was up before them and had the cocoyam cooking in the black iron pot. Warmth when the rain came at night, when the thunder howled its unknowable threats and the children shivered with chill and fear. Coolness in the heat of the day, when Adamo's legs were tired from trying to keep up with the older ones, cool shadow in her arms and her vast body bending over him. Before Adamo knew anything he knew this, his mother's sun and shade.

She gathered firewood and the children beside her gleaned twigs. When she went to hoe the cassava patch, Adamo and the others learned to walk through the fern-thick forest lightly, slipping around the thorns that would tear flesh, placing their feet so. She showed her young how to remain motionless in the snake's presence — not the tight containment of panic, for a brittle branch may snap, but a silent infolding of muscles like a leaf bud.

Afternoons, the girls stayed with their mother to tend the fire and pound the dried yam in the big wooden bowls. But Adamo and his brothers swam in the tepid slime-edged river or climbed the nut palms at the edge of the sacred grove or watched Ofei the blacksmith at his smoky forge turning a new machete.

The days flowed slowly as the river, and when Adamo was no longer a young child, his father taught him what he must know to wrench existence from the forest and yet not turn to vengeance the spirit that animated all things — the tree he felled, the plant he harvested, the antelope whose life he must take to feed his own. The forbidden acts and words were many, and the words and acts of appeasement were many, but Adamo dared not forget, for an offender endangered not only himself but the entire village, and that was the worst any person could do.

'A man is a leaf,' Adamo's father would say in his stern and quiet voice. 'The leaf grows for a while, then falls, but the tree lives for ever. One leaf is nothing. The tree is all.'

Regularly, meticulously, the offerings of mashed yam or eggs were made to the gods of river and forest. The invocations entered into Adamo, for he would speak one day with the same calm voice as his father's.

'Here is food from our hands. Receive this food and eat. Stand behind us with a good standing. Let the women bear children. Let the yams grow. Let nothing evil befall.'

Adamo's father was strong. He knew always what to do. His own father and his mother had been dead for many years, but they were with him. He heard their guiding voices in the night wind. He poured palm wine on their graves, and they drank. They had never left him. When Adamo's mother and father died, they would not leave him, either.

Sometimes it was not enough, and the feared thing happened. Adamo's youngest sister was taken by the crocodile. When the mother turned at the cry, she saw only the blood swirling like flames on the water. Adamo's brother Kwadwo died of a fever, although his wrists and forehead had been bound with costly medicinal charms from Yao the fetish priest. These deaths they mourned each with a terrible stone in the heart, wondering who had been the one to cause by some offence such retribution.

So Adamo learned fear, but the fears were not the greater part. As long as the laws were kept, the palms and the dark river and the red earth were to Adamo like his own brothers, who would not forsake him.

When Adamo was fifteen, a sickness struck the village. That it was smallpox meant nothing to him. But because he was the youngest of her four remaining sons, his mother was determined that Adamo must go until the sickness was over. She had a friend in a village not so far away. He did not want to go, but when his father said it would be best, Adamo went.

His mother's friend welcomed him into her family. Adamo stayed on and on, at first unquestioning, then with a faint anxiety, finally desperate to return home. But always the answer was the same.

'We have heard nothing, Adamo. You are doing good work here — stay.'

Sunrise gave way to mid-day, and mid-day to sunset. Adamo had no notion that he had lived in this other village for a year. But one day when he went to wash himself in the river, he heard his mother's voice. The voice, gentle and persistent, spoke inside his head.

*Adamo — where are you? Adamo — where are we?*

That night he put his machete and his cloth and the knife which his father had given him into a bundle and walked out, without a word, along the bush trail that led back to his village.

The thorn bushes and liana vines by day were green nets that could snare only an unwatchful traveller, but at night they changed, became formless and yet solid, a heaviness of dark before the eyes. Anything a pace away seemed non-existent, as though the world stopped where the foot fell. Adamo had no light. A man needs a light, not so much against the outer darkness, as to be sure that he himself is really there. With his bare feet, Adamo could feel the path. He stumbled over tree roots, slipped on the decay of last year's growth, grasped at branches and found his hands held ferns, insubstantial as spider-webs. But although he feared, he never doubted that he would reach his village, for his mother's voice drew him on.

*Adamo — where are you? Adamo — where are we?*

When the dawn birds had only begun, he came to the village. The huts were there; the street stood dusty and pale in the daybreak. A few monkeys, crying like children, were perched on the forge of Ofei the blacksmith. The palm branches in the sacred grove lifted and swayed in the faint wind of morning, and beyond the village the brown river moaned as it had done eternally.

That was all. Otherwise, silence. Adamo stood at the edge of the forest, looking at his village and knowing, without thinking it, that no one was there.

Then he heard a voice high and quavering as a bird's — an old woman's voice. Soon she came out of one of the huts, walking stooped over, a mud-coloured cloth around her waist, but none around her breasts, for the parts that had once proclaimed her womanhood and had made milk for her children now hung flat and leathery, not worth covering any more. Adamo recognized her.

'Grandmother——' he said, for although she was not his grandmother, it made little difference.

The old woman stopped and peered around, as though she had been momentarily expecting a voice, but now that it had come she was confused and did not know how to reply. Then she saw him.

'It is——' she hesitated. 'Man or spirit, I cannot tell.'

He told her his name, and although she pretended to recognize him, he felt sure she did not. He asked her then about his family, scarcely knowing whether he could believe her or not, for her mind was light, almost departed. But she answered clearly enough.

'They are gone,' she said, in the strangely gloating way the old have, as though the whole course of events could have been avoided had the young paid heed. 'They are either dead or gone. There was a sickness — a long time ago, I think, although I cannot remember so well. Many people died. I do not know who died. There were too many to remember. The others left. Went away. My own family was all dead, but the others tried to persuade me to go with them. I wouldn't go. No, I wouldn't go. Go away, I told them, go away and see what happens. I will stay where I belong, in my village. So they went. I never thought they would really go. But they did.'

Now Adamo began to shiver as though a chill had made each of his muscles work against the others. He questioned her patiently, precisely, saying over and over the names of his mother and his father.

'I am not sure,' the old woman said. 'I think — wait — that would be Afua, the daughter of Bona Ampadu?'

'That is the woman. My mother.'

'I think' — the old woman struggled to remember — 'I think she died. She and her husband. And — was it? — two daughters and four sons.'

'Three sons,' Adamo said dully. 'If they died, it was three sons. I am the other.'

'At least you have come back,' the old woman said pettishly. 'Not like those cowards who ran away. I told them, but of course they would not listen. If we die elsewhere, I said, how are the spirits of our ancestors ever to find us? Tell me that, I said. But they would not listen.'

Adamo, staring at her, did not believe. He could not believe that the spirits of all the dead any longer remained in this place, as the old woman hoped. It seemed to him that the living who had gone from the village had taken with them the ancestral spirits, for their own protection. Whether his parents were alive or dead, they were gone — they had somehow been taken away. The village to him now was deserted as it could not have been had it been empty only of tangible life. The chain that linked endlessly into the past had been broken.

Adamo stood looking at the huts, at the old woman, seeing nothing. Then he turned and ran through the village until he reached his father's hut. He entered and lay down on the floor, not violently but quietly, like a man settling himself for sleep. He was determined to die because he could not think what else to do. Dead, he might find his people.

When the third morning came, his rigid limbs stirred stiffly, his head turned, his nostrils dilated because he smelled food. A betrayal, although she had meant it well. The old woman had crept up to the hut door in the night and left a bowl of goat milk and a dish of fried plantains. Adamo, sobbing despair at his body, rose shakily from the hut floor and bolted the food.

So his belly committed him to life. He went to the river and washed. Then he talked to the old woman and spent the rest of the day gathering firewood for her. When he had accumulated a large pile of dry branches, she assured him it would be enough, for she would not live long. Adamo took both her withered hands in his, looked one last time into the vague and watery eyes that were nonetheless the eyes of one of his people, and walked back into the forest.

He never knew how far he went or where. He drank from

brackish pools, scooping the lime-green scum away. Fevered, he shouted and burned, and when the evil yielded he lay down and covered himself with palm boughs while the sweat lasted. A bush rat crossed his path and he killed it with his machete and ate it, sucking even the frail red bones. He came to villages where he was fed as a madman, but no one had seen his people — they had not passed this way. Adamo found a stony road and followed it until his feet were crusted with hard mud formed of the dust and his blood.

When finally he came to a town, his weariness was overcome by his astonishment, for the full streets jangled with lorries and the shops shone with a greater wealth of new knives and patterned cloth than Adamo had known existed. He strolled and gazed. A few people laughed, but he did not realize they were laughing at him, wide-eyed and filthy, his loincloth in shreds.

In an open field at the edge of the town, men were walking to and fro with guns. At dusk, when the soldiers were sitting outside the long huts, gossiping and rolling dice, Adamo ventured closer. One of the men was cleaning a white leather strap fixed to a drum. The drum was fascinating to Adamo. He knew many drums used by his people, but this kind he had never seen before. He touched it curiously with his fingertips, and the soldier, laughing, handed him the sticks and showed him how to use them.

Adamo and the drum found one another. His fingers sensed some way of expressing what his mind and speech could only grope after and fail to grasp. The strange drum uttered to him the voice he now heard only in dreams, the sorrowing of someone once inexpressibly dear to him, someone whose face he could not now visualize however hard he tried.

When the soldier reached out for the sticks, Adamo would not relinquish them and the soldier grew angry and alarmed, for he could see an officer approaching. He grabbed Adamo roughly by the shoulder.

'Here — wait a moment,' Captain Fossey said. 'He's not bad. Who is he?'

Adamo was startled by the alien voice, for he knew no English. He had seen white men before, but only at a distance. He wanted to run, but the soldier caught his wrist.

'He thinks you would make a drummer. He would teach you. How would you like to stay with us, bush boy?'

So it was that Adamo, who was not aware that he was an African, found himself a private in a West African regiment, having agreed to serve for five years his country, whose name he did not know.

He was given khaki shorts, a jacket with brass buttons, heavy boots, a red fez with a black tassel. He was given food, too, three times a day. But he had no idea what was expected of him, so he did everything wrong, and the men who gave commands became angry. Adamo slept badly, and his dreams filled him with emptiness, like a starving man's belly bloated with air.

One evening a short sturdy man with an enormous stomach clumped into the barracks and unslung his pack onto the cot beside Adamo's. He gave the boy a quizzical glance.

'Where from you?'

Adamo did not speak any pidgin, so he could only shake his head. The other man laughed and spoke in his own tongue, which was Adamo's as well.

'We have men of ten different tongues in this army, bush boy. And the white officers don't speak any of them. You must learn English now, if you want to get along. I myself will teach you.'

Adamo's stiff smile loosened, became real. He rose, stretched, towered, held out both his hands.

'Yes — you will teach me,' he said, still shyly but with certainty, for now he saw this was what was meant to happen. 'You will tell me, and I will learn everything that must be done.'

The others yelped with laughter. 'Manu is the clever one! Hear the Big Drum who drums his own praises. Watch out, boy, he'll have you cleaning his kit and thanking him for the privilege.'

Manu was the regimental bass drummer. His nickname came not only from his instrument but from his paunch and his jovial pomposity. He had just come back from leave. He told them the news of his family, and Adamo listened, too, for the hearty voice and belched laughter seemed to be for him as well. Then Manu began to scold the others.

'What have you done for this boy, scoundrels? Nothing. Lartey, when you joined the army, I saved you a thousand times — have you forgotten? Listen to the Big Drum, you small and little drummers——'

And so, with their duties assigned by Manu, they began to show Adamo what to do, and to protect him from his mistakes. When he did not understand Captain Fossey or Sergeant Sarpong, the others translated unobtrusively, and after a while he recognized the standard commands himself. He cleaned Manu's boots and even polished the brass on the great drum. The bandsmen took this as a joke, and Manu himself sometimes chortled in the depths of his throat, but Adamo did not mind. 'Big Drum' seemed too familiar a name, so he called Manu 'uncle'.

From Captain Fossey, who in Adamo's eyes was the head of the army, the boy learned how to play the parade drum. From Sergeant Sarpong, the regimental drum major, a gaunt and haughty giant of a man, he learned how to march, how to sling his drum at the proper angle, how to watch the baton signal without appearing to do so. The daily drill was not boring to him. With each repetition, Adamo became more confident.

When he finished his basic training, and was proficient enough as a drummer, Adamo was issued with the bandsman's scarlet bolero trimmed with gold, and the square leopardskin apron the regimental drummers wore. He took fanatical care of his uniform and spent hours in cleaning and polishing.

The day came when Adamo was permitted to march with the regimental band, a drummer among the drummers. First came Sergeant Sarpong, tall as a tree, his baton aloft. Then the ranks of drummers, Adamo marching beside rangy Afutu and Botsio with his wrinkled face. Behind them came the Big Drum, Manu, wearing atop his uniform his magnificent mottled leopardskin. Then came the brass section, the horns blaring and bursting with the march tunes. And after the band, the close ranks of soldiers, the clacking boots, the bright bayonets. All the young warriors who now were not strangers to Adamo.

Captain Fossey was pleased at the speed with which Adamo learned.

'I can always tell a promising youngster,' he confided to his colleagues. 'Keen as mustard, he is.'

Captain Fossey's tour of duty here had not been particularly encouraging. He was a ginger-haired, slightly plump Englishman of lower-middle-class origin, a man who had risen from the ranks. This in itself was bad enough, but the bandmaster also had the uncomfortable suspicion that his fellow officers regarded his branch of military activity as not quite manly.

Sometimes Captain Fossey looked at the lanky loose-limbed African bandsmen and thought that they would never in their hearts understand precision. When he heard their deep laughter he wondered uneasily what they were laughing at, and when he went back to his quarters he would strip to his pink flesh and weigh himself on his bathroom scales.

He was a bachelor. The alternate complaining and tittering of the wives at the Club filled him with alarm. How could a man commit himself to regular performance with one of those? A duty, even if only for pride's sake — that was the appalling thing. He did not intend to marry.

Adamo became Captain Fossey's prize. He gave the boy encouragement and praise, for he was under the impression that this was what Adamo needed. Adamo, who had picked up a fair amount of pidgin English, would beam in evident gratitude and produce the first phrase Manu had taught him, a phrase of exceptional efficacy.

'I t'ank you, sah,' he would say in his heavy voice, so much at odds with his watchful, uncertain eyes. 'I t'ank you too much.'

And Captain Fossey would smile, his pale mouth parting slightly, his ginger moustache upturned.

The bandmaster often detailed Adamo to do some little job for him — an hour's work in his garden or an evening spent in helping Fossey's old steward-boy to beat the carpets. These tasks Adamo performed eagerly. He never refused Captain Fossey's shilling or two, but the Englishman had the feeling that the money was not important. Loyalty was the word that rose to Fossey's mind, a sense of personal loyalty. Captain Fossey had never had loyalty directed towards his person before.

He so far relaxed his guard as to mention Adamo to Captain Appiah. Appiah was one of the few African officers in the regiment. He did not like the British officers to make conversation with him, for he felt they were being patronizing. But if they did not speak, he resented their snobbishness.

'That young drummer of mine — Adamo,' Captain Fossey said. 'Lot of your people must be like that, Appiah. No education, coming straight from the bush, but by gum, all he needed was a chance in life.'

Captain Appiah's tense face brooded. He had grown up in the city and had done extremely well in secondary school. He did not like to hear himself equated, as he fancied Captain Fossey was doing, with Adamo. Your people, indeed.

'I do not think he was looking for a chance in life,' Captain Appiah said.

'What do you mean?'

Appiah was not sure himself what he meant. He had observed Adamo on the parade ground and had seen the boy's pleasure in the endless repetitions of the drill. He knew that Adamo followed regulations to the letter. But he could not help wondering how Adamo interpreted the rules he so scrupulously obeyed.

Once when Captain Fossey was ill, Captain Appiah took kit inspection for him. When he came to Adamo, he nodded in satisfaction. Everything was neat, in order, polished. Appiah was about to walk on, when his own curiosity or some obscure malice against Captain Fossey made him stop. He spoke in Adamo's tongue so there would be no misunderstanding.

'This' — indicating the buckle on Adamo's pack — 'and the boots, and the brass buttons. You clean these things. Do you know why you must do so?'

'Sah?' Adamo's eyes widened.

Captain Appiah repeated his words. He did not, as Captain Fossey might have done, imagine that Adamo would make some remark about discipline or the smartness of the company. On the contrary, he expected Adamo to reply that he did not know or that he merely did what he was told. But the young drummer, standing tall in his flawless uniform, did not answer in this way either.

'So all things will go well,' Adamo said calmly, as though there could have been no possible doubt about the matter.

Less and less did Adamo enquire in the palm-wine bars and thronged streets for word of his family. He did not often think of them now. At night in the barracks, after he took off his boots and folded his clothes carefully in the prescribed way, Adamo would lie on his cot and listen to the breathing of men all around him. Then, reassured, he would sleep.

Adamo was not talkative, but he liked it when the others talked to him. Lartey, restless as a scurrying cockroach, always searching for morsels of gossip, sometimes settled briefly beside Adamo while he worked. One afternoon Lartey began to complain about Captain Fossey.

'Again he tells me I am no good, not a soldier. I don't say I am the bravest man in the regiment. I play a drum. I am not a man for rifles. But what is he? Remember when a detachment was sent to stop the riots upcountry? Our big man heard that the band was going to be sent, too, and you should have heard him. What if a spear happened to slit a drum? Terrible! He was so worried about the drums he would place his hands over his own belly whenever he spoke of it. Then, when we were not sent, he said what a pity — we would have given heart to the men.'

Lartey spluttered with laughter, and Adamo laughed too, companionably. Although he and Lartey had the same mother-tongue, Adamo was never quite clear about the other man's meaning, but he took it on faith, sensing from the voice tone what response was expected. Lartey gave him an oblique glance.

'I don't see you in trouble with Captain Fossey, Adamo. You are always trying to please him. You like him so much?'

Adamo looked up, perplexed. 'Like him?'

He had never considered the question. Fossey's skin, which was the palpitating pink of a fresh-killed animal's vital organs, the sour smell his body exuded, the voice so oddly high-pitched compared to the low hoarseness of African voices, the reddish hair which seemed to Adamo a particularly offensive colour, for he associated it with forest demons who were said to be covered with red hair — all these things were unpleasant and even repulsive, but in no way significant. Adamo shrugged and resumed his work.

'He spoke, and many listened,' he said, 'and then I was a drummer among the drummers. His word has power — that I know.'

Lartey looked at Adamo strangely and went away to talk to someone else.

Now when Adamo heard, as he still occasionally did in sleep, the muttering river, the soft slow woman voice, the voices of gods and grandsires, he would be frightened by their questioning and mourning, until they faded and a new voice, high and metallic, alien but not unknown, gained command.

*Here, Adamo. You are here.*

And the man Adamo, sleeping with his legs clenched up to his belly and his long hard arms wrapped tightly around his chest, would sigh, his limbs and muscles unfolding like leaves, and would mercifully cease to dream.

Captain Fossey went on leave each year, but he returned. Once, coming back with a resurgence of ambition, he decided that the regimental band could play at Club dances, and for months he sweated with his troops through campaigns of waltzes, slow foxtrots and even the African highlife tunes. Dutifully the bandsmen blew and beat a dreary path through the ballroom music, but when they played highlife their verve astounded the officers and wives. Captain Fossey was plied with compliments which he accepted as his basic due although he was aware that the troops had actually taken over while he acted merely as a kind of armchair general.

Adamo developed a skill in highlife which became the boast of the entire band. When a number was finished he would throw down his sticks and collapse over the kettle drum in laughter and exhaustion, while Manu clapped him on the shoulder and Lartey whistled and in the background Captain Fossey's voice tinkled high above the hubbub — 'Jolly good, Adamo. Well done.' In the years of Adamo's service, the learning of highlife was the most important innovation that occurred.

One afternoon Captain Fossey sent for Adamo. The bandmaster sat in his office, his puffy hands fiddling with an assortment of papers on his desk. Adamo stood smartly to attention.

'I wanted to see you,' Captain Fossey began, pulling a few hairs out of his ginger moustache, 'because I'll be leaving soon. Posted back to England.'

He wondered if Adamo would express regret at his leaving. The boy looked puzzled but that was all. Annoyed at himself for having bothered to think of it, Captain Fossey continued more brusquely.

'A lot of officers are being posted, with independence coming up. You'll have your own chaps as officers, God help you. Thought I'd better get this settled before I go. Your five years' service time is up this month.'

Adamo's face retained its composure. He stood very straight, his big hands loose at his sides, his patient eyes waiting.

'Yes, sah.'

Adamo's comprehension of English was slight at the best of times, but now, with Captain Fossey's apparent agitation, he could not understand one word. He was anxious and upset because he sensed these feelings in the bandmaster. But he was still confident that the way would be revealed and he would discover what was expected, what task would be required to restore the harmonious order of things.

Captain Fossey sighed. Having hankered for England so long, he now found he did not want to return. He remembered the damp and the cold, the cockiness and terrifying poise of the English bandsmen. Nostalgically, he recalled the ease of his life here, the devotion of men like Adamo. Would Adamo show the same loyalty to the next bandmaster?

'You can always sign up again, but I don't know that I'd advise it, Adamo. Army's liable to undergo all sorts of changes. One just doesn't know what will happen. Men promoted far too fast, from the ranks. I shouldn't say it, perhaps, but there it is. You've shown a talent for high-life. Not long ago I met the leader of a local highlife band, and — well, actually, I put in a word for you. He's short of a drummer. You can find him any evening at the Moon Club.'

It seemed to Adamo that the matter could not be such a heavy one after all, for Captain Fossey had calmed now. Adamo relaxed also and was enabled to catch words here and there, like small slippery fish in the hands. Moon Club — he knew that place. It was full of soft mocking girls and gaudy men whose knife eyes Adamo did not trust. Then he understood the command. That place was to be henceforth forbidden.

Captain Fossey glanced up expectantly. 'Well, what do you say?'

'Yes, sah,' Adamo said agreeably. Then, after a pause and because the officer seemed to be waiting for something more, 'I t'ank you, sah.'

The bandmaster smiled and waved a nonchalant hand. 'Oh, that's all right. You deserve it, Adamo.'

When Appiah, who was now a major, handed over the discharge papers, Adamo frowned questioningly.

'I beg you, sah — what dis t'ing?'

'Discharge papers,' Appiah said irritably, for he was over-worked these days. 'You know, you applied for them through Captain Fossey.'

He looked up, about to dismiss the man curtly, but when he saw Adamo's face he changed his mind and spoke in Adamo's own language.

'You are free to leave the army now. You signed on for five years, and the time is over. Captain Fossey said he thought you could get work with a highlife band. That's all. You can go.'

Slowly, Adamo put the papers in his pocket. Then he saluted and left Major Appiah's office without a word.

He walked back to the barracks, and it was almost night. Tribes of white egrets were flying back to the baobab trees where they slept. Through the clash and clatter of the city's cars and voices, the families of frogs in the nearby lagoon could be heard beginning the throaty trilling that would go on until morning. The thin screeching of the cicada clan came from the *niim* branches now stirring with the first breeze of evening. The bandsmen had left the barracks for dinner. Adamo entered quietly and sat down on his cot.

He sat without moving, his arms limp at his sides. Finally he rose and pulled out his kitbag. He went through it, touching its contents lightly with his hands, pocketing a few things apparently at random, leaving others. Then, as though tiring of it, he shoved it away and went out of the barracks, as deliberately as he had entered. And now, outside, it was dark.

Adamo walked across the parade ground, down a road fringed with well-trimmed bougainvillaea and gardens that boasted weak-coloured zinnias. His feet seemed heavy to him, not from his boots, for he had somehow forgotten that he wore boots, but as though they were encrusted with mud formed of dust and his own blood. His head hurt and his shoulders ached. No wonder, for he had been walking such a long time. He reached out one of his hands — that hard-skinned hand was Adamo's — and the plumed *niim* leaves came away in his fingers. He scattered the leaves on the road, some on this side, some on that side, as though they had been the sacred *summe* leaves scattered in the grove. He thought he cried out, but his voice made no sound.

There were no voices to be heard, neither around him nor inside his head. There were no people in this place, no known voices. None to tell or guide, none even to mourn. Only his own voice which had strangely lost the power of sound, his silent voice splitting his lungs with its cry.

Captain Fossey's bungalow was set in a slight hollow, surrounded by flowering hibiscus with pink tongue-like petals. Adamo knocked, and when the steward-boy came, Adamo asked to see the officer.

Fossey came to the door in his bath-robe, a flowing sea-green silk. He was annoyed at being disturbed while dressing, but when he saw it was Adamo, his expression became a little milder, even anticipatory. His first thought was that Adamo had obtained the job and that he was coming now to express his gratitude.

It was his last thought as well, for within a second Adamo's knife had pierced the pink flesh of Captain Fossey's throat.

Major Appiah touched with distaste the iron bars of the cell door. *Iron, cold iron, is master of men all.* A line from something in school. This iron was slimily warm to the fingers. The whole place was stifling, the damp air foul with the stench of sweat and urine. Major Appiah tapped on the cell bars once more. The man lying in the cell lifted his head.

The officer searched Adamo's face, but Adamo was not there. The face might have been shaped of inert clay. All at once it mattered to Major Appiah to know.

'Adamo — why? Why?'

Adamo's voice was slow and even, and he spoke in his own tongue.

'He would have made me go. Now he is gone.'

Then Adamo's face, curiously striped by the iron bars, lost its empty look and his voice was a quick high cry of pain.

'What did I not do? All he spoke was done, that no evil would come. Was it not enough?'

Appiah could not reply, for Adamo's desolation was unreachable. Adamo stood silently for a moment. Then he cried out again, almost incredulously, as though he refused what he spoke.

'My father's knife — to spill his power? My hand, mine?' The voice faltered. 'Oh, what may follow? You will tell me what I must do. I would not bring harm upon them all — tell Manu I would not do that. I will do whatever you say, whatever must be done. Only——'

In the anguished eyes a question burned and trembled. Finally he was able to express it.

'I will stay?'

Major Appiah had come to tell Adamo when the trial would be held, perhaps even to prepare the man for the inevitability of the verdict. But he said none of these things, for he saw now that they could make no difference at all. Adamo would discover soon enough what ritual would be required for restitution. Perhaps even that made little difference. It was not death that Adamo feared.

'Yes,' Major Appiah said, and as he spoke he became aware of a crippling sense of weariness, as though an accumulation of centuries had been foisted upon himself, to deal with somehow. 'You can stay, Adamo. You can stay as long as you live.'

He turned away abruptly, and his boots drummed on the concrete corridor. He could bear anything, he felt, except the look of relief in Adamo's eyes.

# A Gourdful of Glory

You could walk through the entire market and look at every stall, but never would you see calabashes and earthen pots any better than those sold by Mammii Ama. She was honest — true as God, she really was. You might claim that there were as many honest traders here as there were elephants, and Mammii Ama would understand your meaning, and laugh, and agree with you. But she would let you know she was the one old cow-elephant that never yet died off.

She was a petty trader. A few market women grew rich, and became queen mammies, but Mammii Ama was not one of these. She got by. She lived. Nobody ever got the better of her, but she wasn't one to cheat her customers. She handled good stock. She wasn't like some of those shifty mammies who bought cheap and sold at the regular price the gourd with the faint seam of a crack right in the bottom where you wouldn't notice it until the soup began to leak out. She never sold flawed pots and bowls, either, a bit damaged in the firing so that they broke if you laughed in the same room with them. Such a trick was not Mammii Ama's way. The odd cull, maybe, she would admit. A few could always slip into a lot. You know how it is. A trader woman has to live, after all.

The cockerels, piercing the dawn grey with shrill and scarlet voices, awoke no earlier than Mammii Ama. Expertly, she bunched her fish-patterned cloth around her,

bound on a headscarf of green and glossy artificial silk, and
was ready for the day. She puffed the charcoal embers into
flame, plonked on the tin kettle, brewed tea and ate some
cold boiled yam.

Comfort was still lying curled up on the straw mat. One
always hated to waken a sleeping child. Mammii Ama
gently shook her grand-daughter, and Comfort sat up, dazed,
like a parrot with all its feathers ruffled. She was soon
dressed; not yet five years old, she wore only a shamecloth,
a mere flutter of red and beaded rag around her middle and
between her legs.

Then they were off. Wait — a last thought. Did Adua
sleep peacefully? Was she covered? If you sweated, sleeping,
you got a chill in your belly and you had pain passing water
for evermore. Quiet as a watch-night, Mammii Ama padded
across the hut to the iron cot where her snoring daughter lay.
Adua was properly covered — the blanket was drawn up to
her neck, and all you could see of her was her head with its
wiry hair that she was always straightening with hot pull-
irons, and her face, breathing softly and brown under its
matting of white powder from the night before. Mammii
Ama did not understand why her daughter daubed herself
with talcum until she looked like a fetish priestess in a
funeral parade. Many things about Adua were difficult to
comprehend. The high-heel shoes, for instance, which hurt
and were all but impossible to walk on. Teeter this way,
lurch that — a fine business. The woman's ankle-bones
would snap one of these days — but try to tell her. And the
palaver about the name — a lunacy. Adua called herself
Marcella, and insisted that everyone else do the same. It
was not like the grand-daughter's name. Comfort — a
decent name. A mission name, true, but it had lived here a
long time, until it seemed to have been African always. But
Marcella — whoever heard of such a name? Mammii Ama

226

couldn't bring herself to speak it. She called her daughter
'moon woman' or 'choice of kings', and Adua, who was —
you had to admit it — very vain, liked to hear those names
as she preened herself.

Still, she was a good daughter. She brought home money
— worked all night for it. A club girl, she was, at the
Weekend In Wyoming, and Mammii Ama loved her more
dearly than life, and felt for her a shy and surprised pride,
for the daughter was certainly a beauty, not a cow-elephant
like her mother.

Mammii Ama looked once more on the powdered and
sleeping face, then she was gone, shutting quietly behind her
the packing-case door of the mudbrick shanty.

Mammii Ama took the child's hand while they clambered
onto the crowded bus. She paid her fare, and the bus, with
a rumble like the belly of a giant, jolted off down the road
and into the city.

The market was already filling with sellers. The best
hunter got an early start, Mammii Ama would say. You'd
never catch a fat cutting-grass by sleeping late. As she spread
out her wares in front of her stall, Mammii Ama sang.
She sang in pidgin, so that every passer-by, whatever his
language, would understand.

> '*Mammii Ama sell all fine pot,*
>   *Oh oh Mammii Ama.*
> *She no t'ief you, she no make palavah,*
>   *Oh oh Mammii Ama——*'

And the girl child, squatting in dust as she arranged just-so
the stacks of brown earthen bowls, the big-bellied black
cooking-pots, added to the refrain her high and not-quite-
true-pitched voice.

'Oh oh Mammii Ama——'

Everywhere there were voices, and sweet singing bodies. Everywhere the market women's laughter, coarse and warm as the touch of a tongue. It was still early, and the morning cooks had not yet arrived to buy vegetables and meat for the Europeans.

Moki was already perched atop his firewood. He wiped the rheum from his eyes with an end of his dirty turban. He was old, and his eyes ran mucus, especially in the morning. He was not a Muslim, but his nephew, who died of a worm in the guts, had been one, so Moki always wore a turban in memory of him. No one knew where Moki came from. He didn't know himself. He knew the name of his village, but not the country where it was, and he knew the names of his people's gods. He had come here who knows how long ago, with a Hausa caravan, and had somehow lost the trader who hired him to carry headload. Now he sold pieces of firewood, which he gathered each evening in the bush.

'Morny, Mistah Moki! I greet you!' Mammii Ama called, and the old man fake-bowed to her as though she were a queen mother.

On the other side, a Hausa man was hanging up his white and black wool mats and huge pointed hats and long embroidered robes which only men tall as the Hausas could wear. Sabina the cloth-seller snapped at a small boy who pissed beside her stall, complaining that he was spraying her second-best bolts, draped outside to catch the eye. The small boy's mother threw a coconut husk which caught him on the ear, and he ran off, leaking and howling.

T'reepenny, who looked more ancient than the gods, creaked and trembled up to Mammii Ama's stall. Her hands, bony as tree roots and frail as grass, lugged along the bucket of gourd spoons, half of them broken. She had no stall. She had no money to rent one, so Mammii Ama allowed her to sit beside the calabash-and-pot stall with her bucket. She only said one word, ever. Maybe she only knew one. 'T'reepenny', she would quiver and quaver. 'T'reepenny, t'reepenny', over and over like a brainfever bird, as she held up the gourd spoons for all to admire. She was pleased if she got one penny. Only from white women, rich and gullible, had she ever received as much as three.

With the wares arranged, Mammii Ama was light in heart. Now she began to recall last night's rally. She had gone with the others in the Association of Market Women. They all wore new cloth, in the party's colours, red and white and green. What a thing it had been! Her well-fleshed hips remembered their jigglings and marvellous convolutions in the parade. Her shoulders and hearty arms remembered the touch of others' arms and shoulders as the market women marched. Four abreast, they entered the meeting-place like a charging army, like an army with spears of fire, with rifles fashioned of power and glory. And they all shouted together — loud as a thousand lorry horns, loud as the sea — 'Free-Dom!'

And he had been there, the lovely boy they loved so well, the Show-Boy. He spoke to them of the day that was coming, the day of freedom. And they shouted with one voice, and they cheered with one voice. They were his women, his mothers and his brides.

'Hey, you Sabina!' Mammii Ama shouted. 'Were you at the rally?'

'Naturally,' the shriek came back. 'Didn't you see me, Mammii Ama? I was at the back, in between Mercy Mensah and that old Togo woman, whatever her name is.'

'I was at the front,' Mammii Ama said loudly, but with modesty.

'I was there, too,' Moki chipped in.

Everyone laughed.

'Wha-at? I never knew you were a market woman, Moki,' Mammii Ama bellowed.

'When you get to my age, it's all the same,' Moki replied evenly. 'Man — woman — what does it matter? We all eat. We all die.'

An outburst of chitter-chatter. 'Don't tell me that story, Moki!' 'Maybe it's an old muzzle-loader, but I'll bet it still fires!' And so on.

'What did you think of it, Sabina, the rally?' Mammii Ama continued, when the gust of ribaldry faded.

Sabina shrugged. She was thin, and her mouth always turned down, as though she had just swallowed a piece of rotten fish.

'Well, it's a lot of talk, if you ask me,' she said. 'Free-Dom. Independence. All right — the white men go. So, then? We'll still be haggling over tuppence at our stalls, my friends.'

Mammii Ama jumped to her feet and shook her head and both fists at Sabina.

'Ei! Somebody here is like a crocodile! Yes, somebody acts like the crocodile who crawls in the mud of the river. He lives in the river mud — and he thinks the whole world is only river mud. Oh, blind! Blind!'

She appealed to the others.

'Free-Dom — it's like the sun,' she cried. 'You have to crawl out of the river mud or you can't see it.'

Moki muttered and went on cleaning his eyes. Old T'reepenny nodded her head. She agreed in this way with everything Mammii Ama said. She didn't understand, but she agreed. Whatever Mammii Ama said must be right. The Hausa man stared — he spoke no Ga.

Sabina went on shrugging, and Mammii Ama grew so furious she rushed over to Sabina's stall and burst into fresh argument. She grew inspired. She no longer cared about

Sabina. Around her, the market women gathered. They cried 'Ha — ei!' when she paused for breath. They swayed and chanted to the rhythm of Mammii Ama.

'Go call all de market woman!' Mammii Ama cried, this time in pidgin, to captivate a wider audience. 'Tell dem say "Free-Dom"! Go call all de market woman — say, you no go sell befoah five minute. You sell Free-Dom dis time. What dis t'ing, what dis Free-Dom? He be strong, he be fine too much. Ju-ju man he no got such t'ing, such power word. Dis Free-Dom he be sun t'ing, same sun he be shine. Hey, you market woman, you say "Money sweet — I be poor woman, nothing with, on'y one penny. I no 'gree dis Free-Dom, I no be fit for chop him." Oh — oh — I t'ink you be bush woman, no got sense. I no 'gree for you. I tell you, dis Free-Dom he be sweet sweet t'ing. You wait small, you see I tell you true. Market woman all dey be queen mammy den.'

Moki stopped his eye-wiping and waved a piece of firewood, roaring encouragement to his friend Mammii Ama. The Hausa man uttered sombre cries in his own tongue — "Allah knows it! Has not the Prophet himself said the same? It will be shown at the Last Day!" T'reepenny, carried away by excitement, grasped a gourd spoon in either hand and executed a sort of dance, back bent and stiff-kneed, all by herself, until her unsteady breath gave out and she sank down beside her bucket once more, chirping her mournful word.

Sabina, feeling herself outnumbered, began to weep, begging them all not to forget her unfortunate past. If she seemed sour, she sobbed, they knew why.

Mammii Ama immediately grew sympathetic. She broke off and put an arm around Sabina's shoulder. A terrible thing it must have been, she agreed. Enough to mark a person for life.

Sabina had once had a wealthy lover — well, not wealthy,

perhaps, but certainly nicely fixed. A clerk, he was, a man in a government office. He always seemed healthy, Sabina used to say. He seemed so strong, so full of life, so full of love. How that man would do it! Again and again — why, half a dozen times in a single night, that was nothing to him, Sabina said, simply nothing.

Then one night, his heart swelled and burst, and he died, just like that. He was with Sabina at the time. They had gone to sleep, still together. At least, she had gone to sleep. A little later, feeling cramped and trying to turn, she had wakened to find a dead man there. Dead as a gutted fish, and his eyes wide open. Sabina got a baby that night, it turned out, and she went around saying her child had been given her by a dead man. She was sure of it. She screeched and cried. A child begotten by a corpse — who could stand the thought? No one was surprised when the baby was born dead.

The women clucked softly. Mammii Ama, ashamed of her attack, soothed and soothed in her full mother-voice.

'There, my red lily. Cry, then. It is nothing. I am a fool; I have a head like a calabash, empty.'

Into the hush-hushing throng of women ran Comfort. Her face was frightened and excited.

'Mammii Ama! Mammii Ama! A white woman has come to your stall!'

And Mammii Ama looked amazed, dumbfounded, only partly in mockery of the child. Hastily she hitched her cloth up around her, and flew back.

'Ei — what a madness!'

She went running along like a girl, like a young girl at her first outdooring. She carried her weight lightly, and her breasts bounced as she bounded over gutter and path, over smouldering charcoal burner, over the sleeping babies with blackflies at their nostrils' edge.

232

'Who is the young virgin fleeing from her seducer?' Moki shouted, as she approached. 'Oh oh Mammii Ama!'

The white woman was thin and tall. She had very little flesh on her, just yellow hide over bones, and her eyes were such a pale blue they seemed not to be there at all — only the jelly of the eyeball, nothing to see with. She was holding a brown earthen bowl in her hands.

Mammii Ama regained her breath.

'Madam — I greet you,' she said with hoarse cheerfulness.

The white woman smiled uncertainly and looked over her shoulder. Mammii Ama looked, too, and it was Ampadu standing there.

Ampadu was a clerk. He had a good job. One heard he had influence. He was a really educated man — he knew not only reading and writing, but also the work of account-books and typewriters. Mammii Ama, who could neither read nor write, and who kept her accounts in her head with never a mistake in twenty-four years, was greatly impressed with Ampadu's power over words and numbers. She did not tell him so — in fact, she constantly made fun of him. They were distantly related, and Ampadu, who understood her unexpressed pride in this relationship, took her jibes in an easy-natured way.

She clapped him on the shoulder. He was neatly dressed in a white shirt and grey flannel trousers. How prosperous he looked. And his rimmed spectacles, how well they suited him.

'Ampadu! I greet you!' she cried in Ga. 'How are you, great government man? Do they still say your pen is more active than your love-branch? Hey — you, Moki! Did you know this? When the old chief's young wife wanted a lover, she sent for Ampadu's pen!'

The clerk laughed, but not wholeheartedly. He patted his stomach in embarrassment. Mammii Ama, realizing

Ampadu was accompanying the white woman, began to roll
her eyes and pretended to stagger.

'What's this, Ampadu? What's this? What's all this
about?'

Ampadu held up his hand, like a policeman stopping a
lorry.

'She wants to see the market,' he hissed. 'She's the wife
of my new boss. Mammii Ama, please be sensible, I implore
you. She wants to buy a calabash, God knows why.'

The white woman was growing impatient.

'Ampadu — ask her what she'll take for this bowl, please.'

'Ten shilling,' Mammii Ama replied without hesitation.

'Ten shillings!' the white woman cried, and even Ampadu
looked stunned.

Mammii Ama seized the bowl from her hands.

'See, madam — dis one, he be fine too much. No be
bad one. Look — put you fingah heah — you feel? All
fine — nevah broke, dis one. Ten shilling, madam.'

'How much is the usual price?' the white woman asked
Ampadu.

Ampadu scuffed his shoes in the dust. Mammii Ama
felt quite sorry for him, but she had to try hard not to
laugh.

'Usual price?' Ampadu appeared to search his memory.
'Let me see, what is the usual price? I am sorry, madam —
I am afraid I don't really know. My wife, you see, buys all
the cooking-pots——'

'Ten shilling!' shouted Mammii Ama in a huge voice.
'All time, meka price he be ten shilling! I tell you true,
madam. I no t'ief you.'

'Five shillings,' the white woman offered.

'Nine shilling sixpence — for you.'

They settled at length on six shillings, to Mammii Ama's
well-disguised delight. The white woman then bought a

black cooking-pot and two calabashes. Mammii Ama was amazed. What could such a woman want with cooking-pots and calabashes? Were Europeans living like poor Africans all of a sudden? Mammii Ama felt excited and confused. The order of things was turning upside down, but pleasurably, in a way that provided food for speculation and gossip.

When the white woman was gone, they all discussed it. Who could understand such a thing? Mammii Ama, dusting and re-arranging her stock of pots and bowls, began one of her speeches.

'Hey! Stranger woman, listen to me. Do you feed your man from a calabash you bought in the market? Does your man eat from a bowl made of river clay? Ei! The gourd-vine dances — he shakes his leaves with laughter. Ei! The river fish drown in their laughter. Your own dishes — are they not white as a silver shilling? They are white as the egret's feathers, when he sleeps in the baobab tree. If the fine vessels displease you, give them to my grand-daughter. Yes! Give them to Comfort, the lovely and dear one——'

Mammii Ama turned the last bit into a song, and sang it all day. Some of the others joined the refrain, varying it from time to time for amusement.

> '*Yes! Give them to the woodseller,*
> *Give them to Moki, the lovely one——*'

Mammii Ama added a stanza in pidgin, so everyone around would know she was no longer cross at Sabina.

> '*Meka you dash dem for Sabina,*
> *She fine too much, same been-to gal,*
> *She like all fine t'ing——*'

A week later, the white woman returned, this time alone. Mammii Ama greeted her like an old friend. The white woman bought a gourd spoon from T'reepenny, and haggled with Mammii Ama over the price of another bowl. Finally, Mammii Ama could restrain her curiosity no longer.

'Madam — why you buy African pot?'

The white woman smiled.

'I want to use them for ashtrays.'

'Ashtray! For dem cig'rette?' Mammii Ama could not believe her ears. 'You no got fine one, madam?'

'Oh — I have lots of others,' the woman said, 'but I like these. They're so beautifully shaped.'

Mammii Ama could not credit it.

'An' dem calabash? Madam chop *fu-fu* now?'

'I use the shallow ones to put groundnuts in,' the woman explained. 'For small-chop with drinks. The big ones I'm using for plants.'

'Free-Dom time, meka all African get dem fine dish,' Mammii Ama mused. 'I look-a dem na Kingsway store. Fine dish, shine too much.'

She stopped herself. It would not do, for business, to admit she would like to use fine white dishes. She even felt a little guilty at the thought. Were not her calabashes and bowls the best in the market? But still——

The white woman was looking at her oddly.

'You don't mean to tell me that you think you'll all be given — what did you say? — shiny dishes, when Independence comes?'

Mammii Ama did not know whether she believed it or not. But she grew stubborn.

'I tell you true!' Speaking the words, she became immediately convinced of their absolute truth. 'Market woman, all dey be same queen mammy den.'

'Is that what freedom means to you?' the woman asked.

236

Mammii Ama felt somehow that she was being attacked at her very roots.

'What dis t'ing, what dis Free-Dom? You no savvy Free-Dom palavah, madam. He be strong, dis Free-Dom, he be power word.'

'You're free now,' the woman said. 'We give you justice. I'll wager you won't have it then.'

The woman did not speak pidgin. Mammii Ama could not follow every word, but she detected the meaning. The white woman was against Free-Dom. Mammii Ama was not surprised, of course. Nor was she angry. What else would you expect of Europeans? When she spoke, it was not to the white woman. It was to the market, to the city, to every village quiet in the heat of the sun.

She spread her arms wide, as though she would embrace the whole land. She felt the same as she had once long ago, when she went to meet her young man in the grove. She was all tenderness and longing; she was an opening moon-flower, filled with the seeds of life everlasting.

'Dis Free-Dom he be sun t'ing,' she cried. 'Same sun, he be shine. I no 'gree for Eur'pean. I 'gree for Free-Dom.'

The woman looked thoughtful.

'Your leader seems popular among the market women.'

'Ha — aah! He fine too much. He savvy all t'ing. He no forget we. Market woman all dey come queen mammy. All — all——'

She stuttered and stopped. The Free-Dom speech seemed to have lost something of its former grandeur. Now, Mammii Ama's words would not rise to her heights. Earthbound, she grasped for the golden lightning with which to illumine the sky. She found it.

'Dat time, you t'ink we pay wen we deah go for bus?' she cried. 'We no pay! At all! Nevah one penny.'

The white woman still peered. Then she laughed, a dry sound, like Moki breaking firewood.

'You really think the buses will be free after Independence?'

'I hear so,' Mammii Ama said, truthfully. Then, feeling her faith not stated with sufficient strength, 'Be so! Meka come Free-Dom nevah one penny for we. We go for bus free, free, free!'

Her words had the desired effect. The white woman was staring at her, certainly, staring with wide eyes. But in her face was an expression Mammii Ama did not understand. Who was this stranger, and why did she come here with her strange laughter and strange words and a strange look on her skull-face? Why didn't she go away?

Mammii Ama frowned. Then she heaved her shoulders in a vast shrug and turned back to her stall.

'Hey, you Comfort! Hasn't the village woman come yet with the new calabashes?'

Soon, with the white woman gone, everything was in order, everything was itself once more, known and familiar.

> *'Mammii Ama sell all fine pot,*
> *Oh Oh Mammii Ama!*
> *She no t'ief you, she no make palavah,*
> *Oh Oh Mammii Ama!'*

The white woman did not come again for a long time, and Mammii Ama forgot about her. Things weren't going so well. Both Adua and the child got sick — skin burning all over, belly distended. Mammii Ama went to a dealer in charms. Then she went to a dealer in roots and herbs. She spent, altogether, six pounds four shillings and ninepence. But it did no good. Adua wouldn't drink the brew the herb-dealer concocted, nor would she allow Mammii Ama to give it to the child. When the fetish priest came to the shanty, Adua lay with her head covered by the blanket, not wanting to see him, but afraid to send him away. Then Adua insisted that Mammii Ama take Comfort to the hospital to see the doctor. Mammii Ama was very much opposed to the idea, but one did not dare argue with a sick person. She took the child. They waited three days before they could see the doctor, and Mammii Ama was in a panic, thinking of her empty market stall, and no money coming in. She had a little money saved, but it was almost gone now. Finally, the doctor gave Comfort a bottle of medicine, and Mammii Ama, when they arrived home, gave some of it to Adua as well. Slowly, the sickness went away, withdrawing a speck of its poison at a time. Adua went back to work, but Comfort was still too weak to help in the market.

That was always the way — sometimes you had luck; you were well; the coins in the wooden box grew; you bought a little meat, a little fish, a bowl of lamb's blood for the stew. Then — bam! Fever came, or somebody robbed you, or nobody needed pots and calabashes that month. And you were back where you started, eating only *garri* and lucky to have anything. You got by somehow. If you couldn't live, you died, and that was that.

But then a great thing happened. Not in the ordinary run of exciting things, like Moki killing a small python, or Sabina getting pregnant again, this time by a live man. No — nothing like that at all. This was a great thing, the greatest of all great things.

Independence.

The time came. Everyone was surprised when the time actually came, although they'd been expecting it for so long. It was like a gift — a piece of gold that somebody dashed you for nothing.

Mammii Ama was so excited she could hardly breathe.

The night before the Day, everyone gathered at the Parliament building, everyone who could dance or walk or totter, even old T'reepenny, who nearly got broken like a twig by the crowd, until Mammii Ama staunchly elbowed a path for her. And there at midnight, the white man's flag came down, and the new flag went up — so bright, and the black star so strong and shining, the new flag of the new land. And the people cried with one voice — 'Now — now we are Free!'

The Day — who could describe it? Commoners and princes, all together. The priest-kings of the Ga people, walking stately and slow. The red and gold umbrellas of the proud Akan chiefs, and their golden regalia carried aloft by the soul-bearers, sword-bearers, spokesmen, guards. From the northern desert, the hawk-faced chiefs in tent-like robes. The shouting young men, the girls in new cloth, the noise and the dancing, the highlife music, the soldiers in their scarlet jackets. The drums beating and beating for evermore. The feasting. The palm wine, everybody happy. Free-Dom.

Mammii Ama sang and shouted until her voice croaked like a tree toad's. She drank palm wine. She danced like a young girl. Everybody was young. Everybody's soul was just born this minute. A day to tell your grandchildren and their children. 'Free-Dom shone, silver as stars — oh, golden as sun. The day was here. We saw it. We sang it and shouted.'

The day, of course, like any other day, had to finish sometime. Mammii Ama, exhausted, found her way home through the still-echoing streets. Then she slept.

The next morning Mammii Ama did not rise quite so early. The tea and boiled yam tasted raw in her mouth. She swallowed her cold bile and marched out.

Only when the bus drew to a stop did she remember. She climbed on, cheerful now, full of proud expectancy.

She was about to push her way through the standing people near the door, when the driver touched her arm.

'Hey — you! You no pay yet.'

She looked at him shrewdly.

'Wey you say? You t'ief me? I no pay now.'

'So? Why you no pay?'

Mammii Ama folded her arms and regarded him calmly.

'Free-Dom time, meka not one penny for-we. I hear it.'

The driver sighed heavily.

'De t'ing wey you hear, he no be so,' he said crossly. 'Meka you pay you fare. Now — one-time!'

Some of the other passengers were laughing. Mammii Ama scarcely heard them. Her eyes were fixed on the driver. He was not deceiving her — she could read it in his tired, exasperated face.

Without a word, she took out the coin and dropped it in the metal fare-box.

That day the white woman visited the market again. Mammii Ama, piling bowls in neat stacks, looked up and saw her standing there. The white woman held up a calabash and asked how much.

'Twelve shilling,' Mammii Ama said abruptly, certain that would be enough to send the woman away.

To her utter astonishment, however, the woman paid without a murmur. As Mammii Ama reached out and took the money, she realized that the calabash was only an excuse.

'How were your Independence celebrations?' the white woman smiled. 'Did you have a good time?'

Mammii Ama nodded but she did not speak.

'Oh, by the way——' the white woman said in a soft voice. 'How did you get on with the bus this morning?'

Mammii Ama stared mutely. She, the speech-maker, was bereft of speech. She was more helpless than T'reepenny.

She did not have even one word. She could feel her body trembling. The fat on her arms danced by itself, but not in joy. The drummer in her heart was beating a frenzy. Her heart hurt so much she thought she would fall down there in the dust, while the yellow skull of the woman looked and tittered.

Then, mercifully, the word was revealed to her. She had her power once more. Her drumming heart told her what to do. Snake-swift, Mammii Ama snatched back the calabash, at the same time thrusting the coins into the woman's hand.

'You no go buy from Mammii Ama! You go somewhere. You no come heah. I no need for you money.'

She felt a terrible pang as she realized what had happened. She had parted with twelve shillings. She must be going mad. But she would not turn back now. She took another belligerent step, and the yellow menacing skull retreated a little more. She spoke clearly, slowly, emphasizing each word.

'I no pay bus dis time,' she said. 'Bus — he — be — free! You hear? Free!'

Inspired, Mammii Ama lifted the gourd vessel high above her head, and it seemed to her that she held not a brittle brown calabash but the world. She held the world in her strong and comforting hands.

'Free-Dom he come,' she cried, half in exultation, half in longing. 'Free-Dom be heah now, dis minute!'

The sun rolled like an eye in its giant socket. The lightning swords of fire danced in the sky.

She became calm. She knew what was what. She knew some things would happen, and others — for no reason apparent to her — would not. And yet, there was a truth in her words, more true than reality. Setting down the calabash, she re-adjusted her fish-patterned cloth above her breasts. She looked disinterestedly at her former customer. The white woman was only a woman — only a bony and curious woman, not the threatening skull-shape at all.

She watched the white woman go, and then she turned back to her stall. She picked up the calabash and set it with the rest. An ordinary calabash, nothing in it. Where was the glory she had so certainly known only a moment before? Spilled out now, evaporated, gone. The clank of the coin in the fare-box echoed again in her head, drowning the heart's drums. She felt weary and spent as she began stacking the earthen pots once more. A poor lot — she would be lucky to get ninepence apiece. They seemed heavy to her now — her arms were weighted down with them. It would continue so, every day while her life lasted. Soon she would be an old woman. Was death a feast-day, that one should have nothing else to look forward to?

Then a voice, hoarse as a raven's, began to sing. It was Moki the woodseller, and as he sang he beat out the rhythm with one of his gnarled sticks. Nearby, others took up the song. Sabina, singing, wrapped her cover-cloth more tightly and swaggered a little in front of her stall so they could see her belly was beginning to swell with the new, good child. The Hausa man donned one of his gilt-beaded hats and waggled his head in mock solemnity. Ancient T'reepenny shuffled in her solitary dance.

Mammii Ama, looking from one to the other, understood their gift and laughed her old enduring laughter and sang with them.

> '*Mammii Ama sell all fine pot,*
> *Oh Oh Mammii Ama——*'

She was herself again, known and familiar. And yet — there was something more, something that had not been before. She tried to think what it was, but it eluded her.

243

She could feel it, though. So that the others might know, too, she added to her old chant a verse no one had ever heard her sing before.

> *'Mammii Ama, she no come rich.*
> *Ha — ei ! Be so. On'y one penny.*
> *She nevah be shame, she no fear for nothing.*
> *D' time wey come now, like queen she shine.'*

And they caught the rhythm, and the faith, and the new words. Mammii Ama straightened her plump shoulders. Like a royal palm she stood, rooted in magnificence, spreading her arms like fronds, to shelter the generations.

**THE END**

# Afterword

BY GUY VANDERHAEGHE

Readers change, but books with life in them survive readers' changes. When Margaret Laurence's *The Tomorrow-Tamer* was first published, the emerging nations of Africa were much in the news and much on the conscience of the West, and it was assumed that the stories in this collection offered "sociological" and "political" insights into post-colonial Ghana. Now, in a different climate, assumptions have reversed. Concerns about "cultural appropriation" and "authentic voice" foster doubts whether a white, middle-class liberal, a mere sojourner in Africa, could possibly render the continent and its inhabitants accurately. Regardless of where one stands in this controversy, an awareness of the arguments surrounding it subtly shape and colour one's response to *The Tomorrow-Tamer,* and influence what one seeks and, consequently, finds between its covers.

Of course, it has to be recognized that Laurence herself broached these topics now so hotly debated. Discussing her African novel, *This Side Jordan,* in her essay, "Gadgetry or Growing: Form and Voice in the Novel," she volunteered remarks which apply equally to *The Tomorrow-Tamer.*

> I actually wonder how I ever had the nerve to attempt to go into the mind of an African man, and I suppose if I'd really known how difficult was the job I was attempting, I would never have tried it. I am not at all sorry I tried it, and in fact I believe from various comments made by

African reviewers that at least some parts of the African chapters have a certain authenticity. But not, perhaps, as much as I once believed.

In a typically honest and direct manner, Laurence was admitting how difficult it was for the outsider, the "stranger," to accomplish what she had tried to do, and admitting how limited she felt her success had been. While stopping short of a disavowal of the African books and what they contained, she suggested that their real importance lay in the lessons she had learned writing them.

> I had decided I could never get deeply enough inside the minds of African people – or, at least, I'd gone as far as I personally could as a non-African – and had a very strong desire to go back and write about people from my own background, people whose idiom I knew and whose concepts were familiar to me.

Yet *The Tomorrow-Tamer* deserves better than this. It is more than a literary signpost which set Laurence's feet firmly on the road home to Manawaka, and more than a piece of reporting, a record of Africa and Africans at a decisive moment in their history. No, these stories have lasted because they are profound and moving meditations upon the words "change" and "stranger," and because they are a living testament to Laurence's gift for embodying in the flesh of her characters such poignant abstractions.

The word *stranger* obviously awakened in Laurence strong feelings. A passage from Exodus, "Thou shalt not oppress a stranger, for ye know the heart of a stranger, seeing ye were strangers in the land of Egypt," is quoted in "The Rain Child" – a verse which years later she returned to for the title of her collection of essays, *Heart of a Stranger*, in which she reflected,

> for a writer of fiction, part of the heart remains that of a stranger, for what we are trying to do is to understand

those others who are our fictional characters, somehow to gain entrance to their minds and feelings, to respect them for themselves as human individuals, and to portray them as truly as we can. The whole process of fiction is a mysterious one, and a writer, however experienced, remains in some ways a perpetual amateur, or perhaps a perpetual traveller, an explorer of those inner territories, those strange lands of the heart and spirit.

The whole cast of "The Rain Child" is, for instance, a cast of strangers. There are the obvious ones, foreigners such as Hilda Povey, futilely trying to coax an English rosebush into bloom in an inhospitable environment, while her compatriot, Violet Nedden, doubly exiled because she recognizes that in Africa she is an alien teaching an "alien speech," finds herself dreading retirement in a Britain which has, in the years of exile, become nothing more to her than an "island of grey rain." Then there are the "outcast children." Yindo the garden boy, a Dagomba from the northern desert, forced to speak a hesitant pidgin because no one understands his language. Ayesha, the former child prostitute, returned from Lagos because someone there recognized her speech as Twi. Finally, Ruth Quansah, raised and educated in Britain, an English girl with a black skin, ignorant of the language and customs of her homeland, rejected by her African classmates and, eventually, by her English friend, David Mackie, who has taken up the task of "showing Africa to her as she wanted to be shown it – from the outside." Her father, Dr. Quansah, knows his daughter's pain because he is suffering it too. As he confesses to Violet Nedden, "I still find most Europeans here as difficult to deal with as I ever did. And yet – I seem to have lost touch with my own people, too."

This isolation, this losing touch, this failure to connect, for Laurence crystallizes the essence of the stranger. Knowing the frustration of her own struggle to enter fully the minds of her own characters, to *connect* with them, and through them to establish a connection with her readers, gave Laurence insight and sympathy for the alienated. She knew, as every writer does, how hard-won and desperately fragile all such ties are.

In *The Tomorrow-Tamer* change is seen as a threat to precarious ties of every kind. Any alteration in the equation necessarily produces an alteration in the result, and the result most often is an individual cast adrift in a cold and comfortless universe. This is most likely to be the plight of the more vulnerable African, but it is a fate which can befall the European too. The European narrator of "The Drummer of All the World," who knew Twi better than he did English at the age of six, who was suckled by an African nurse, who learned all the proverbs and parables of Ghana, and, when his missionary mother lay sick, who prayed to the Ghanaian gods, returns after an education in England to find a country transformed by the rush to independence. "The old Africa was dying, and I felt suddenly rootless, a stranger in the only land I could call home," he laments.

Political change is a destroyer and orphan-maker, but an even greater danger is religious change. Among Canadian writers working in the last half of the twentieth century, Laurence was an anomaly – she took religion seriously, and nowhere in her fiction is this seriousness more evident than it is in *The Tomorrow-Tamer,* a god-driven and god-haunted book. Will Kittredge, trying to explain to his friend Danso why the missionary, Brother Lemon, does not want to live in the middle of an African shanty town, says that the people there are a threat to Brother Lemon and everything he is. But, as Danso points out, that only makes it even. In this world of shades and omnipresent gods, a loss of faith means a rending of the most fundamental and meaningful connections, not only a separation from God, but a psychological separation from the community of all believers. Or, as Ludwig Wittgenstein put it, "If you have no ties to either mankind or to God, then you *are* an alien."

The link between change, strangerhood, and loss of faith is nowhere more clearly drawn than in the title story of the collection. There the arrival of strangers (European engineers and administrators, urban African workers) to construct a bridge near a small secluded village has dire results. At each step in the construction the villagers are certain that the gods will exact a terrible punishment for the sacrileges committed. When their holy grove is destroyed by earth-moving equipment they are left utterly bewildered.

> So the grove was lost, and although the pleas were made to gods and grandsires, the village felt lost, too, depleted and vulnerable. But the retribution did not come. Owura did not rise. Nothing happened. Nothing at all.

In their bewilderment, there are always those who will seek new allegiances, new meanings, new spiritual links. Kofi, a young villager chosen to work on the bridge, attempts to interpret the modern steel miracle in the light of what he has been taught by the fetish priests and the elders. In a discussion with the other villagers, Kofi declares that there is something in the bridge, something as strong as the old god Owura. He goes further and decides that

> The other bridgemen might go, might desert, might falter, but he would not falter. He would tend the bridge as long as he lived. He would be its priest.

Having taken this leap into apostasy, he ventures an even more daring one. Standing high on the exposed steel of the bridge he is granted another vision. When he sees for the first time the new road that connects his village to the outside world, the desire to be the priest of the bridge withers inside him. A more secular wish replaces it, a wish to leave the village, rejoin the bridgemen, and continue the work of building bridges. Suddenly he is filled with a sense of his own power.

> Exultant, he wanted to shout aloud his own name and his praises. There was nothing he could not do. Slowly, deliberately, he pulled himself up until he was standing there on the steel, high above the forest and the river. He was above even the bridge itself. And above him, there was only the sky.

It is as if Kofi has, in a matter of months, compressed a journey which took Europe centuries to complete. In that moment of self-exultation, he becomes, psychologically, a European. Significantly, it is also the moment of his death, a death interpreted by the other villagers according to the old religion. The bridge sacrifices its priest to appease the river god.

In the imaginations of characters such as Kofi, or Adamo in "The Voices of Adamo," in their struggle to make sense of a perplexing, ever-changing world, we can find analogies with their creator's own struggle to write truthfully and honestly. In their attempts to understand a foreign civilization they mirror Laurence's own attempts to enter the mind of the fictional "other." The Kofis, the Dansos, the Adamos, the Tettehs, are doubtless driven to do this through necessity, but upon reflection we may conclude that so are we.

Change makes strangers of us all. *The Tomorrow-Tamer* is, after all, ironically titled. There is no taming tomorrow. Over two thousand years ago Heraclitus stated, "Everything flows and nothing stays." More than most writers, Laurence felt this truth in her very bones, and it was to the image of the Heraclitean river that she turned for the beginning of *The Diviners*, the last of her novels.

> The river flowed both ways. The current moved from north to south, but the wind usually came from the south, rippling the bronze-green water in the opposite

direction. This apparently impossible contradiction, made apparent and possible, still fascinated Morag, even after the years of river-watching.

Margaret Laurence knew that life is like the river, fluctuation and contradiction. But she wished to remind us that the exigencies of a world in flux do not exempt us from a simple human duty, the duty to imagine and re-imagine, to strive with compassion to plumb the hearts of our fellow strangers. This, more than anything else, is what *The Tomorrow-Tamer* is about.

# BY MARGARET LAURENCE

**AUTOBIOGRAPHY**
*The Prophet's Camel Bell* (1963)
*Dance on the Earth* (1989)

**ESSAYS**
*Long Drums and Cannons:*
*Nigerian Dramatists and Novelists 1952-1966* (1968)
*Heart of a Stranger* (1976)

**FICTION**
*This Side Jordan* (1960)
*The Tomorrow-Tamer* (1963)
*The Stone Angel* (1964)
*A Jest of God* (1966)
*The Fire-Dwellers* (1969)
*A Bird in the House* (1970)
*The Diviners* (1974)

**FICTION FOR YOUNG ADULTS**
*Jason's Quest* (1970)
*Six Darn Cows* (1979)
*The Olden Days Coat* (1979)
*The Christmas Birthday Story* (1980)

# New Canadian Library
## *The Best of Canadian Writing*

## TITLES BY MARGARET LAURENCE IN THE NCL

*A Bird in the House*
Afterword by Isabel Huggan

*The Diviners*
Afterword by Timothy Findley

*The Fire-Dwellers*
Afterword by Sylvia Fraser

*A Jest of God*
Afterword by Margaret Atwood

*The Prophet's Camel Bell*
Afterword by Clara Thomas

*The Stone Angel*
Afterword by Adele Wiseman

*This Side Jordan*
Afterword by George Woodcock

*The Tomorrow-Tamer*
Afterword by Guy Vanderhaeghe

*NCL — A Series Worth Collecting*